INSPECTOR FRENCH:
THE AFFAIR AT LITTLE WOKEHAM

Freeman Wills Crofts (1879–1957), the son of an army doctor who died before he was born, was raised in Northern Ireland and became a civil engineer on the railways. His first book, *The Cask*, written in 1919 during a long illness, was published in the summer of 1920, immediately establishing him as a new master of detective fiction. Regularly outselling Agatha Christie, it was with his fifth book that Crofts introduced his iconic Scotland Yard detective, Inspector Joseph French, who would feature in no less than thirty books over the next three decades. He was a founder member of the Detection Club and was elected a Fellow of the Royal Society of Arts in 1939. Continually praised for his ingenious plotting and meticulous attention to detail—including the intricacies of railway timetables—Crofts was once dubbed 'The King of Detective Story Writers' and described by Raymond Chandler as 'the soundest builder of them all'.

T0016822

Also in this series

Inspector French's Greatest Case
Inspector French and the Cheyne Mystery
Inspector French and the Starvel Hollow Tragedy
Inspector French and the Sea Mystery
Inspector French and the Box Office Murders
Inspector French and Sir John Magill's Last Journey
Inspector French: Sudden Death
Inspector French: Death on the Way
Inspector French and the Mystery on Southampton Water
Inspector French and the Crime at Guildford
Inspector French and the Loss of the 'Jane Vosper'
Inspector French: Man Overboard!
Inspector French: Found Floating
Inspector French: The End of Andrew Harrison
Inspector French: Fatal Venture
Inspector French: Golden Ashes
Inspector French: James Tarrant, Adventurer
Inspector French: A Losing Game
Inspector French: Fear Comes to Chalfont
Inspector French and the Affair at Little Wokeham

By the same author

The Cask
The Ponson Case
The Pit-Prop Syndicate
The Groote Park Murder
*Six Against the Yard**
*The Anatomy of Murder**

*with other Detection Club authors

FREEMAN WILLS CROFTS

Inspector French: The Affair at Little Wokeham

COLLINS
CRIME
CLUB

COLLINS CRIME CLUB

An imprint of HarperCollins*Publishers*
1 London Bridge Street
London SE1 9GF
www.harpercollins.co.uk

HarperCollins*Publishers*
Macken House, 39/40 Mayor Street Upper,
Dublin 1, D01 C9W8, Ireland

This paperback edition 2023
1

First published in Great Britain by Hodder & Stoughton Ltd 1943

Copyright © Estate of Freeman Wills Crofts 1943

Freeman Wills Crofts asserts the moral right
to be identified as the author of this work

This novel is entirely a work of fiction. It is presented in its original form
and may depict ethnic, racial and sexual prejudices that were
commonplace at the time it was written.

A catalogue record for this book is
available from the British Library

ISBN 978-0-00-855424-8

Set in Sabon Lt Std by Palimpsest Book Production Ltd, Falkirk, Stirlingshire

Printed and bound in the UK using 100% Renewable Energy
at CPI Group (UK) Ltd

All rights reserved. No part of this publication may be reproduced,
stored in a retrieval system, or transmitted, in any form or by any means,
electronic, mechanical, photocopying, recording or otherwise, without
the prior written permission of the publishers.

MIX
Paper | Supporting
responsible forestry
FSC™ C007454

FSC
www.fsc.org

This book is produced from independently certified FSC™ paper
to ensure responsible forest management.

For more information visit: www.harpercollins.co.uk/green

Foreword

When I had finished my last book and the time came to start the next, I called at 16 Alford Terrace to see French, to discuss with him which of his cases I should now deal with. I found he was in hospital. After a good deal of trouble I was allowed to see him.

'Hullo,' he greeted me. 'Nice of you to look me up.'

This was embarrassing, since I had only come for what I could get. I said how sorry I was to see him there.

'What happened?' I asked.

He glanced at the door and lowered his voice. 'Spot of trouble in the black markets. Difference of opinion over bringing some of them in.'

I naturally pressed for details, but he was not communicative.

'After the war,' he murmured vaguely. 'It's all a bit hush-hush at present.'

'But I want another book,' I protested.

'That's all right,' he smiled. 'You never told them about that affair at Little Wokeham. One of my best cases.'

'But that's pre-war and pre-Rollo too.'

'All the better. They'll be glad to forget the war and they won't weep about Rollo.'

The story which follows is what he told me.

F.W.C.

CONTENTS

1

Anthony Mallaby

When, much against his will, Anthony Mallaby settled down to practise in the tiny village of Little Wokeham near Guildford, Surrey, the idea that he could ever become a willing accessory to the crime of murder had never penetrated his consciousness. That he, who had always been so law-abiding, should live to see the day when the uniform of a policeman should fill him with indescribable dread, was an absurdity which in that earlier life before the hideous affair occurred he would have dismissed with the ridicule it deserved. Yet the incredible thing had happened. He, Anthony Mallaby, had compounded a crime for which the law of his country prescribed death, and should the facts he was trying to hide become known, there would be no doubt as to his condemnation. Yet no one was more genuinely anxious to live an honourable life and to help his friends and neighbours than was he.

What fatal weakness, he asked himself again and again, was there in his make-up, that when the test came he should choose the course which he not only knew to be wrong, but which in the event of discovery would inevitably bring on him this ghastly retribution? And through what trick of malevolent fate was it that this should happen when for the first time for many years the prospect of a happier life had risen above his horizon?

For Anthony Mallaby's life had not been a happy one. He was, he knew it and he no longer burked the fact, a failure. Not his fault admittedly, but none the less a failure for that. His childhood had been all that could have been desired, at least while his solicitor father was alive. He had done well at school and better at college, and, deciding on medicine, had passed his finals with brilliance. At that time he was looked upon as a coming man in the mental and neurological fields which he had determined to make his own. Then came illness, a long slow wearing complaint. After hovering for weeks between life and death he had recovered, the wraith of his former self. Gone for many a long month was his energy, gone for ever was his ambition. When able once again to practise he took some voyages as a ship's doctor and then bought the tiny practice at Little Wokeham. It gave him enough work to keep him occupied, all he could do in fact, but it utterly failed to fill his life. As the years passed he had slowly regained strength, though by the time he felt fit enough to take up his former studies he had found it was too late to do so. Now at forty-three he knew what he was. Bitterly he had given up hope of ever tasting success.

Though the hamlet of Little Wokeham was within thirty miles of Piccadilly Circus, it had remained delightfully unspoiled by the march of progress. Set on one of the lower levels of the Green Sand Ridge, its scattered groups of houses toned in with the oaks and firs and bitches of its surrounding heath. In a way it was an outpost of civilisation. Trains and buses gave it the cold shoulder, and those residents who yearned for high life, as represented by the cafés and cinemas of Guildford, had to walk a mile for a conveyance or take their own cars. Perhaps for this reason, it was very much a self-contained community, with its church, its chapel, its village hall, post office, two excellent inns (both with good sleeping accommodation), and even its petrol pumps, symbolically placed at its entrance as an indication to the traveller that here was a place which had not been afraid to move with the times.

Dr Mallaby soon made a very pleasant circle of acquaintances. He was retiring to the point of shyness, but he was generally liked, and whether he dropped in to the bar of the Three Swallows or called at a neighbour's house, he was greeted with smiles and made welcome. He lived at Green Gables, a cottage at the head of the village, and was looked after by an elderly housekeeper, Mrs Hepworth. She was an efficient if somewhat austere woman, and made him comfortable in a monosyllabic and rather gloomy way.

When Mallaby had been for eight years at Little Wokeham a new factor had come into his life. Hurst Lodge, one of the largest houses in the immediate vicinity, which had been empty during his residence, was let. It was in bad repair and an army of tradesmen erupted over house and grounds. Then, this visitation passing, the new residents arrived.

The affair caused a sensation in the village. The landlord of the Three Swallows redecorated his front and wondered if the gentlemen—if there were such—could be interested in his private bar. For the first time in living memory Mrs Bentham, the postmistress and keeper of the one general shop the place boasted, altered the display in her window. Mr Yardley of the garage polished his petrol pumps and thought with satisfaction that they were well placed for vehicles going to the Lodge. Even Mrs Hepworth thawed sufficiently to regale the doctor with her impressions of the family, gained from discussions with the village intelligence corps, together with observations from behind the surgery curtains, undertaken while her employer was on his rounds.

It appeared that the name of the family was Winnington and that it consisted of an old man, two younger men and a young woman. Further research revealed the facts that the old man was Mr Clarence Winnington, the younger men Mr Bernard Winnington and Mr Richard Horne, the former's nephew and secretary respectively, and the woman Miss Christina Winnington, niece to Clarence and sister to Bernard. In the opinion of the village they were 'gentry', and would probably prove valuable acquisitions. A staff of servants was installed, with a hard-featured man named Josephs at its head, and he dealt ably with the succession of optimistic milkmen, bakers, laundrymen and others who called with messages of goodwill.

It did not at first seem to Dr Mallaby that the new arrivals would make any personal difference to himself. But they had not been in residence a week till he was rung up from the Lodge. 'Mr Winnington's compliments,' said a stately voice, afterwards discovered to belong to Josephs, the butler. 'He is not feeling too well today and would be grateful if you could make it convenient to step round.'

A couple of hours later Mallaby stepped round—in his rather elderly Vauxhall. He was taken to the library, a charming room with a view of low tree-clad hills in one direction and in another a peep of the village, smothered in greenery. On a couch lay a tall thin man of about seventy, with heavy overhanging eyebrows, a great mass of untidy white hair, and a not too good-tempered expression.

'How are you, doctor?' he said, holding out his hand as Josephs announced 'Dr Mallaby.' 'Excuse my not getting up, but when I feel off colour like this I find I am better if I stay quiet. Won't you sit down?'

For a few moments they chatted about the district, and then came to Clarence's health. He suffered, it seemed, from indigestion, and when Mallaby had made his examination his honesty and worldly unwisdom came out in his verdict. Instead of insinuating that the case had been bungled and that he was going to put it right, he declared that he didn't think Winnington's former medical adviser's treatment could be improved on and that he would send some similar medicine. He could see that his patient looked disappointed, but he would make no concession to such human weakness. A few more remarks and he stood up to go.

At that moment the door opened and a woman of about thirty entered. Instantly Mallaby felt attracted to her. She was not particularly good-looking, in no sense a beauty, but she seemed to radiate an atmosphere of charm, of honesty and sympathy and kindliness, which went straight to the doctor's heart.

'Oh, sorry, Uncle Clarence,' she said. 'I didn't know you were engaged.'

'Come in, Christina. This is Dr Mallaby. My niece, Miss Christina Winnington.'

She shook hands with a friendly smile.

'What a delightful country this is,' she said. 'After the part of the Midlands we were in, it's like heaven.'

'Yes,' agreed Winnington, 'we wanted to be near, but not too near Town, and I think we've just hit the proper mean.'

'It's a pleasant neighbourhood,' Mallaby admitted, 'particularly if you're fond of walking.'

'Oh yes,' Miss Winnington answered with fervour. 'I'm having a grand time exploring, and I've fallen in love with the heath.'

For five minutes they stood chatting, and then Mallaby thought it advisable to remember an engagement. Again when she shook hands there came that engaging smile.

Some days later, when Mallaby was paying the old man another call, he met her in the hall on his way out.

'Oh,' she said, walking over, 'tea's just coming in. Won't you stay?'

With a feeling of distinct pleasure he accepted. Old Winnington, he fancied, was rather surprised to see him in the lounge, though he welcomed him civilly enough. His manner, however, grew cordial when a chance remark revealed the fact that Mallaby knew the West Indies.

'When were you there?' he asked. 'I was governor of Trinaica for twenty years. I've just retired.'

'Then I must have been there during your term,' returned Mallaby. 'But I think I exaggerated when I said I knew the island. When I was a young man my health broke down, and during convalescence I took a number of voyages as a ship's doctor. We called several times at Trinaica and I've been over most of the island. I don't know it in the sense of having lived there.'

'Ever met Dr Brook?'

Mallaby smiled. 'The M.D. at Queenston? Oh yes. A nice fellow. He took me to the club on several occasions.'

'I envy you both,' put in Christina. 'The one thing I want, Dr Mallaby, is to travel: to see places like Trinaica. What a feast of memories you must have to look back on.'

'Sentiment, all pure sentiment,' Winnington grunted. 'No place out there as pleasant as this: is there, doctor?'

'They appeal in a different way, of course,' Mallaby returned diplomatically, 'but I can thoroughly appreciate Miss Winnington's view.'

As he spoke the two other members of the household entered the room. Bernard Winnington, Christina's brother, was a good-looking man. He had better features than his sister, though he did not look so amiable. His face in repose bore an anxious expression, and though he laughed and chatted easily enough, Mallaby imagined he was not happy. Horne, the other man, was introduced by Winnington as 'my secretary'. He was a quiet, efficient-looking man of about thirty-five, not very striking in any way, but seemingly of a good type. Mallaby took to them both.

He was somewhat at a loss to understand why a retired man like Winnington should require such a superior secretary. A chance remark revealed the explanation. Winnington was writing a history of his family. He was evidently one of those people who glory in genealogies, particularly when they can trace their own descent through many generations. Winnington's ancestors, it appeared, had fought at Crécy, at Trafalgar, at Omdurman and at Mons, as well as occupying all sorts of other distinguished positions. Mallaby, who also came of an old family, felt that the man had some excuse for perpetuating the record.

He was amused by the reactions of the four persons towards the project. Old Winnington evidently took it with extreme seriousness, in which view he was backed up by Horne, doubtless for the obvious reason. On the other hand, while Bernard's and Christina's remarks were models of correctitude, he was satisfied that both spoke with their tongues in their cheeks.

Mallaby paid several other visits to Hurst Lodge, but it was some time before he had an opportunity of talking alone to Christina. Then one day when he was crossing the heath after a call on a patient, he overtook her with two of her dogs. Their ways lay together and they fell in side by side.

It was upon this occasion that for the first time their talk grew intimate. With her kindly manner Christina broke down Mallaby's shyness, and he told her of his life, his early ambitions, his long illness and slow recovery, ending, as it had, in his present backwater. She said little in reply, but he felt her sympathy, and as he spoke he felt happier than he had done for years.

'I'm afraid,' he said as they parted, 'I've been talking too much about myself, but when you were so kind as to listen, I just couldn't resist it.'

'I feel you have paid me a compliment by telling me,' she returned gravely.

This meeting was followed by others, not designed by either party and at comparatively long intervals. But as the months passed a gradual change came over Mallaby, and at last he realised that what he thought could never happen to him had taken place. He had fallen in love. How, he thought, could anyone who saw Christina Winnington do anything else? She was not like anyone he had ever met. So kind, so good, so understanding, so sensible. Why, just to be in her presence was like a healing salve on a throbbing sore; it brought him peace, banishing that substratum of bitterness which always lay more or less consciously at the core of his being.

Nearly nine months after the Winningtons' arrival at Hurst Lodge a tremendous event happened to Mallaby. He received a letter in an unknown hand, and when he tore it open his drab surgery suddenly became a brighter place. It read:

> HURST LODGE,
> THURSDAY.

Dear Dr Mallaby,

We hope you will come and dine with us quite informally on Saturday at 8.00. Just the family!

Yours sincerely,

Christina Winnington.

Mallaby stared as if the words were written in letters of gold.

'She likes me!' he thought. 'If she didn't, she wouldn't have asked me.' In his humility the idea filled him with a joyful and wondering surprise.

He was as nervous as a boy going for his first aim vote when he drove up to Hurst Lodge on Saturday evening. He found the prospect of dining with Christina intoxicating, but his diffidence made it also a little alarming. Devoutly he hoped he would do her—and himself—justice.

He found the quartet in the lounge. They were certainly striking-looking people. Clarence with his tall frame, strong face and mass of white hair, was even now a fine figure of a man, and in his prime must have been positively impressive. Bernard also had an air of distinction, though somehow he looked just a little gone to seed. Horne, polite and smiling, gave an extraordinary impression of competence, as if he would quietly though unhesitatingly deal with any conceivable situation which might arise. And Christina! Mallaby caught his breath as he saw her for the first time in a dinner-frock. Why, she was beautiful! In her sports clothes he had not realised it, but now he knew that she was by far the most charming-looking woman he had ever seen.

Their greetings were cordial enough, if somewhat offhand, but before they settled down to conversation two other persons entered the room. These were the Plants, whom Mallaby had met on various previous occasions. Mrs Plant and Christina were sisters.

Bellissa Plant was a large slightly untidy woman with a look of Christina, a caricature, as Mallaby told himself. Both appearance and manner proclaimed her soft and easy-going, but she seemed kindly and the two sisters were obviously very fond of one another.

Her husband, Guy Plant, was of a different type. Thick-set and powerfully built, he had a dark saturnine face, with hard eyes and a rat-trap mouth. He looked a man of ruthless determination, and not too pleasant at that. An ugly person to cross, thought Mallaby, hoping he should never be called upon to do it. His manner, however, was pleasant, but Mallaby noticed that though he smiled frequently, his eyes never once softened.

From chance remarks on previous meetings Mallaby had learnt a good deal about these two. Plant, it seemed, was in shipping and had an office in Queen Victoria Street.

What his exact position was had not emerged, though with such a face it could not be otherwise than important. He and Bellissa had been married for six years and had one son, now just gone to a kindergarten. They lived on the southern outskirts of Weybridge and seemed to have plenty of money. All this, Mallaby felt, might have been expected, but what had considerably surprised him was to learn that before her marriage Bellissa had been her husband's secretary.

About Horne, Mallaby thought there was a minor mystery. He had been, he had once said, a journalist working in Fleet Street on the staff of one of the big dailies. From his personality it was impossible to believe he had been unsuccessful. Why then had he left so promising a job for one which was an obvious backwater?

As the meal progressed, and still more markedly in the lounge after it, Mallaby glimpsed for the first time an unexpected factor in the household. There was an undercurrent of strain in the atmosphere. It was an impression rather than a clear-cut manifestation, though none the less convincing for that. Beneath the apparent easy and happy life at Hurst Lodge all was not well. With the exception of Horne, who seemed completely at ease, every single member of the circle was affected in one way or another. With Clarence Winnington it took the form of a testy irritation and an insistence on getting his own way in every immaterial trifle. Bernard's features, when he was not actually speaking, relapsed into an expression of anxiety as if he were facing some urgent and wearing problem. It was the same with Plant. He seemed also to be bearing a secret burden of care. Mallaby indeed wondered whether there was not in his eyes a trace of actual fear.

Both women were also affected, though to a lesser degree. With Bellissa it seemed mere unhappiness, but with Christina doubt and misgiving appeared predominant.

More than once Mallaby took himself to task for allowing his imagination to run away with him, but he could not rid himself of the thought that there was a spectre in the life of Hurst Lodge. The suggestion that Christina might be unhappy was like a physical pain, but even if he knew how, he was not in a position to help her.

When the evening was over and he drove home he took with him a good deal to think about. With Christina he was more hopelessly in love than ever. Her grace, her beauty, her kindness were a marvel. Her smile when he was leaving had turned his heart to water. For her he would do anything and suffer anything in the world.

There was joy in his mind, but it was mingled with despair. No woman living as she lived would marry the penniless—or almost penniless—doctor of a community like Little Wokeham. What had he to offer Christina? Nothing but poverty and renunciation! No, Christina was not for such as he.

Yet he wondered. Was she really happy? Wealth and luxury were powerful advantages, but peace of mind might be more important still. Could it be that residence at Hurst Lodge carried with it some condition which would make Christina glad to exchange it for a home of her own, even though a poor one by the world's standards?

A faint tinge of hope mingled with Mallaby's doubts as he put away his car and let himself silently into his house.

2

Christina Winnington

To Christina Winnington one of the greatest assets of Little Wokeham was its heath. Five minutes' walk from Hurst Lodge she could take her stand on a certain small hillock, rotate on her own axis through three hundred and sixty degrees, and not see a human habitation. Houses there were, of course, but they were blocked out by a plantation of pines, close and solid, a heavy serrated wall of dark green. For nearly a mile in two other directions the heath ran on, open and wild and primitive, with its miniature hills and valleys and plains covered with heather and bracken, gorse and birch, pine and an occasional clump of oak. Traversing it in all directions were innumerable sandy tracks and paths, all very similar, all charming and irresistible alike to horsemen and hikers. How these paths came into being and remained so well trodden Christina could not imagine, for she seldom met other users, and her uncle's suggestion that they all led eventually to public-houses seemed to her demonstrably untrue.

Her appreciation was added to by the joy the heath

gave her two cocker spaniels. For them it was paradise. Christina loved to see them dash about, enthralled by the scents of hares and rabbits, so completely immersed in their business, so wholehearted in their delight. As she tramped along one morning in the week after Mallaby had dined at Hurst Lodge, she contrasted their present rambles with the heart-breaking walks on the chain which were all that she could give them in their last home in the suburbs of Sheffield.

To herself the change to Little Wokeham had been almost as great. Indeed, as she looked back on her life it seemed to have been a series of changes, each more fundamental than the last.

The first was the death of her mother. It occurred when she was seven, with Bellissa two years older and Bernard a sturdy urchin of ten. Their old nurse then took charge, a conscientious woman, but hard and matter of fact. Christina missed the companionship she had been accustomed to, and learnt to keep her feelings to herself. That was a change, and a big one.

It was fifteen years to the next. During this time she and Bellissa lived on with their father in their old home near Newton Abbot in Devon, Bernard joining them for Ms vacations till he came down from Oxford, when he left to enter a solicitor's office in Town. Their father Marmaduke Winnington was what used to be known as a country gentleman, a type now almost extinct. Having inherited a considerable sum, he had grown easy-going and careless of money, and his daughters had learnt to avoid the subject of finance.

When Christina was twenty-two the pleasant monotony was interrupted and a bitter experience brought another change into her life. A young neighbour fell in love with her and asked her to marry him. She was fond of him and she agreed. Then, a week before the wedding, he was killed while motoring.

For the time being her own life seemed to be at an end, and then two more blows fell on her, so pressing and heavy that her loss became correspondingly dwarfed. The first was her father's death; the second, the discovery that he had been living on his capital and that only a pittance remained to be divided among his children.

Bernard, who had never taken his professional duties seriously, was earning only a microscopic salary. However, by joining forces the three were able to take a tiny house in Pinner. Bellissa studied shorthand and typing and eventually got a job in the Yellow Star Line offices, while Christina kept house for the trio.

For five years they lived together, not unhappily, and then still another change befell them. It came through Guy Plant, the accountant of the Yellow Star Line and Bellissa's chief. Bellissa had by this time been promoted to be his personal secretary. She was of a very different type from the average girl clerk, and Plant fell in love with her and asked her to marry him.

The proposal presented Bellissa with a time-honoured dilemma. In her new limited sphere the match would be a fine one for her. The drudgery of the office would be ended and her material future would be assured. On the other hand, if she were to refuse she could scarcely remain in Plant's office and he might make it difficult for her to get another job. The arguments for acceptance were strong.

Against it there was only one: she did not love her suitor. She told herself that this need not matter, mutual forbearance and esteem could lead to happiness. She knew also that it might bring misery and disaster.

For a week she hesitated, then her easy-going character won. She took the line of least resistance. Three months later they were married.

The loss of Bellissa's contribution made things difficult for the other two, and Christina had just determined to look out for a job when a new and unexpected factor arose in their lives. Clarence Winnington, their father's brother, retired from his governorship in the West Indies, came home, and opened his house to them.

It was many years since they had seen their uncle, who had not till then evinced any particular interest in their existence. The first news they had from him was an invitation to dine at the Savoy. Slightly surprised, they accepted without suspecting an ulterior motive. That he had an ulterior motive they soon discovered. First, as he admitted sardonically, he wanted to see what they were like. Then, as apparently they satisfied his criteria, he made them a sporting offer. He was alone in the world and lonely. He wanted to settle down in England. If they would come and live with him, running his house and helping to entertain his guests, he would provide a comfortable home and a hearty welcome.

'Another thing I must tell you before you make up your minds,' he went on, 'because it's a factor which you should consider. While I've been abroad I've collected in one way or another a bit of money; in fact, rather more than a bit. If you can see your way to do what I ask, I'll leave you a third each: I don't want to make distinctions, so one-third will go to Bellissa. When succession duties are paid, that will mean about twenty thousand apiece. Well, think

16

it over and come and dine again in a week and let me know what you've decided.'

They thought it over, not during the coming week but during the next half-hour, and then agreement was reached. Subject to their being free to leave at any time they desired after the expiration of one year—in which case they would forfeit the legacy—they accepted his terms. So long as they fulfilled their contract they would be free to order their lives as they thought best. Finance was to be his concern, excepting for their personal expenses, which they could meet out of their own money. Christina would have an entirely free hand with the house and servants, but Bernard was to leave his office and spend most of his time with the others. Clarence had been lent a house at Sheffield, but this was only a temporary convenience. They would look about till they found some place which they really liked, and in the choice Clarence promised to consider their preferences as well as his own.

To be near Bellissa, Christina at once voted for Surrey or Hampshire, and as both Clarence and Bernard wished to be within easy reach of Town, this was agreed to. A lengthy search discovered Little Wokeham and Hurst Lodge, to which in due course they moved.

The brother and sister had early found that there was to be another member of the household. Clarence had advertised for a literary assistant, and Richard Horne had applied and been engaged. He came to Sheffield shortly after the others and was soon immersed in researches for the family history.

Christina took to Horne at once. He was quiet and unassuming, and yet quite a personality. He slipped easily into their household arrangements, gave no trouble, and with his ready smile was always anxious to render a service. He had a sense of humour which she found a great asset, and his eminently sane outlook helped her to keep things in their proper perspective.

Christina presently realised that the job she had taken on was no sinecure. Hurst Lodge was a biggish house, and even with the stat? of servants under Josephs it took a good deal of running. Clarence was fond of company and people were constantly dropping in for meals and having to be put up. Bernard, on the other hand, was up against the difficulty of finding enough to occupy himself. Though he looked after his uncle's guests as well as the outside of the establishment and dealt with accounts and correspondence, time hung heavy on his hands.

The real snag in the new arrangement was not, however, the work. It was Clarence himself. They soon found out that to put up with him and his idiosyncrasies was about as much as they could manage. He was arbitrary and domineering and given to sarcasm, which Christina always considered an unpardonable offence. Being so important a man in his West Indian island seemed to have had a bad effect on him, and now that he was once again a private individual, he had no one but his niece and nephew on whom to vent his spleen. More than once Christina regretted that they had joined with him; then, when she faced the alternative, the advantages of the partnership appeared so overwhelming that she was content to remain where she was.

Her views were shared by Bernard.

'Sometimes when the Old Devil makes one of his smart-alick speeches I feel I could take the poker and bash in his head; then I think, well, the price might be rather high for a moment's pleasure. Fortunately he's over seventy and I don't think his heart's any too good. Has to go slow on a hill, you know: begins to pant.'

She shuddered. 'Horrible to consider it like that.'

'Not a bit of it. You don't suppose he wanted to benefit us when he asked us here? He was thinking of himself, first, last and all the time. We only get his money when he can't use it any more himself, and we work jolly hard for it. Do be reasonable, Christina.'

'I admit it's worse for you than for me. I have the house as an interest and I'm fond of the garden, but you haven't much to keep you going.'

'Better than that rotten office in Town, at all events. Besides, I'm—how do you put it?—reacting advantageously to my environment. Things aren't so bad since I got to know those Montgomerys. They're fond of racing, and you know, it's rather sport. We've been at two or three places together and we're going again shortly.'

'But that's expensive surely? I don't see Father's money running to it.'

Bernard winked slowly. 'Ah,' he said somewhat cryptically, 'there's more in most things than meets the eye. Do you know that I've made forty-seven pounds and ten shillings over and above my expenses already? That's a worthwhile game.'

'You won't always win.'

'No, my little optimist, I won't. If I win on the balance it'll do me. And I'm pretty safe about that. Bert Montgomery knows a man in the Clevedon stables, and now and again for a consideration he ups and outs with a pretty valuable tip.'

'I don't see how you can believe in that,' Christina

returned primly. 'If the stableman really knew anything about it, he'd bet himself.'

'Ha ha!' Bernard laughed. 'Clever little girl. Knows a thing or two, doesn't she? Of course he would—if he had the cash. As he hasn't, he sells for a small cert and lets the buyer take the risk.'

Christina could seldom vanquish her brother in argument, and now she did not try. She merely said she was sorry he had begun to bet and expressed a pious hope that it would not lead to disaster. He grinned.

'Don't you wish it would, so as to prove you right,' he mocked, and changed the subject.

To Christina one of the great advantages of her new job was its proximity to Bellissa. Little Wokeham was only fifteen miles from Weybridge and the sisters saw a good deal of each other. Christina could ask any guests she chose to Hurst Lodge, and Bellissa was constantly coming for lunch or dinner or spending the night. Bellissa's marriage had unfortunately not proved very happy. If Clarence was difficult, Guy Plant was at times actually offensive. He was mean about money, and though as accountant of such an important company his salary ran into four figures, Bellissa had a constant struggle to make ends meet. Their personal relations also had deteriorated. She charged him with not keeping his bargain as to their conditions of living, and he accused her of having married him solely for his money. Outwardly things were still normal, but Christina knew that trouble might come at any moment.

These various reactions were what had caused the feeling of strain in the family atmosphere which Mallaby had noticed when he dined for the first time at Hurst Lodge.

Christina was perfectly conscious of the effect she had

produced on Mallaby during these last months. At first he had seemed to her an old fogy, though a rather nice old fogy. He reminded her of her father and the type of people she used to meet at her home. Like her father, he was good and kind and ineffective. She thought of him as an innocent old lamb who didn't know enough to come in out of the rain and who obviously wanted a woman to look after him. In short, he aroused her maternal instincts.

But when they had their walk and he told her the history of his life, she realised that she had misjudged him. He was not really weak and ineffective. It was his deprecating manner which had produced the illusion. As she saw more of him she began in a slightly condescending way to grow fond of him.

Not indeed then nor for a considerable time after did the idea of marrying him occur to her, but eventually she began to think she might do worse. She could, she knew, guide his actions into any direction she chose. Again and again she wondered whether marriage would lead to their mutual happiness.

It was Bellissa who first made the matter seem one of practical politics. She was talking one day about her own marriage.

'I don't know what's come over Guy recently,' she complained. 'His temper's fiendish. Nothing that I can say or do is right.'

'Worse than before?'

'Much worse. He's got something on his mind, but he won't say what it is. I've asked him twice, and each time he has gone completely off the deep end.'

'Poor Bellissa! Hard luck.'

'It's money, I think. At least, I'm finding it harder than

ever to run the house. I simply can't get out of him what is required.'

'You don't know how the business is doing?'

'It couldn't be that; he's got a fixed salary. I sometimes wonder if he's got another establishment.'

'Oh, Bellissa, don't say such a thing!'

'Perhaps I oughtn't to. I admit he's never given me any reason to suspect it. I don't know, Christina: sometimes I feel that if it wasn't for the boy I'd leave him.'

'My dear, is it as bad as that?'

'It's my own fault. I should have known—I did know, when I saw how he treated the staff. That was before he—wanted to marry me. I knew he could be horrid if he wanted to.'

'But that's different. Anyone that's any good can be that.'

'Not necessarily. Your old doctor friend couldn't: not if he found someone trying to murder him. Oh, if I had only married someone like him things would have been different.'

'He could never make the money that Guy does.'

'So much the better. It's money that has been a curse to Guy. Why don't you marry your doctor, Christina? Things can't be any too pleasant for you here.'

'They're not really. But you know our position. Living on our expectations, though it comes as a bit of a shock to put it like that. Yet it's the truth.'

'But he wouldn't cut you out of his will if you married. He hasn't cut me out.'

'I don't know. Your marriage made no difference to him; it was done before he came home. But if I were married he'd have to get someone else to run this house. I don't really know where he'd find anyone else to put up with him: I mean, unless he left her his money.'

Bellissa swung round and faced her sister. 'Don't be a fool, Christina! Don't sell your happiness for cash. I've tried it, and it doesn't work. You know if you married Dr Mallaby he'd do exactly as you said in everything.'

'He hasn't asked me, and if he knew I was heir to twenty thousand he wouldn't.'

Bellissa made a rude retort. 'If he had any say in it you're more of a fool than I took you for.'

This conversation made a deep impression on Christina. Wearily she took stock of her position. Was she, like Bernard, really only waiting till her uncle should die to get her twenty thousand? Yes, in honesty that was what it came to. And she knew in her heart that Bellissa was right about the value of money. Yet—twenty thousand was twenty thousand.

Then she told herself that things were not so bad as she was making out. She was doing all she could to make her uncle's life easy for him, and the payment for the work was what he had himself suggested. The money she hoped for was being honestly earned. Putting up with his domineering ways and hurtful sarcasms was part of the service required.

But would marriage with Anthony Mallaby resolve her difficulties? As Bellissa had said, she believed that if she chose she could bring it about. Of course her uncle might not cut her out of his will, but if he did, she would still have her own pittance to add to Mallaby's income. Would she be happier so? She did not know.

Her advantage, however, was only the smaller part of it. What about his? She felt sure he loved her and wanted to marry her, but she could not give him love in return. Would it be fair to offer him anything less? Of course she

23

could do something for him. He was lonely and wanted a companion. Well, she could give him companionship. He wanted looking after. She could make him comfortable and, she thought, happy. Would that be enough?

The question was terribly difficult and Christina could not see her way clear. Almost inevitably she temporised. As the weeks passed she remained pleasant and friendly to Mallaby, but avoided anything which might bring matters to a head.

In the meantime all four members of the household were becoming old inhabitants of Little Wokeham, and all were agreed in at least one thing: that the more they knew of the place, the better they liked it.

3

Guy Plant

Bellissa Plant had been correct when she told Christina that her husband was in some kind of trouble and that she imagined it was financial. The truth was that he did not know where to turn for money.

One evening a few weeks after the sisters' conversation and over a year after the Winningtons had moved to Hurst Lodge, Plant was seated in the deepest armchair in the study of his house on the outskirts of Weybridge, painfully taking stock of his position. Having ascertained just where he stood, his eyes were now staring before him into vacancy and his fingers trifled with the pad on which he had jotted down his figures, while he tried desperately to find some way out of the difficulties which beset him.

Guy Plant had not been intended for a business career. His father was a doctor in general practice in the country near Liverpool, and the old man's idea had been that his son should follow in his steps. He had taught the boy a good deal about medicine, particularly the routine of a country practitioner's life. But while Guy readily absorbed his teaching—as he did any information which came to him—his special aptitude for figures was not to be denied, and when the time came to make a definite choice, he decided for finance rather than medicine. Having qualified as a chartered accountant, he entered the accountant's department in the Liverpool office of the Yellow Star Line. His superiors, impressed by the young man's ability and grit, transferred him first for three years to their Marseilles office, and then to a good position at their headquarters in London. In this latter job he did excellent work for several years. As a result of the successful reorganisation of an unsatisfactory subsidiary business, he was promoted to second in command, and when his chief retired upon age-limit five years later, he succeeded him.

For a time his energies were devoted to improving the efficiency of his department, but when this had been brought to as near perfection as seemed possible and his work became largely routine, he grew tired of it and looked about for some other interest.

He found it through the conversation of a stockbroker friend with whom one day he was lunching. This man described how from following political trends he had been able to forecast first the fall and then the rise of a certain foreign government's stocks. The expected fall having taken place, he had bought to the limit of his ability. Presently the rise had followed and he had sold with a four-figure profit. If his friend had told the story in the hope of a commission he was disappointed. Plant wanted to repeat the trick himself. He was not particularly anxious to make more money; his tastes were simple and his salary ample for all his requirements. But the idea of pitting his brain against the market thrilled him. He began an intensive study of international finance.

For several weeks no trends such as his friend had observed suggested themselves; then he thought that a rise in oils and petrols was likely. He estimated the amount, sat back, and waited to see what would happen. Within the period he had forecast oils rose by very nearly the percentage he had guessed.

This disaster, for to him it was nothing less, confirmed his faith in his own ability. Now he felt satisfied that his superior intellect would enable him to foresee coming events more clearly than other men. For many more weeks he watched and studied; then he thought that a change of government in one of the South American republics, which he believed imminent, would raise the value of its stocks. He bought with every penny he could raise. The government fell, a more stable one took its place, the stocks appreciated, and Plant cleared a substantial sum. A few weeks later he tried again and scored a further success. The second and third of his disasters!

It was at this time that, already a little bored with his new hobby, Plant first began to notice his secretary, Bellissa Winnington. Up till then women had played but a small part in his life, but now, perhaps for this very reason, he fell devastatingly in love. His cautious nature would have liked to avoid matrimony, but he soon found that no progress with Bellissa was to be hoped for on other lines and presently he proposed. He was astounded and his desire was whetted when she did not immediately accept, but asked for a week to think it over.

His delight when eventually she consented was intense, and for a time he lived in a heaven such as he had not believed existed. Together they searched for a house, fixing at last on Ivy Cottage, in the southern suburbs of Weybridge. The painting and papering, the furnishing and the various other preparations, passed as an entrancing dream. Then came the wedding and the honeymoon in Italy.

It was during the honeymoon that the first pangs of doubt arose in Guy Plant's mind. Somehow being with Bellissa did not prove the joy he had expected. She was kind and pleasant, but he soon saw that this was due to her easy-going nature rather than to any particular liking for himself. Gradually he realised that he bored her, and then at long last that his presence was actually irksome to her. No longer could he hide the fact that the foundations of his happiness were laid upon sand.

While this was true, Bellissa's intentions had been of the best. She was out to make him a good wife, and had he accepted what she could give him and treated her with affection, their married life might have been successful enough. That he did not do so was his misfortune, if perhaps not altogether his fault. He found his discovery, with its revulsion of feeling, too bitter to hide. He felt cheated and grew harder and more self-centred, more sardonic, less pleasant to his subordinates and to her. He drew away from her in their home life, retiring in the evenings to his study and taking little interest in her affairs. While outwardly they remained on good terms, the possibility of real sympathy and understanding between them slowly died.

Under these circumstances it was perhaps inevitable that when the sharp edge of his disappointment had worn off he should have recourse again to his Stock Exchange operations. The excitement took his thoughts off domestic affairs. He was now less careful before he plunged, and he began to back fancies instead of considered opinions. The inevitable, of course, happened. He began to lose. His natural caution warned him to take no more risks, and for a time he did draw in his horns.

Then occurred the return of Clarence Winnington to England, the setting up of the Hurst Lodge establishment, and more important to Guy Plant, the disclosure of the fact that on Clarence's death Bellissa would, unless her uncle changed his mind, inherit the sum of twenty thousand pounds. This profoundly altered his outlook. He knew that, owing to Bellissa's easy-going character, twenty thousand left to her was twenty thousand left to him.

Somehow, with this sum in the background his Stock Exchange losses shrank in importance. Again he began to indulge in what was practically gambling, sometimes making a few pounds, but usually losing. Then in a moment of recklessness he plunged, buying a large block of Mexican shares which he could not cover, in the expectation that they would rise and that he could sell at a profit. Under normal conditions his action would probably have been justified, but unhappily a tornado wiped out the expected profits and he was faced with a ruinous loss. To meet it he had to borrow, and now he could not repay the loan. This was the disastrous fact that he was considering as on this evening, over a year after the Winningtons had moved to Hurst Lodge, he sat in his study taking stock of his position.

What an incredible fool he had been! He had meant to amuse himself, to relieve his boredom, to have a little excitement, and then to stop before he became in any way involved. Why had he not stopped? He did not know, except that the thing was more insidious than he had realised.

Irritably he pulled himself up. This kind of thinking would get him nowhere. Regrets were useless. He must have money or he would go under.

Money! The more Plant thought of it, the more the idea of his wife's legacy forced itself into his consciousness. Twenty thousand! If he had a twentieth of it his difficulties would be over.

All the same, there was no help here. Even if Clarence Winnington did not alter his will, which he might easily do, he was a hale and hearty man showing no symptom of an early decease. The fact that he was seventy-two counted for nothing: he might live another twenty years and more. But twenty thousand pounds in twenty years' time would be no use to Plant. He must have the money now. By mortgaging his house and insurance policy he could postpone the crisis for a few weeks. But it would only be a postponement. Without additional cash he was lost.

For the first time Guy Plant forced himself to consider what his failure to raise the money would mean. There was only one word for it: ruin, ruin utter and complete. It would mean personal misery and wretchedness. It would mean bankruptcy, leaving his home, giving up his possessions, losing his job and his salary. It would mean having to start life again at the age of thirty-nine, penniless and handicapped by a wife and son, and debarred from getting the sort of work he could do. He thought of himself more than of Bellissa—not, to do him justice, through mere selfishness, but because he felt Bellissa would find a home

30

with her uncle. For himself death would be preferable: if only he had the courage to commit suicide. But had he? As shrinkingly he looked forward to the possibility, he doubted it.

No, a failure to get the thousand-odd he was in need of would be the end. He simply could not face it. No matter at what cost, he must raise the money.

It was then for the first time that a very horrible idea shot into his mind. Bellissa's legacy! Was there no way in which the existing conditions might be altered, so that he could get it at once?

When he realised what he had really thought, he felt a shock of horror. He, Guy Plant, a . . . Even in his mind he boggled over the word. A *murderer*! Never! It had been an idea only.

He tried to banish it, but it returned. If Clarence Winnington should die without altering his will, Bellissa would get twenty thousand pounds. Directly the death occurred she could, if she asked for it, get an advance on her legacy. And just such an advance would save him, would save her, would save their home and their name and their happiness. A solution of all their troubles: if Clarence Winnington were to die.

The sweat formed on Plant's brow. He must not think of such a thing. It was madness; he must retain his sanity. All the same, he would be saved: if Clarence Winnington were to die!

Relief surged back into his mind as he suddenly saw that his dreadful remedy was out of the question. Even if he wished to, he could not murder Clarence. He would be found out, inevitably and without hope of escape. There was no way in which it could be done secretly.

Again he wiped his forehead. Was there not? Suppose . . .

His eyes took on a look of horror as his idea took shape, developed, and grew with dreadful rapidity from a vague nebulous conception to a feasible plan, increasingly clear-cut in its details. Yes, he now believed that Clarence could be murdered and with complete safety, provided only that there was nothing to suggest the identity of the murderer, because once the police were really suspicious they pried and nosed till they got their proof. Thank heaven, in his case there was something to suggest it. Bellissa's legacy would be like a hand pointing unmistakably to himself. An attempt would mean certain conviction. He dared not risk it.

Unless he had an alibi.

Plant had always been interested in crime stories and he had more than once amused himself by thinking out a perfect alibi. He had devised one which would, he was convinced, prove absolutely watertight and unbreakable. Unfortunately—or fortunately for him, as he now saw—it required two persons: one to commit the crime, the other to impersonate him elsewhere; this other, of course, having no motive or apparent connection with the affair. It was good, but in this case for an obvious reason it was inapplicable: there was no second person who would help him in such a way.

Relief was the predominant factor in Plant's mind as he realised that he could not, no matter how much he might be tempted, seriously consider the murder of Clarence Winnington. But that did not mean that he could do without money. As Bellissa's legacy faded from his view, he turned to another idea with which on various occasions he had trifled.

As accountant of the Yellow Star Line he had unique opportunities. Could he not borrow the needed thousand from the firm's overflowing coffers? Surely his ingenuity should be equal to the task?

Over this problem he now racked his brains. It would be extraordinarily difficult. A few pounds he could get easily enough and no one would be any the wiser, but when it ran into hundreds it was a different matter. The trouble was that all sizeable amounts were dealt with by cheque through the bank. He could sign a cheque in favour of some imaginary person and no doubt could get it countersigned, but he did not see how he could collect the money. Even if he were to retain the cheque, forging on it an endorsement and the bank's rubber stamp, he could not get the cash. It would remain in the bank and his books would simply be wrong.

His most hopeful line seemed to be in connection with the weekly pay roll. Some thousands of pounds were paid out in cash every week. The procedure was to send a cheque for each pay centre to the bank, from which the money required for that centre would be obtained, taken to the centre, and distributed by the pay clerks. The amounts of these cheques continually varied, and as the headquarters one was always large, it would be a simple matter to make it out for a bigger sum than was needed. If the director countersigning the cheques should question it, he could say that the extra represented the wages of the crew of a newly arrived ship. Plant was satisfied that there would be no trouble so far.

The allocation and book-keeping would be more difficult, but not, he thought, impossible. It would mean finding a set of pay sheets totalling the amount he required, forging a duplicate set, and getting the sets entered in the books by different clerks. The men would then be paid against one entry while he pocketed the money shown on the other. He believed he could use his position to prevent the fraud coming out. As soon as he was able to repay the money he would destroy the forgeries and himself discover the mistake. Of course, such a scheme would have to be completed before the annual audit, but this was not long over and he had some nine months in which to work.

Here again the difficulty would be to get his hands on the actual cash without arousing his clerk's suspicion. He might meet it by simply giving the necessary instructions in a sufficiently peremptory way, but then again he might not.

Next day when he had completed his routine work he sent for the books which concerned the actual handling of cash, so that he might examine the possibilities in greater detail. It was his habit to look into the working of various sections of his department in this way, so the action created no surprise. To make his check seem more convincing, he included the petty cash. Incidentally, the petty cash would be the easiest account to manipulate, and as it ran into fairly big figures he decided that, before dismissing it, he would estimate the number of weeks it would have to be cooked to bring him in the required amount.

As he looked down the items for the previous week he noticed one, large even for so big a business. It was for £1. 4s. 3d. for carriage collected by an L.M.S. carter for a consignment of ledgers from their Glasgow contractors.

There were scores of items in the week's account, but Plant's eye for figures was such that when, some pages further on, he came to another item for £1. 4s. 3d. he instantly recognised the sum. He was interested to find that it too represented the carriage on a package of ledgers from Glasgow.

He did not, of course, question these entries: he had no reason to doubt their accuracy. All the same, he thought it a coincidence that the packages should have chanced to be of precisely the same weight. However, when on going over the previous week he noticed a similar coincidence, his interest was definitely aroused. This time the items were for carriage on two crates of old records from their Aberdeen branch.

Plant sat back in his chair, thinking deeply. Then he turned to another week and went down the items with care. Once again he found the same thing: similar entries for two packages of officers' sample uniforms from their Bradford contractors.

He returned the accounts without comment, but for lunch he went to a certain restaurant which he only occasionally patronised. As he had hoped, he found there one of the higher officials in the L.M.S. Goods Department.

'I want you,' he said after due greetings had passed, 'to do me a favour. It's a microscopic matter, but confidential. I've found an entry in my books which I want to check. Could you let me have, without giving away that questions have been asked, a list of all last week's deliveries of packages from J. & H. Hudson Bros. of Glasgow to our head office?'

'Shall I write you?' the official asked.

'I'll be here tomorrow.'

'I'll bring it along.'

Next day Plant's suspicions were confirmed. Only one package had been delivered during the entire week.

He spent a quite disproportionate time thinking over the matter. There could be no doubt who was responsible. From the organisation of the office it could only be one clerk, a man named Arthur Crossley. He was an ingenious sort of fellow, thoroughly competent, and, if a trifle lazy, up till now had been satisfactory enough.

The next day Plant sent for him.

'Oh, Crossley,' he said, 'doing anything special this evening?'

'No, sir,' the man returned, evidently both surprised and relieved.

'This return that you make out,' Plant picked up a paper, 'is wanted early this month, tomorrow in fact. I'm too busy to look into it now, so I wish you'd bring it down to my house tonight. Do what you can to complete it, and I'll run through it with you then. You know where my house is?' and Plant explained.

It was an unusual, though not an unprecedented request. The return was not required, but if a question arose Plant would say that he had been expecting an interview with the Chairman next day, when a matter covered by it might come up.

There was a haggard look in Plant's eyes as that evening he reached his home.

4

Arthur Crossley

It was Arthur Crossley's inveterate habit of boasting which first brought him into trouble. From his earliest years he had sought to impress his friends by stirring tales of his prowess. Like Iago, none had made so many journeys or seen so many wonders as he had.

Otherwise Crossley was a harmless and indeed an estimable young man. He was steady and hard-working and well-mannered. His mind was quick and ingenious, which made him efficient at his business, if slightly impatient with his slower-witted colleagues. It was true that he frequently showed a tendency to take the line of least resistance, which indicated a fundamental weakness somewhere in his character.

His father, a bos'n on one of the Yellow Star Line ships, had given him as good an education as he could, and his influence had secured him a start as junior clerk in the firm's accounting department. Young Crossley had there done reasonably well, having been promoted twice in ten years. During this period his father and mother had died, leaving him alone in the world. He now had a bed-sitting-room in a narrow street in Chelsea, and as he paid regularly, gave little trouble and was always polite, his landlady thought the world of him, and, for fear of losing him, made him as comfortable as she knew how.

In spite of his easy manners, Crossley was not a good mixer and often in the evenings he felt lonely. He had tried to fill his free hours with various interests. He belonged to a gymnasium and a tennis club, he went to the pictures one night a week, and on Sundays he usually took a long cycle-trip into the country. But often his excursions were taken alone, and on these occasions he felt he was not getting all he could out of life.

When he fell in love, therefore, he did it abruptly and overwhelmingly. Jessie Howard queened it at the cash-desk of the restaurant he patronised for his midday meal, and when she first appeared he thought he had never seen such beauty. She was indeed a pretty girl, with her pale clear complexion, her dark hair and eyes, and her dainty yet competent air. She was not like so many in her position, a bored and slightly resentful money-changing automaton. When Crossley put down his check she glanced up and smiled as she gave him his change.

Crossley was intoxicated. He could not get that smile out of his mind. His lunches, which up to now had been dull enough, became the great event of his day. He hurried at breakneck speed from the office in the hope of getting a place from which she was visible, seated at her cash-desk like a beneficent and condescending prisoner in a small high-sided dock. He tried to leave the restaurant during a pause in the outgoing stream, so as to have a moment comparatively alone with her. This was not easy for it was a large place, but the first time he managed it he made with fear and trembling a halting remark. She replied with a brighter smile than ever.

The affair moved according to precedent. One evening, taking his courage in both hands, Crossley hurried from the office to the restaurant, and settling down to shadow the door, strolled about within its sight.

It was well after eight before she appeared. He was not a bad actor, and his start of surprise when they met would have deceived anyone less interested. That night she had an engagement and was in a hurry. To Crossley it did not matter, for in the few moments of their talk a date for the pictures had been made. Their visit was the first of many.

If during these evenings Arthur Crossley had kept to the literal truth, no harm would have resulted. Jessie Howard was a good and sensible girl and knew the value of money as well as anyone. But in Crossley's telling, his job grew more important and his salary greater than they really were. Jessie naturally did not see, when she was trying to please and amuse her companion, why some of this wealth should not be spent on her, and when he appeared to consider the cost too closely, she let him know that she thought him mean.

If anyone else had thought him mean it would not have mattered, but he was now so completely in love that Jessie's good opinion was for him the most important thing in the world. The obvious solution was to admit that he had been romancing and to tell her the truth, but unhappily he lacked the courage. He therefore turned to the alternative, to make more money.

This decision was easy to reach, but extraordinarily difficult to put into practice. For weeks he puzzled unsuccessfully over the problem.

Then an incident occurred which suggested a plan. It was his duty to pay small sums from the petty cash, and one day among other items he settled a cartage charge of two pounds with the vanman concerned. As he carried the receipt back to his desk he noticed that two of the sheets had stuck together. Beneath the receipt was a blank form.

For a time he did not envisage the possibilities which that form suggested, but soon the obvious idea occurred to him. Gradually he saw that here, with what was practically complete safety, two pounds were to be had for the picking up.

Simultaneously he realised that his action would be stealing. He fought against the idea, trying to banish it from his mind. The more he did so, the more enticing it appeared. Two pounds! That would cover a number of shows with Jessie, and perhaps a little dinner as well. Which, he asked himself, would he rather take, the microscopic risk or have Jessie turn him down for meanness?

The struggle was bitter, but the issue was not really in doubt. That evening he took the receipted waybill and the blank form home, and after some preliminary practice he produced a copy, identical save for the date, which he put five days later. When that date came round he put the forged receipt with the others, entered the amount for the second time in his books, and pocketed the money.

Though his conscience continued to give him some nasty jars, he was not afraid of discovery. It was unlikely that any immediate examination would be made into the petty cash, but if it were, he was still safe. There was a receipt for every penny that had gone out, and if either of the duplicate items was questioned, it would be found that a package of that description *was* delivered, for which the cost had been the figure given. It was unlikely to the last degree that every figure in his list would be followed up to its source, but again even if it were, he could plead that the mistake had not been his.

Those extra two pounds made an immense difference to his pleasure during the next week or two. Jessie beamed on him and life altogether became kinder and more rosy. But two pounds will not last for ever, and when the money was spent, the very fact that he had been so lavish made it all the harder for him to revert to previous conditions. Once again his problem grew acute.

His booty had been due to the happy accident of the extra form, but he could not hope for such a miracle to happen a second time. He gave the affair days of anxious thought, then decided there was only one thing to be done. He would duplicate his entries of certain other items, though without supplying corresponding receipts.

This was definitely dangerous. If one instance were discovered he could say he had made a mistake and entered the same figure twice, but if suspicion were aroused and investigation revealed other instances of the same thing, these could not be so easily explained. However, it was unlikely that such a close investigation would be made. In any case, Jessie's goodwill had become more than worth the risk, and he proceeded to carry out the plan.

Matters were in this state when he was thunderstruck to receive orders to take his books in to the chief himself, who was about to make one of his periodic examinations of how the work in his department was being done.

For the rest of that morning Crossley felt physically sick. Clinging desperately to hope, he reminded himself that there was nothing in the petty cash book to arouse

41

suspicion, and that though Plant might follow up a few items for his own satisfaction, he would never go through the whole of those in any one period. There was really no reason for fear.

All the same, his relief when the books were returned to him without comment was so great that he all but collapsed and gave himself away. Then as a couple of days passed and he heard nothing, his hopes grew to certainty; he was safe, not only for the moment, but for a considerable time to come. A second investigation was unlikely for several months, and long before the audit he would have found some way out of his difficulties. If the worst came to the worst he would have an accident. He would spill petrol from his lighter on the receipt file and set it on fire. By the time the flames were extinguished, the evidence against him would be gone.

Then came the summons to Plant's office, and for a moment he had a new qualm of fear. He fought it with fair success. When he found what he was wanted for, he realised once again the danger of giving way to panic. Let him act normally and all would be well: to appear frightened was to ask for trouble.

That evening, having duly completed the return, he took his bicycle and rode down to Weybridge. Not only would he enjoy the ride, but he might as well have the train fares, which he would enter up in his petty cash book. He found Ivy Cottage with a little difficulty, hid his bicycle behind a shrub inside the drive gate, and walked to the door.

He was admitted by a pleasant-looking maid who said Mr Plant was expecting him. She led the way up a single flight of stairs to a door in the back wing, threw it open, and announced him.

The room was small, but comfortably furnished as a man's sitting-room or study. Two deep chairs were drawn up to a cheerful fire, and a shaded standard lamp diffused a mellow light. In the window, now heavily curtained, was a flat-topped desk. Beside it stood a vertical file cabinet, and two of the walls were covered with bookshelves. In one of the easy-chairs sat Plant.

'Come along, Crossley,' he said pleasantly, but without getting up. 'Take a pew.' He pointed to the other armchair. 'Help yourself.' He indicated a box of cigarettes on a small table.

Crossley thanked him and lit up. This was a new and much more attractive chief than he had yet known. He had often read that men who were unapproachable in their offices could be very different in private life. It was a pleasant discovery.

His satisfaction was short-lived. Between the armchairs stood a small table on which lay a newspaper. Very quietly Plant reached forward and lifted the newspaper. Then he stared steadily and inquiringly at his guest.

Crossley's eyes dropped to the table, and as he saw what lay upon it an icy terror gripped him. There were three pieces of paper; the cartage receipt, his forged copy, and a list of the other payments he had doubled.

For some moments neither man moved; then Plant said softly, 'Well? What about it?'

Crossley found the question an anticlimax. What did it mean? The thing was known. There lay the evidence, and nothing that he could say would explain it away or make any difference. He was finished. Dismissal, of course, was a certainty, but perhaps even dismissal would not meet the case. He had left himself open to prosecution, perhaps even to—

Plant spoke more sharply. 'Well? What have you to say? I'll hear any excuse you have to offer.'

In a semi-stupor Crossley wondered why the man was talking like that. What could he answer? What excuse was there? This was ruin. At the very best, with this on his record, he would never get a clerk's job again. Then a pang, hideously sharp, shot through his mind. It was the end—with Jessie. Never again would he dare to see her, never—

Once more Plant's incisive voice broke into his musings.

'A serious matter, Crossley! Fraud, forgery, theft! To be put into a position of trust, to betray that trust, to steal the firm's money. A bad business. Theft and fraud are bad enough, but at forgery the judge always goes off the deep end.'

Crossley, white-faced and filled with anguish, stared without attempting a reply. Then a wave of self-pity swept over him.

'You couldn't—just this time—overlook it, sir?' he stammered. 'I've had—my lesson.'

Plant shook his head. 'If it was a matter between you and me I might, though I should be wrong. But as trustee for a public company I have no choice. How did it come to happen? Not, I'm afraid, that it can make any difference.'

Crossley seemed to himself to have dropped out of the affair. As if someone else was speaking he heard himself reply: 'I—I—got fond of a girl. I wanted to give her a good time.'

'Tell that to the judge, just as you've told it to me. It may make him take a more lenient view.'

Once again silence fell, and then Plant moved abruptly.

'I asked you to come down here to see if you had anything to say. If you haven't, I must ring up the police.'

Crossley stared at him dully. What was the good of all the talk? If the thing had to be, let him get on with it. In silence he shook his head.

Plant turned towards the telephone. Then he sank back again in his chair. He looked long and appraisingly at the huddled figure beside him.

'You're in a tight hole, Crossley,' he said at last. 'What would you do to get out of it?'

Crossley stared. To get out of it! What was the man raving about?

'I—I don't understand, sir,' he muttered hoarsely.

'Well, it's clear enough. If I could overlook and forget this, what would you do to earn it?'

Then the words did mean something! Overlook? Forget? A dreadful excitement rose in Crossley's mind.

'Do?' he cried in a strangled voice. 'Why, *anything*! Anything, willingly and thankfully.'

'Don't make promises you may not be able to keep,' Plant said grimly. 'But there is a way in which it might be overlooked.'

Crossley's eagerness grew painful. He hung breathlessly on the other's words.

'I'll be quite frank with you,' went on Plant. 'I can,' he smiled rather cruelly, 'because you're not in a position to give me away. The fact is that you're not the only one to dabble in crime. There's a little matter I want to pull off, and if you care to help me I'll forget about'—he pointed to the receipts—'these.'

Crossley could not believe his ears. His chief, the respected if unloved accountant of the Yellow Star Line, dabbling in crime! Impossible!

'Tell me, sir,' he gasped.

'You would have nothing to do with the affair directly.' Plant was now speaking in his ordinary matter-of-fact tones. 'You wouldn't even know what the crime was. In the unlikely event of discovery you'd of course be for it as well as I, but even then your ignorance would count in your favour. But I don't want you to go into it blindly. Don't imagine you'd get off. You wouldn't. You'd catch it hot. I want you to realise that.'

Crossley was speechless. He could only nod.

'What you'd have to do would merely be to help me with an alibi. On a certain evening you'd come down here secretly. I'd let you in and you'd sit in this room for two or three hours—while I was out. You'd have to move about occasionally, type at intervals, smoke to scent the air, turn off and on the wireless, and answer the telephone in my voice if it rang. The idea is that the servants, who are beneath and who would hear you, would swear I was here all the time. That's the lot. Or rather no, it's not the lot.' Plant bent forward and dropped his voice. 'If you did it well, I'd not only overlook this, but I'd give you a little of what you helped me to get. I'd give you something to spend on your young lady—one hundred pounds!'

Sweat stood in great drops on Crossley's forehead. A hundred pounds! If Plant offered anything like that the crime must be a pretty bad one. If it came out, to help with the alibi would surely mean prison. There was the moral side too. For the rest of his life he would have it on his conscience. It would be different to the petty cash affair; that he had slipped into, but this would be a deliberate choice.

Deliberate choice? What nonsense! What choice had he? As far as prison went, he was offered the chance of it as against the certainty. The moral side he need scarcely worry about; this new affair could not really be worse than what he had already done. No, he had no choice left.

When he thought of the other side of the picture his heart leaped. A hundred pounds! What could he not do for Jessie with a hundred pounds? Why, he could even ask her to marry him! In halting but eager language he agreed. He would do whatever Plant wanted.

Then a cold wave of doubt swept over him. If Plant was that sort of man, could he trust him? Might he not help with the alibi and then be given away?

'But would I—? Don't think me offensive, sir, but it's so important to me. If I did this, would I be—safe?'

For the first time Plant smiled his unmirthful smile. 'Safe that I wouldn't go back on you? You're quite right to ask that, and your question is not offensive. We'd each be absolutely safe from the other's treachery. You'd be safe, because you'd only have to tell about the alibi to get me arrested. I'd be safe, because you could only explain your knowledge by admitting your fraud and forgery. So we've both got no choice but to play straight.'

Crossley saw it. He was saved, but at a cost, a hideous cost. All the same, as he rode back to Town his feelings were mixed, and as he thought of Jessie, satisfaction at the evening's events began to outweigh his forebodings.

5

Christina Winnington

'Letter from Bellissa,' remarked Bernard Winnington as he laid an envelope on the table beside Christina one morning a few days after Arthur Crossley's unhappy interview with Guy Plant. 'Funny neither of you girls seem able to get the telephone habit. Why on earth does she trouble to write when she can talk to you at any hour of the day or night?'

They were breakfasting alone, an unusual experience at Hurst Lodge. Clarence had a touch of bronchitis and was staying in bed, and Horne had gone to Haltwhistle to try to trace the burial-place of a Winnington ancestor who was believed to have done great things in the Border wars.

'They want us to alter the date of the party from Thursday to Saturday,' said Christina, looking up from her letter. 'Guy has to go to Paris and won't be back till Saturday morning.'

'Just like him,' grumbled Bernard. 'We should alter our plans to suit his convenience. He doesn't suggest altering his to suit ours; no blooming fear!'

'It's easier for us. One day's the same as another here. His business appointments may be outside his control.'

'Then let him stay away. Who wants him here anyway? You don't and I don't, and I bet Bellissa doesn't.'

The party was a small family affair to mark Clarence Winnington's seventy-third birthday. He had, he explained, always given a party on his birthday, and this was the second to take place at Hurst Lodge. In the West Indies, where he had no relatives, outsiders had been asked, indeed it appeared to have been almost a state function, but last year it had been a purely family affair, and this time outside his immediate circle only Dr Mallaby was being invited.

Christina put down the letter and helped herself to coffee.

'Why do you dislike Guy so much, Bernard?' she asked. 'He's never done you any harm.'

'He hasn't because he's never had the chance. But I bet the date'll be altered. The Old Devil likes him. He kowtows, and that goes down.'

'I don't see why he shouldn't be polite to his wife's uncle.'

'He doesn't give two hoots about his wife's uncle, as you know very well. It's his wife's uncle's sixty thousand he grovels before. But it's all the same to me. I don't care whether the dam' party is on Thursday or Saturday or two years hence or never.'

'Bellissa seems to want it changed too.'

'Naturally. She's learnt by this time what it's healthy for her to want. But why Guy cares to come is a mystery to me. Likes to see his wife wearing jewels, I suppose. The Old Devil's persisting in that idiocy? He's having them down?'

Christina shrugged. 'Yes, same as last time.'

To make his celebration as impressive as possible, Clarence was bringing down from London his late wife's jewels, which were to be worn by his nieces. They were really exquisite pieces of work, worth a fortune, and were only brought out on very special occasions. He was, he had told Christina, dividing them between her and Bellissa in his will, and if they could agree as to what each would like, he would add a codicil confirming the selection.

'I think he's potty. It's not safe to keep first-rate stuff like that in a house that a burglar could walk into at any point. Besides, who are they intended to dazzle? There will only be ourselves.'

Christina laughed. 'You've got out of the wrong side of the bed this morning and no mistake. What's the trouble?'

His brow darkened and he looked away. 'Nothing,' he answered sulkily.

'Don't talk nonsense, O my brother. Seriously, what is it? Anything I can do to help?'

He hesitated. 'You're a good sort, Christina. Just a spot of passing trouble.'

'Money?'

'Well—yes. But don't worry. I'll manage somehow.'

'Tell me.'

She persisted, and at last, very unwillingly, he told her. He had gone with his friends the Montgomerys to a roulette club and had dropped a packet: more than he could afford.

It threw a sidelight on Christina's character that no word of criticism passed her lips. She told him that she could not pay his debt: she hadn't the money. But she could pay an instalment on it, and would be glad to do so.

He was grateful, though he point-blank refused to take a penny.

'Just like you, Chris, but I'll be all right. You'll see. I'll touch Montgomery for it, and if he doesn't come up to scratch I'll have nothing more to do with him.'

Half an hour later Christina took her sister's letter up to Clarence. The old man looked almost regal, with his fine features and his mass of white hair, as he lay propped up on pillows and wearing a startling black-and-gold dressing-gown. She greeted him with a smile.

'Morning, uncle. Breakfast all right?'

'Not much to go wrong with tea and toast. Besides, Josephs knows what his place is worth. What's that you've got there?'

'A letter from Bellissa. Guy has to go to Paris on Thursday week. He wants to know if the party could be put off till Saturday?'

'Wants to stay over Sunday, I suppose. Well, why not?'

'No reason that I know, but it's a matter for you.'

'Everything that is done in this house is a matter for me. I've no objection, so if you haven't either, we may consider it settled.'

'I don't know if Dr Mallaby can manage Saturday; he's accepted for Thursday. I'll ring him up.'

'You needn't worry overmuch. You may take it from me that he'll be able.'

Christina refused to be annoyed. 'How's the chest today?' she went on pleasantly.

'If I were to give my opinion, I'd say it was better. But of course I'll not know till the doctor comes.'

Conversation with her uncle was always rather heavy going, and Christina soon found she had household matters

51

to attend to. She met Mallaby accidentally in the hall when a little later he made his call, and asked him about the change of date.

'Quite the same to me, Miss Winnington, thank you so much,' he answered. 'I'm not engaged on either evening.'

She passed on with a pleasant word. She could picture her uncle's sardonic smile when she mentioned it. She longed to tell him that his factual forecasts were usually as correct as his imputations of motive were false. Then she remembered that a remark like that would delight him. It would show he had hurt her, and it would give him an opportunity for more sarcasm.

Before the party Christina had another interview which considerably interested her. After dinner that evening she and Horne sat alone in the lounge, Bernard having gone out and Clarence being still in bed. Horne she had found both pleasant and well informed, though reserved. He never spoke of himself or his affairs, except once to say that he had been a journalist in Fleet Street before taking on Clarence's job. Christina and Bellissa in talking this over had imagined he had somehow come to grief professionally, as a man with ambitions would never have given up such a position for a dead-end like Clarence's. This evening for the first time he broke his reserve and told Christina of his life.

'How did your researches in the north progress, Mr Horne?' she asked him as they settled down. She had no sympathy with her uncle's work, and the question was dictated by politeness rather than interest.

It appeared that he had had a successful expedition. He had found the ancestor's grave in a tiny cemetery on the Scottish side of the Border, and had unearthed some interesting family particulars from worm-eaten old books in the adjoining church.

'It sounds a find, and for the purposes of the book well worth the journey. But I'm afraid I couldn't get up the necessary interest to make me do it. I don't mean take the journey,' she added hastily; 'I was referring to writing the book.'

He smiled. 'To be quite candid, I don't think I could either, even if it concerned my own family. But one does a lot when one's paid for it.'

'Yes, but—' She hesitated, uncertain as to whether she was showing too great interest.

'But—' He smiled again.

'I was going perhaps to be impertinent,' she admitted. 'What I was going to say was that you surely could do far more valuable work than this?' He grew more serious and at first she thought she had offended him. Then he spoke, so earnestly that she saw the fact was far otherwise.

'It's good of you to take so much interest in my affairs. I appreciate it immensely. I'd like to tell you what I'm really here for, if I may. I haven't spoken of it before for reasons which you'll immediately appreciate.'

'I would take it as a compliment if you did,' she answered, 'but I don't want to force a confidence.'

'You're making it look as if it was a mountain instead of the molehill that it is,' he returned. 'But I'd like to tell you. My Fleet Street job was principally on the political side, and everything had to be written up to support the policy of the paper, which was ultra-conservative, while I myself am halfway to being a Socialist. It was against the grain all the time.'

'I can well understand that,' said Christina warmly. This somehow was not what she had expected. 'But couldn't you have transferred to some other paper more in accordance with your views?'

He shrugged whimsically. 'I doubt if there is one,' he declared. 'I'm not a complete Socialist, still less a Communist. I don't think either would suit this country. I want a half-and-between policy, so I naturally fall between two stools and am hated impartially by both sides.'

She made sounds indicative of interest. 'What exactly do you advocate?'

'I want private property to remain as it is, and I want enough freedom to be left to ensure maximum individual effort. But I also want the profit motive to be taken out of the direction of a number of our basic industries: I should have them run by corporations. And of course I want a central planning board.'

'But can you take out the profit motive without killing individual effort?'

'I should only remove it in the case of what are now the owners. Without criticising them individually, with them it has led to abuses against the nation. In the case of the workers, technical staff and management, I should leave it as at present.'

'I'd like to talk it over with you. It's a new idea to me.'

'I'd love it. But that really wasn't what I wanted to tell you. When I was on the paper I got an idea for a book, a novel on this subject. It would describe the kind of society that I have in mind. Probably I'm talking through my hat, but I think it might be valuable. Well, the point is that I couldn't write it when I was in Fleet Street. My work was too constant, and besides I was too much upset by the strain of always writing against my feelings. But I couldn't afford to give up the paper: I have no private means. So you can guess that when I saw Mr Winnington's advertisement it seemed like the answer to a prayer. I simply leaped at it. I do Mr Winnington a good day's work, all honest and above board. Then I turn over to my novel. I've always pretended to go to bed early and drifted off before the rest of you. I don't really. I write till the small hours.'

'Oh!' said Christina, thrilled by this account of effort and stress, 'how splendid! Have you done much? Of the novel, I mean?'

'The first draft's finished.' Though he still spoke diffidently, there was something both of enthusiasm and of triumph in his manner. 'I'm now revising. It'll take two or three months yet before I've got it as I want it.'

'I hope you'll let me read it when it's ready?'

His face lit up. 'How good of you! I *should* be pleased. I didn't dare to hope for such a thing.'

'But why not? I should be tremendously interested.'

The discussion had given Christina quite a different impression of Horne. Without formulating any definite conclusion, she had vaguely supposed that he was at Hurst Lodge for some rather questionable reason. Now the mystery was explained, and to his outstanding credit.

At last Saturday came, the day of the party. Clarence's bronchitis was better and he was in great form, evidently looking forward to the celebration. Everything was in readiness. The jewels had arrived and were locked in the safe in the library. An elaborate seven-course dinner was in preparation, and after much urging Bernard had agreed to propose his uncle's health.

Christina had feared the evening would prove an ordeal, but when the time came she found herself enjoying it. Everyone seemed to be on his or her best behaviour and the feeling of stress had largely gone out of the atmosphere. Clarence could be a very charming host when he chose, and on this occasion he did choose. Bernard had at least temporarily forgotten his financial embarrassments and talked and joked like his old self. Possibly as a result of his confidence to Christina, Horne seemed much more one of the party, and kept up his end of the conversation with unwonted brilliance. Even Mallaby was less pessimistic than usual, and interested everyone with tales of his sea experiences. Bellissa was obviously happier than for weeks. Only Guy was silent, almost morose. He appeared to have some weight on his mind, and Bellissa's remarks about his bad temper recurred forcibly to Christina.

Dinner passed without incident, but later that evening Christina had an experience which gave her furiously to think. The party had adjourned to the billiard-room. Clarence, Bernard, Guy and Horne were playing a hundred up and the other three were chatting while they waited for their turn. The talk turned on English landscape-painting, when Mallaby raised a question about the details of one of the pictures in the gallery upstairs.

'You can't see it properly by artificial light, of course,' Christina said, 'but I think we could settle the point if you cared to come up.'

'I'd love to.'

'Will you come, Bellissa?' Christina went on, rising.

'No. I'm too lazy. You take Dr Mallaby.'

It was when they reached the top of a short flight of steps leading to the gallery that it happened. Christina somehow caught her foot in her long evening-frock. She stumbled and instantly found herself grasped in Mallaby's arms. As quickly, when he found she had regained her balance, he released her.

He apologised, she smilingly thanked him, and for a moment it looked as if the incident was closed. But it wasn't. The contact seemed to have broken down the doctor's self-control, and she presently realised that she was listening to a proposal.

She was a good deal taken aback. Though she knew she attracted him and had weighed the pros and cons of marriage with him were he to ask her, she had lately come to the conclusion that such was not his intention. Now she felt undecided. The arguments for acceptance appeared no more cogent than those for refusal, and her feelings were not strong enough to override her reason.

'I haven't much to offer you, I'm afraid,' he went on while she was still wondering how she should reply. 'I'm no longer young and I'm not wealthy nor likely to become so. I cannot hide the fact that professionally I'm a failure. I can give you little more than affection and respect and reasonable comfort.' He paused, then went on: 'I didn't intend to speak. I thought that you were not for such as I. I was carried away by what happened, and now I'm glad that I was. What do you say, Christina? Can you contemplate the idea?'

On the spur of the moment she simply could not decide, and in the end she followed Bellissa's example and asked him for a week in which to think it over.

Shortly afterwards the party broke up. Mallaby drove off in his car and Horne went up to bed. The others, Christina, Bellissa, Bernard and Guy, followed Clarence to his library, where the jewels were taken off, checked over, put in the cases and locked in Clarence's safe. Bellissa then followed her sister up to her room for a chat before bed. Christina told her about Mallaby.

'So it's come at last! I thought it would sooner or later. What are you going to do about it, Christina?'

'I'm not sure. I feel like accepting, but I'm not satisfied that it would be fair to him. I question if I could make him happy. My brand of affection is perhaps not enough. I think I would always be fond of him, but I don't believe I'd ever love him.'

'Why not tell him that and let him decide?'

'That wouldn't be fair either. He'd feel bound to renew his proposal. He's that sort.'

'It is difficult,' Bellissa agreed; 'I daren't advise you. As I've said before, I've learnt in my own experience that it's a mistake to marry for money, but of course that doesn't apply here. I should think if you can give him genuine affection it would meet the case. It should offer a good chance of happiness, at all events.'

As that night Christina weighed the issues she came gradually to agree. In the morning she had practically made up her mind to accept Mallaby when the week came to an end. She told Bellissa her probable decision when they went out during the morning for a walk on the heath, but Bellissa had apparently been pondering the matter also, and now her opinion had altered. To Christina's surprise, she immediately began pouring cold water on it.

'I think,' she declared, 'your question has pretty well answered itself. If you're so doubtful about the marriage as all that, it means that you're better out of it.'

'I don't agree with you,' Christina returned. 'If I am doubtful, it means that I'm not trying to solve it by my feelings, but by my reason.'

'If you really wanted it you'd have no doubt at all,' Bellissa insisted. 'Besides, there's another point. Suppose you married him and Uncle Clarence died and you came in for your money.'

'Well?'

'Well, don't you see? That money would open a new world to you. Suppose you met someone then that you knew was the right man. That would be misery for you.'

'Not very likely at my time of life. In any case, it might happen just as easily if I didn't get the money.'

'No, it mightn't. The money would lead you into new surroundings and you'd meet new people. But there, I don't want to influence you. It's a matter for yourself only.'

Christina of course knew this very well, and she was annoyed with herself for her indecision.

The day passed normally, the various members of the household following their individual bents until about five o'clock they all gathered in the lounge for tea. There Christina was disappointed to find that Bernard, who had been out all day, had lunched well rather than wisely. He was by no means drunk, but he Was excited and inclined to be quarrelsome. Clarence looked fastidiously superior; however, Bernard did not notice it and there was no actual unpleasantness.

It was after tea, when they were sitting round the fire, that an incident occurred which, though it seemed entirely trifling at the time, turned out afterwards to have been fraught with serious consequences for all concerned. At this time Clarence and Horne had left the lounge, only

Bernard and Guy remaining with the sisters. The talk turned on military strategy, and Guy referred to Mr Churchill's description of the battle of Blenheim in his *Marlborough*, which he had just finished. Bernard had read a different account of the engagement, and a mild argument arose between them as to the disposition of Tallard's forces just before Marlborough's breakthrough. Bernard began to sketch.

'No,' said Guy, looking over his shoulder, 'according to Churchill that's not quite correct. He gives a plan of that very part of the action. Let me show you.'

He took his fountain-pen from his waistcoat pocket, but it had run dry.

'Blow!' he said; 'this thing's empty. Lend me yours a moment, Bernard.'

Bernard passed over his pen and Guy began to sketch. As he did so Horne re-entered.

'Ah,' he said, seeing what was happening, 'the battle of Blenheim? You've been reading *Marlborough*?'

Before Guy could answer Josephs entered.

'You're wanted on the telephone, Mr Bernard, if you please.'

With a word of apology Bernard followed him out. Horne and Guy continued discussing the battle, eventually agreeing on the point at issue and changing the subject.

In a few moments Bernard reappeared. He was evidently full of some new subject and had forgotten about Blenheim.

'Just heard that Archie Ainsworth has been smashed up in a car accident,' he told them. 'Not exactly serious, but he'll have to lie up for a while. Reckless beggar; I've often told him he was asking for it.'

Both incidents passed from Christina's mind as a little

later she went up to dress, and her thoughts returned to her own problem: what answer she should give to Anthony Mallaby. Bellissa's remarks had influenced her unconsciously, and now she was more in doubt as to her decision than ever.

6

Guy Plant

When Arthur Crossley left Ivy Cottage on that evening some ten days before Clarence Winnington's birthday party, Guy Plant remained seated in his chair, his eyes staring unseeingly at the fire and an expression of horror stamped on his features.

Now that he had taken his dreadful decision, he was seized by an overwhelming revulsion of feeling. Murder! The very idea revolted him, made him feel physically sick. The actual deed would be ghastly enough, but its possible sequel simply did not bear thinking about. The slightest oversight in his plans, the briefest relaxation of his watchfulness, a careless word, an unguarded look, almost a guilty thought: any of these would be sufficient to arouse suspicion. And if the police once really suspected him, he was doomed. They would not let the matter rest till they got him.

Even if he escaped that crowning disaster, he would pay dearly for what he was about to do. His peace of mind would be gone. Always in the background fear would be crouching, waiting for an opportunity to spring up and paralyse his will and lead him to destruction. Moral considerations as such mattered little to him, but deep down in his heart he knew that in this matter a guilty conscience would mean that never again would he know real happiness.

He shuddered. Was this ghastly project really necessary? Was there no other way of escape?

His thoughts swung back to the alternative and his heart hardened. Like Crossley, he felt that he was not confronted with a choice between evil and good. The choice was between possible and certain ruin. After all, if he killed Clarence the chances of discovery were small. Care in the working out of his scheme, an admittedly terrible ten minutes, then reasonable watchfulness, and he should be safe. Safe! Free from his load of debt. Free from the certainty of ruin. Even comparatively wealthy! No, there could be no doubt as to his decision.

The expression of horror passed from his face and his habitual look of keen efficiency took its place. Still he stared unseeingly at the fire, but now his busy brain was grappling with his plan. In general outline it was settled, but minor details required to be worked out. Usually he thought on paper, continuously jotting down the ideas which crowded into his mind. Now that would be dangerous. He must proceed by memory alone.

His scheme was founded on the fact of the approaching birthday party and Clarence's decision to have his jewellery worn by his nieces. It was desirable, though not absolutely essential, that the affair should take place on a Saturday evening. The crime would be committed on the following night, Sunday, and during the day he would find some opportunity of making certain arrangements with Clarence, so that the old man would unwittingly fall in with his plans.

Plant spent a considerable time thinking of where Bellissa should be on that Sunday night. If she came up to his study and found Crossley impersonating him, it would be the end. Should she not remain away from home for that weekend?

It was true that Bellissa rarely came to his study; he had never made her visits welcome. But through the crookedness of fate she might chance to do so on that particular evening. He could no doubt work out some plan to keep her away, but if suspicion were aroused, his having done so would markedly strengthen it.

He presently reached the conclusion that under no circumstances dare he risk her finding Crossley. How was the danger to be avoided? Bridge at a friend's house would be ideal—he did not himself play—but it involved approaching the friend. Bridge at his own house, which would be easier to arrange, would not be sufficiently certain. At last he thought of a plan, though it was by no means as good as he should have liked.

Before going further he decided to deal with a matter which normally should have come last on his list. In any case, it could not become urgent until after the commission of the crime, and he devoutly hoped it never would do so. This was a way of escape if, in spite of all his precautions, suspicion were aroused and the police got on to his track. He had already worked out a tentative scheme for such a flight, and he believed that, in spite of any hue and cry which might be raised, he could manage to evade the watch at the ports, get out of the country, and lie hidden abroad.

To arrange it would not only be a test of his skill, but the knowledge that such a safeguard was in readiness would stiffen his nerve when he came to the actual deed.

Of the items necessary, the first was the alteration of his passport. Though he planned to get out of the country without using this travellers' aid, he was aware that he could not settle down anywhere abroad without one. He had held a passport for many years, but obviously that he would now require must not bear his name. They were extraordinarily difficult documents to alter, but he thought he could do it. As a boy he had been interested in letter and figure problems of all kinds, and he had often thought how easily his name lent itself to manipulation. Now he proposed to manipulate it.

The name *GUY PLANT* was printed by hand in small sloping capitals, done with a fine pen. Plant began by experimenting with nibs and inks till he had obtained a combination giving him lines exactly like those on his copy. Then very carefully and after much practice he began to alter the letters.

The first was the most difficult. The *G* of Guy had to be changed to the *R* of Roy. With a sharp penknife, he scratched out the top left corner and lower part of the *G*, utilising the remainder as part of the *R* which he printed over it. The *U* was easier to deal with, a curved line across the top, carefully joined to the uprights, making it into an *O*. The *Y* remained unaltered.

The surname presented much less difficulty. The addition of a lower loop changed the *P* into a *B*, two horizontal lines and the *L* became an *E*, the *A* and *N* stood, and only the *T* had to be dealt with. This was easily managed by scraping out a little of the left end of the crossbar, lengthening it towards the right and adding two horizontal strokes below it. He was now *ROY BEANE*.

For the first time in his life Plant found it to his advantage that he wrote an illegible signature. He made a few judicious additions to that beneath the passport photograph and was satisfied that it would read almost anything.

His work, of course, would not pass muster before a real examination with microscopes and infra-red ray photography, but he believed it would satisfy any hotel people or gendarme who might casually inspect it.

He gave a lot of thought to the question of forging a date of entry into France, which, owing to his knowledge of the language, was the country he proposed to make for. In the end he decided not to attempt this, but to pay flying visits to Paris at short intervals until he was sure that all chance of suspicion had died down. This would give him a genuine entry stamp reasonably near the date of his showing the passport. Admittedly the latter would bear an exit stamp from France of later date, but unless suspicion were aroused the old stamps would not be checked up. If he were really suspected, a discrepancy in the dates would not matter, for the obvious reason that the forgery itself would be discovered.

Considerably encouraged by the success of his preliminary effort, Plant turned to the preparations for the murder itself. He was projecting a business interview in Paris, and he now wrote fixing this for the Friday following Clarence's birthday. On reaching home he told Bellissa that the appointment had been settled for him over his head, and asked her to see if she could have the party moved from the Thursday to the Saturday. They had a standing invitation to stay at Hurst Lodge, and she was also to ask if they might remain till Monday so that he might have a ramble over the heath on Sunday. He knew she would be glad to stay, as indeed she immediately admitted.

During the following week he continued his preparations. The next item gave him considerable trouble. He wanted to find some office work with the following rather exacting requirements:

1. It must be something which only he could do.
2. It must involve a lot of typing.
3. It must be something which required time and thought and which he might therefore prefer to do at home, away from the interruptions of the office.
4. It must be wanted shortly after the Sunday of the murder.

At last he thought of the very thing. A confidential report was required by his Chairman on a scheme for altering the pension basis of the higher officials of the Company. Only he could prepare it. He was accustomed to type—not very skilfully—such drafts himself, from which fair copies were made at the office. It was pre-eminently a matter for undisturbed thought and one which under ordinary circumstances he probably would handle in the quiet of his home.

The only snag was that it was not needed for some weeks after the Sunday of the murder, but he saw how he could get over this. He was having an interview with the Chairman on the Wednesday of the murder week, and he would think up some points to discuss with him before completing the final draft. This, he thought, would be absolutely natural and could not possibly lead to suspicion.

As occasion offered he now secretly drafted and typed

the report so as to have it ready before he went to Paris, locking it away in his study desk.

The next thing he required was an anonymous letter. This he prepared in the time-honoured way. He bought a cheap letter block, and wearing gloves and with a nib which did not suit his hand and a bottle of poor ink he printed it in rough block lettering. It read:

Mr Winnington. If you want to stay alive look out for Mr Bernard. He took too much at the Three Swallows and let out he was going to knock your block off for the money coming to him. I dont care a dam for him or for you but I dont want to see murder done if I can stop it. So look out.

This effusion he also locked away in his desk.

His next proceedings were more complicated. First he bought four second-hand suitcases and left them in the cloakroom at Charing Cross. At a theatrical supplies shop he obtained a pair of plain glass horn-rimmed spectacles, as well as a suit of old uniform. On the Saturday, a week before the party, he packed his shabbiest gardening clothes in his oldest suitcase, together with a small sack, and on his way to the office deposited it in the cloakroom at Blackfriars Station. After work, instead of going home he lunched at a restaurant, and then, taking out the suitcase, he walked to Cannon Street Station, changed in a lavatory, and left the suitcase in the cloakroom there. With his disreputable clothes, his cap worn on one side, his glasses, his dirty hands and nails—soiled by fingering some garden loam he had brought—and the sack, few would have recognised him as the dapper accountant of the Yellow Star Line.

In the East End, far away from his usual haunts, he made a number of purchases. First he bought a pair of thin rubber gloves and a couple of blocks of soft rubber, a small piece of cloth, some birdlime and a washleather bag. Then he visited three second-hand clothes dealers. In one he purchased a dark-grey hat of soft felt, which could be made fairly respectable or completely disreputable according to the twist of the brim. In the next, a large and superior establishment, he had the luck to find a reversible coat, dark on one side and lightish on the other. In the third he selected a pair of well-worn rubber-soled shoes one size too big for him: he wore sevens and these were eights. He explained that they were for his brother, who could not come for them himself. At a ship-chandler's he added to his collection sixty feet of fine line and a ball of stout cord, and at a working plumber's twelve 9-inch lengths of 1-inch gas-pipe and a single piece of heavy 1-inch lead water-pipe. All these articles he squeezed into the sack, still further adding to his disguise by carrying it over his shoulder.

Returning to Cannon Street, he got out his suitcase, changed back to his normal attire in a lavatory, packed the sack and its contents into the suitcase, washed his hands and left for home.

That evening after dinner he retired to his study, as indeed it had now become his custom to do. There, having silently locked the door, he set to work on his purchases. Dividing his rope into four 15-foot lengths, he bound these together in pairs to make two double lengths, inserting his gas-pipes at intervals between the strands of each pair to form a rope ladder. This he rolled up and locked away. Then he carefully brushed the dark side of the overcoat,

69

at the same time smearing dirt on the light side. The shoes he padded up with old handkerchiefs so that he could wear them with reasonable comfort. Lastly he trimmed the soft rubber blocks for insertion into his cheeks, thus altering the shape of his face.

His immediate preparations were now complete, but three more matters had to be attended to before he left London. On the Wednesday evening he met Crossley at a prearranged point in a Soho backwater and coached him in his duties for the following Sunday evening. Then before leaving the office on Thursday he called his secretary.

'I'll not be back till Monday,' he told her. He instructed her about certain matters, continuing: 'I'm considering drafting out my report on that pensions scheme during the weekend; I want to discuss it with the Chairman when I see him on Wednesday. I wish you'd get out some stuff for me,' and he explained what he wanted. 'You might send it to my house so that I'll get it on Saturday.'

The third matter was equally easy. By scraping together all his resources he managed to collect a hundred pounds. This he changed into single notes, sealing them in an envelope. At the same time he filled in a receipt form for Crossley to sign.

That Thursday afternoon he caught the six p.m. plane from Croydon, and by half-past eight was at the Hotel Ambassador in Paris. Having bought some papers and borrowed a directory, he busied himself during the evening in making a list of furnished apartments and noting the addresses of a few theatrical requisite suppliers.

Next morning he first completed his official business. Then in the afternoon he spent a couple of hours inspecting the rooms on his list, and was lucky enough to find a comfortable bed-sitting-room in a quiet street off the Rue Singer in Passy. This he engaged, paying a month's rent in advance.

'My name is Beane,' he told the landlady, 'Mr Roy Beane of London. I am an author, and I wish to stay in Paris for a few weeks to get local colour for a book I am writing. I'm not sure when I shall want to move in, but I take it you'll be ready for me when I come?'

The landlady, pleased to receive payment without contributing her quota of work, agreed with enthusiasm.

On Saturday morning at a theatrical supplies shop Plant purchased another suit of old uniform. Having packed it in his suitcase, he went out to Le Bourget and returned to London by the midday plane. He drove home, saw that the information from his secretary was there, and picking up Bellissa, went on to Hurst Lodge.

During the drive he mentioned a change of plans. 'By the way, Bellissa, I'm terribly sorry after the fuss I made, but I can't stay at Little Wokeham till Monday after all. I have a report to make out during the weekend, and I'll have to go home after tea on Sunday to do it. But you needn't come till Monday; in fact, if you don't mind, it would be better for you to wait. It would make my going off seem less of a change.'

Bellissa, easy-going by nature and by training accustomed to carry out her husband's wishes, agreed. As he knew, it was what she preferred. When later he announced his intention, there were polite murmurs of regret, but no real interest. Thus another fence was taken.

The next twenty-four hours were for Guy Plant a period of almost unbearable strain. Try as he would, he could not banish from his mind the ghastly spectre of what he was about to do. Care also was needed not to betray his mood by a syllable, a movement, a glance, which might be remembered and afterwards brought up against him. The effort seemed to interpose a barrier between himself and the others, cutting him off from their real companionship. He could scarcely bear to look at Clarence, and when the old man spoke to him pleasantly and asked his advice about an investment, he felt he simply could not proceed with the affair. It was only by barking back to the alternative that he was able to steel himself to carry on.

One difficulty, perhaps his greatest, had to be surmounted while at Hurst Lodge: without arousing suspicion, to induce Clarence to fall in with his plans. Here his foresight in having the dinner transferred to the Saturday justified itself, for it was not till Sunday morning that he could find an opportunity. After breakfast, when the four men were sitting chatting over the lounge fire, Clarence went to the library to work at his book, just as Plant had expected he would. As it was Sunday, Horne was not in attendance. Presently Plant began feeling in his pockets. Then he got up.

'Damn!' he said, 'I've left my cigarettes upstairs. I won't be a moment.'

'Have one of mine,' said Bernard, holding out his case.

Plant shook his head. 'Thanks, but I'd better get my own while I think of it. Don't want to be without them all day.'

He strolled slowly out of the room, then hurried to the library, knocked, went in and closed the door behind him.

The old man was seated at his desk and looked up, apparently slightly surprised at his visitor. 'Well, Guy? Want to see me? What can I do for you?'

'I've got a serious and confidential matter to discuss

with you, Mr Winnington, concerning the family,' Plant answered gravely, 'but because it is so confidential I don't want anyone to know we are having a talk. It's really rather important, and if you could see me this evening I'll run down again. Could you be here alone after dinner, say between nine and ten? I'd come to the window and you could let me in.'

Clarence was curious and wanted to know then and there all about it, but Plant explained that he did not wish the others to guess that he had been the source of information, which they certainly would if the two were known to have been closeted together. Clarence then reluctantly agreed and Plant, taking his cigarette-case from his pocket, returned to the lounge. He had been away no longer than it would have taken him to go to his room, and he was satisfied that no suspicion that he had not done so had been aroused.

Everything was now in train for the evening, and Plant directed his energies towards acting as normally as he could till it was time to leave. For a little longer they smoked in the lounge, chatting desultorily and glancing at the Sunday papers. Then he and Bernard went for a tramp on the heath, Bernard leaving him to keep a lunch engagement, while Plant returned to Hurst Lodge.

The afternoon dragged appallingly, but at long last there was tea. Aeons of pointless conversation followed before he could go off to get his car. Then, after more vapid remarks, came the blessed moment for which he had been waiting all day, when he could drive away and be alone.

The intensity of the relief that he found in solitude frightened him. Was this what his whole life was to be, continual fear and effort and struggle? No, he told himself, once get the hideous affair over and all would be well. It was this looking forward to what was to come that was so irksome. Directly it was done he would obtain relief. So he tried to reassure himself, though with a sad lack of conviction.

It was during the drive home that, when feeling for his handkerchief, Plant discovered that he had put Bernard's pen into his pocket with his own. He knew from its feel whose it was, for he had noticed when he had borrowed it to make his battle of Blenheim sketch that the pocket clip was broken off. A momentary feeling of annoyance passed through his mind as he saw that he would have the trouble of sending it back. He could understand how he had come to pocket it. His action had been automatic and resulted from his attention being fixed on trying to act normally. Obviously Bernard had also forgotten it, first because he was absent from the room when the sketch was finished, and second because when he did return his mind was filled with his friend's accident. The incident, of course, was unimportant, and in the stress of more urgent matters Plant quickly forgot it.

It rained as he drove home, but it proved only a shower. In due course he reached Ivy Cottage and had supper. His cook, Mrs Miggs, was remaining in, but the other girl, Ellen, had gone out for the evening. So much the better. Mrs Miggs would make a perfect witness. She was highly reliable-looking and always spoke with such an air of conviction that no one could possibly doubt her testimony. Ellen, on the other hand, was a scatter-brained creature whose statement, if she could be made to give one, would carry little weight.

'I've got some work to do this evening,' he said casually as he went upstairs after supper, 'and I don't want to be disturbed. If anyone calls, just say I'm not at home. I've switched the phone through to the study and I'll deal direct with any calls.'

Mrs Miggs' manner showed that she thought this quite normal. 'Very good, sir,' she returned. 'I'll see to it.'

Plant breathed a sigh of relief. So far he had done well. The only preparations which could be traced to him were innocuous. The only person whose knowledge might be dangerous, Clarence himself, would not come forward with his information.

Zero hour was now fast approaching, and Plant began to get ready for his grim errand. First he put on the large-sized shoes, the coat with the soiled grey side outwards, the hat with the brim twisted at all angles, and the spectacles. He slipped the rubber pads into his cheeks, and the anonymous letter, the lead pipe, the piece of cloth and the birdlime into his pockets. Then, very softly opening the window—luckily it was a calm night— he let down the rope ladder and made it fast to the window mullion with a hook he had prepared.

At half-past eight operations were to begin, and when he had finished it was just twenty-seven minutes past. Now that the affair was actually upon him, his nervousness had vanished and he was once again his cool and competent self. Crossley was the one weak link in the chain, but Plant believed he had so terrified him with the consequences of failure that this link would hold.

Suddenly he glanced up. There in complete silence was Crossley's head, rising jerkily above the window-sill. The young man glanced in, stopped climbing, and stared at his chief with an expression of doubt which rapidly changed to consternation.

'Come on, you ass,' Plant whispered softly. 'Who do you think it is?' He felt a thrill of intense satisfaction. No better test of his disguise could have been devised.

'You've made a job of it,' said Crossley, also in a whisper. 'For the moment I wasn't sure.'

'Plant nodded. 'Then carry on as we arranged,' he breathed. 'Only Mrs Miggs is in the house and I've told her I'm not to be disturbed. I've locked the door, all the same. Don't forget the four main things: to type, to poke the fire at intervals, to turn on and off the news summary, and to smoke continuously.'

'Not much chance of my forgetting.'

'Good. Where's the bicycle?'

'Behind a shrub just inside the gate.'

Silently Plant climbed out of the window, and feeling foot by foot for the rungs, descended the ladder. He found it much more difficult than he had expected, for his body fell back and his feet swung out in front, scraping hard against the wall. However, by taking it slowly he reached the ground without disaster. A moment later he found Crossley's bicycle, wheeled it out, switched on the lamp and rode off into the night.

7

Guy Plant

Plant pedalled along rapidly, though not fast enough to attract attention. Until the previous week he had not ridden a bicycle for over twenty years, but in view of tonight's expedition he had had a few evening runs on Crossley's. He had found himself in surprisingly good training.

The night was well suited to his purpose. It was cold, so that he could ride in a coat without becoming over-heated. Since the shower on his way home there had been no rain, though the moon was still obscured by clouds. He could thus see trees and other large objects, which would later enable him to find his way without a light, but objects which should remain decently veiled, such as the items of his disguise, would be invisible. He had plenty of time to do the fifteen miles and need not exert himself unduly.

The choice of his route had been rather a problem. The main road was of course the most direct, and in the heavier traffic he would be more likely to be overlooked. On the other hand, he would be continually illuminated by car headlamps, and the chance of being observed by cycling policemen was therefore greater. For this reason he had decided to keep to byroads, and now he was glad he had done so. He met few cars, fewer pedestrians, and, so far as he could tell, no police. The unaccustomed motion and the need for a sharp lookout kept his mind occupied and prevented him brooding too much over what lay before him. When he did think of it he reminded himself of how quickly the dreadful business would be carried through. In a matter of minutes he would be returning, safe, and with the menace of debt and ruin removed.

At ten minutes to ten he reached the outskirts of Little Wokeham. He had had a satisfactory run. No untoward incident had occurred, and he was convinced that no one had observed his passage. To the north of Hurst Lodge, the direction from which he was approaching, the land was cultivated, the village and heath lying southwards. A farm lane ran up from the road along the Lodge boundary, and into this he turned. It did not lead to any houses and at this hour of a cold night was likely to be deserted. There was of course a certain risk from amorous couples, but he thought these would keep to the even greater seclusion of the heath. In any case, even if he were seen, there was still his disguise.

He knew the ground well, having been over it many times. Now he extinguished his lamp and pushed the bicycle behind a convenient shrub. He walked on up the lane till he reached a gap in the fence which he had noticed on a previous visit, passed through, and stealthily approached the house. His way lay across the grass to a path which ran from a tiny lake in the grounds straight to the library window. On neither grass nor path did his footprints show. Presently he was close to the building. Here he stopped, straightened his hat, reversed his coat to show the respectable side, and took the spectacles off his nose and the pads out of his cheeks.

The library was lighted up, but the curtains were drawn. He crept softly along the gravel path to the french window. The curtains did not exactly meet and he was able to peep into the room. Clarence was seated at the fire and the clock on the chimney-piece showed two minutes to ten. So far, so good! Now for a horrible ten minutes and then—safety!

In spite of his assurance, as Guy Plant raised his hand to knock at the window, a wave of deadly fear and repulsion swept over him. His heart was beating rapidly and he paused for a moment to regain his composure. After all, it would not be so bad. His plans were cut and dried, foolproof and easy to carry out. In any case, he had gone too far now to draw back. He tapped softly.

He could see Clarence rise and approach the french window. A moment later it opened.

'I left it open for you,' said Clarence.

Plant smiled and laid his finger on his lips. 'We mustn't be heard speaking,' he said quietly. 'I don't want it to be known I came down.'

'You're certainly very mysterious,' Clarence grumbled, but in a low tone. 'Come and sit down. What's it all about?'

He moved towards the fire while Plant closed the window.

'As a matter of fact,' the latter said, 'it's a letter which has rather worried me. I want you to read it and see what you think of it.'

As he had hoped, at the mention of a letter Clarence turned towards his desk.

'A letter?' he said, sitting down. 'Show it to me.'

Plant dropped into a chair beside the desk, and taking out his wallet, extracted the anonymous letter. Without a word he handed it over. Clarence glanced at it and his eyebrows rose. Again as Plant had hoped, he took it by its edges and laid it down on the desk, presumably with the idea of safeguarding any fingerprints it might bear. He began to read it carefully.

'You see,' said Plant, standing up and moving behind him. With his left hand he pointed to the paper, while with his right he gripped the lead pipe. 'It's a forgery. Look at the joins between the horizontal and vertical strokes and you'll see what I mean.'

Everything was going exactly to plan. Clarence leant forward to examine the document more closely, and at the same moment Plant struck. Without a sound Clarence collapsed forward over the desk; then, rotating in a way which made Plant physically sick, he slouched to the ground and lay motionless. Blood welled slowly from the wound. It marked the pipe, but to Plant's relief did not stain his hand.

With his pulse pounding like a sledge-hammer in his temples Plant stood gazing at the motionless figure. The head was dented, so much so that death was assured. For a moment Plant felt paralysed, then he pulled himself together.

His first care was to wipe the pipe in the dead man's clothes. Then, once more pocketing it, he drew on his rubber gloves. He tiptoed to the door leading to the hall. It was locked. He did not want Clarence's prints to be found on the key, so he rubbed key and handle with his gloved fingers.

Half of his dreadful plan had now been carried out. Clarence was dead and the twenty thousand was already, or shortly would be, Bellissa's property. The second part still remained: the diversion of suspicion from himself and the members of the household.

Clarence's desk was placed in the window; not the french window, but another. The chair stood with its side to the light and facing the fire across the desk. The windows were of the casement type, with steel-framed leadlights, carried on wooden lintels, sills and mullions. The panes were about five inches by eight in size.

Plant now took out his piece of cloth and his birdlime and carefully coated one side of the cloth. Then he went out by the french window, and having retraced his steps for some distance down the gravel path, turned and approached the second window direct. This led him first across the carefully mown lawn and then over a rose-bed which stretched along the wall of the house. Standing on the soft loam, he pressed the cloth on to the pane which covered the handle of the casement behind Clarence's chair. Sufficient light passed through the curtain to enable him to do this accurately. Having made sure it was sticking tightly, he folded his handkerchief into a pad, held it in the middle of the pane, and struck it with the end of his lead pipe. Gradually he increased the force of the blows till at last the pane broke. The cloth and birdlime prevented the pieces from falling, and though the blow made a dull thud, he felt sure it could not have been heard beyond the library. If it were, it would be attributed to Clarence—at least till later.

Lifting away the cloth and broken glass, Plant inserted his hand through the hole, turned the handle and pushed the window open. He climbed in, shut the window after him, and standing close against it behind the curtain in the corner at the back of Clarence's chair, he tramped several times on the same area. He moved the large waste-paper basket as if he had used it to cover his feet, which showed below the curtain. Then he stepped forward to the point at which he had struck Clarence. He wrapped the sticky cloth with its bits of broken glass round the lead pipe and placed both on the floor, where he could get them when he was leaving.

His next proceeding he found more difficult than any which had preceded it. Setting his teeth, he stooped over the body and began to search for Clarence's keys. The very touch of the corpse gave him cold shivers, and it was all he could do to roll it over to get at the under pockets. But he dared not pause. When he had found the keys he forced himself to roll it back as it had fallen. Then, crossing to the safe, he opened it, quickly emptied the various jewel-cases into his washleather bag, and closed the safe door. The keys he left swinging from the lock. Lastly he carefully reassumed his disguise.

His scheme was now complete, and having picked up the lead pipe and cloth, he stood looking round him to make sure that nothing had been forgotten. Then just as he was moving off to the french window he stopped, frozen, staring in horror. There on the desk was the anonymous letter! He had forgotten it!

It might not, of course, have given him away, but then again it might. It would at least have shown that this was not the mere burglary his plan was intended to suggest.

The police were horribly efficient about things of the kind. The nib, the ink, the paper; any one of them might have proved a clue. Worse still, he had taken the paper from his wallet with his bare fingers—he had not dared to let Clarence see his rubber gloves—and no doubt it bore his prints.

Shaken and trembling, he picked it up and put it in his pocket. Then, walking to the french window, he fingered that handle and key also with his gloved hands, opened the door portion, slipped out, closed it softly behind him, and set off down the gravel path.

The worst was over! It had not indeed been as bad as he had anticipated. Now he had only to complete his plan and the nightmare would be at an end. He had simply to avoid mistakes and oversights. If he did so, and of course he would, he need have no fear. So far nothing he had done could be traced to him. A little further effort and he might rest with an easy mind, knowing he was safe. Reasonably satisfied, he concentrated on the points still to be dealt with. And, first, to get rid of certain embarrassing articles.

Small as was the artificial lake, it had a boat-house and slip. A branch from the path he was following led to these. He took it, and reaching the edge, threw in the lead pipe and cloth. They went down with a soft though satisfying plop. Then, passing through the gap in the fence into the lane, he recovered the bicycle, wheeled it to the road, turned on its light and rode off.

An hour later he pushed it back behind the shrub on his drive, tiptoed to the rope ladder, with some difficulty climbed it and tapped softly at the window. Crossley, seated before the fire, got up and quietly opened it. He looked white and scared. In ten seconds Plant was in the room.

'Well?' he breathed. 'Everything all right?'

Crossley made a gesture of horror. 'The telephone!' he whispered. 'It's been ghastly!'

Plant stared in silence.

'Someone rang up,' went on Crossley, 'a man. He said—' He paused in apparent doubt.

'Well?' Plant whispered fiercely.

Crossley continued haltingly. 'He said, "Is that you, Mr Plant? Horne speaking." I said, "Yes," trying to copy your voice. "I'm sorry to tell you," he said, "that something very serious has happened. Mr Clarence is," and he sort of hesitated, "is dead!" I said, "Dead? Good God!" as you might have, and he said, "It's worse than that. They think he was murdered!" I said, "Good God! Murdered!" He said, "Can you come down? Mrs Plant asked me to ask you." I said, "I'll come at once," and I rang off. I was afraid to talk any longer in case my voice would give me away.'

A cold hand seemed to grip Plant's heart. He ought to have foreseen this possibility, but he had not. Heavily he sat down and then poured himself out a stiff whisky.

'How long ago was this?' he asked.

'About twenty minutes.'

Twenty minutes! If so, he ought to be half-way to Hurst Lodge by this time!

'Do you think the man noticed your voice?'

'I don't think so. He seemed too much upset himself.'

Relief began to steal back into Plant's mind. Crossley had not done so badly. Perhaps it would be all right. But he must hurry, hurry!

'Nothing else?'

'Nothing.'

'You typed and poked the fire and turned on the set?'

'Yes.'

'All right. Get away quickly. Your job's done and you'll get your hundred in a day or two. No, steady a moment. You may as well have it now. Sign that.'

He took the envelope containing the hundred notes from his desk, together with the receipt, and placed them on the table before Crossley. The young fellow opened the envelope and his eyes glistened. Slowly he began to count.

'Nonsense, man,' Plant whispered testily, 'there's no time for that. I assure you they're right. Take them and sign and go.'

Crossley still hesitated, but a gesture from Plant decided him. He thrust the envelope into his pocket, signed, and moved towards the window.

'Right.' Plant hurried him on. 'Out you get. Quick as you can without making a noise.'

Looking relieved, Crossley swung himself out of the window and jerkily disappeared. Instantly Plant plunged into his preparations. Silently but with haste he worked. First he burnt the anonymous letter and Crossley's receipt, breaking the ash with the poker. Then he took off his coat, hat and shoes, making them into a bundle and wrapping them round with the rope ladder, which he drew up as soon as it ceased shaking. Having locked up the bag of jewellery and hidden the bundle in a cupboard, he rang the bell. In due course Mrs Miggs appeared.

'I'm sorry to say I've had bad news about Mrs Plant's uncle,' he told her. 'Got a phone message a little time ago.

He's very ill and I'm going down. I don't know, but I'll probably stay the night. At all events you'll be all right here? Has Ellen come in?'

'Yes, sir. But in any case I'd be all right. I'm sorry for your news.'

Plant shook his head sadly. 'It mayn't be as bad as they suggest,' he said. 'I hope not. Of course with a man of Mr Winnington's age one can never tell.'

'Very true, sir. You'll be back tomorrow, I suppose?'

'Oh yes, sure to be. But I'll ring you up in the morning in any case.'

'Thank you, sir.'

He dared not show impatience, but he could scarcely restrain himself while she talked. However, at last she went off. Waiting only till the kitchen door closed, he seized his bundle, went downstairs, put on a coat and hat and walked deliberately out to the garage. In another couple of minutes he was on the road.

He drove mechanically, his thoughts busy with this unfortunate development. It had scared him stiff at first, but on second thoughts it seemed less serious. There were two dangers, of course; first, that Horne might have noticed something unusual about his voice, and second, that they might now remark on his late arrival. Apparently there was not much fear of the first contingency. Crossley had done remarkably well. As Plant recalled his account of the conversation, he felt that it might have been himself speaking, at least as far as the phraseology was concerned. It was indeed almost a stroke of genius to have rung off on the ground that he was leaving for Hurst Lodge immediately. Yes, Crossley had shown surprising presence of mind. Besides, there was the point the young man had

86

made, that the speaker was himself too agitated to be critical.

Unfortunately that very haste in ringing off made his delay in arriving all the more remarkable. Oh well, some risks were unavoidable. He would say he had had trouble with the car.

On his drive one important matter had to be dealt with. Turning down a by-road, he followed it till it crossed the River Wey. He parked the car some distance from the bridge, then, taking his bundle, walked forward. From the centre of the bridge, after a careful look round, he dropped the bundle into the water. He knew that it would sink—it was with this very object that he had used gas-pipe instead of wood for the rungs—but even if it were found, nothing could be traced to him. Returning to the car, he swung it round and headed for Little Wokeham.

Now nothing connecting him with the crime remained, with the single exception of the jewels. He noted that next day he must move his suitcases from Charing Cross to some other station, locking up his booty in one of them as he did so. There it would be safe until he could remove it to some more secure hiding-place.

As he reviewed all that he had done he grew more and more reassured. His plan was good—practically perfect, in fact, and he had carried it out flawlessly. Suspicion was impossible. Admittedly the jewels were a nuisance. He had not wanted them and he did not propose to turn them into money. Eventually he would leave them somewhere and they would be found and returned. He had not thought out the details of that yet, but he would do so later. For the time being, the apparent theft was necessary to supply a motive for the murder. As he had arranged matters, the police would spend their time looking for a non-existent burglar. A little care, and what he had so well begun would be satisfactorily completed.

Then suddenly Guy Plant's complacency was rudely shattered and he dropped, shuddering, to the very depths of despair.

Once again while feeling for his handkerchief he touched his pen pocket. He was not thinking of pens, but vaguely he noted that only his own was there. For a moment he failed to grasp the significance of this, then it burst on him with devastating clarity. Instantly he stopped the car and began feverishly to search his pockets.

No: it was gone! He had lost Bernard's pen!

The sweat stood in great drops on his forehead as he thought of the only place in which he could have dropped it. Since Bernard had given it to him he had stooped only once . . .

Then he breathed again. Before leaving that ghastly room he had looked at the body, carefully and from all sides. The pen was not there. If it had been, he would have seen it. *It was not there.* Desperately he sought to convince himself. Perhaps when he was taking off his overcoat . . .

He thought with horror and exasperation of the series of minor incidents which had led to this terrifying climax. His own pen going dry so that he had borrowed Bernard's, Bernard having broken the clip of his, Bernard being called out of the room before getting it back, Bernard's friend's accident, which put everything else out of his mind. What an incredible run of ill luck! It looked as if Fate had deliberately willed to entrap him!

'Guy Plant found himself on the horns of an appalling dilemma. Should he go on to Hurst Lodge, which for him might be the gateway to prison and death, or should he forfeit all the benefits of his crime and fly the country before it was too late—assuming he could still get away?

He restarted the car and drove slowly on while he wrestled with the problem. Gradually his panic subsided. After all, the situation was not so bad as he had at first believed. Suppose the worst happened and the pen was found beside the body, he had only to swear he left it somewhere for Bernard—on the hall table, for instance. That indeed would be the natural thing for him to do, and the reason he had not mentioned it to Bernard was the reason Bernard had forgotten to ask for it: that the accident had put it out of both their minds. Besides, there was the alibi.

As he thought of the alibi, Plant's courage surged back. The alibi was unbreakable, absolutely and completely convincing. It proved his innocence, no matter what circumstantial evidence might be brought against him. He had just to keep a stiff upper lip, to stick to his story, and all would be well. He drove on more confidently.

All the same, when he pulled up at Hurst Lodge and saw the outline of a policeman at the door, he had to fight hard to prevent panic again seizing him. That civil-spoken man and all his kind were now his mortal enemies, they were out remorselessly for nothing less than his life. Only his utmost efforts and care could save him. With all his strength of mind he braced himself to meet what might be coming.

8

Anthony Mallaby

Mallaby drove home from Clarence Winnington's birthday party like a giant refreshed with wine. He was in an exalted frame of mind without precedent in his experience. After weeks of thought, of hopes and fears and doubts, he had at last acted. He had taken the plunge and the result was staggering! He could not have believed in such good fortune.

Yet it was only negative. The most he could say was that Christina had not turned him down. All the same, from her manner he had believed that she was inclined to accept! He scarcely dared think of what that would mean. To be able to help her, to share her burdens, to work for her, to plan for her! And for himself! Christina in his home, always there. Christina to come back to when his day was done. No more lonely meals and long silent evenings! Even in this backwater of Little Wokeham with its small interests they could be happy. For small interests were as vital as large ones, and with the relinquishment of ambition there was the coming of peace.

Then the reaction set in. Could he make her happy? Was there any chance that an old fogy like himself could satisfy a woman of Christina's type? What he could offer her in material things would be very different to what she was accustomed to; would not he himself fall as far short in companionship? He knew that material comfort and brilliant conversation did not ensure happiness, but did she? Would she expect more than he could give?

Then he realised why she was considering it. She was not happy at Hurst Lodge. He had long been aware of the strain in the atmosphere, but only recently had he divined its cause. It was Clarence Winnington. He was nothing more nor less than a polished bully. He made the house hateful for all its inmates.

Mallaby shrugged. What concerned him was not her reason, but the overwhelming fact that she was considering giving her consent. To avoid trying to influence her unduly he thought that during her week of reflection he ought not to see her. But there was no reason why he should not write to her. As he lay awake that night he feverishly composed phrases which, while telling her of his love and longing, would also paint a fair picture of what she might expect as his wife. He would tell her everything, cons as well as pros, and she would then make her decision with her eyes open, knowing all the facts.

But on the evening of that very day after the birthday party Mallaby learnt something which filled him with doubt and left him wondering whether it would not be his duty to withdraw his proposal.

He had just finished supper and was beginning to draft his letter when his bell rang. It was Bernard Winnington. 'Come in,' Mallaby said warmly as Mrs Hepworth

91

announced him. 'I hope Mr Winnington is none the worse for his labours last night?'

'Unfortunately no; wish he was,' Bernard answered surprisingly.

Mallaby glanced at him sharply. His voice was slightly thick and he distinctly lurched as he crossed the room. On one or two previous occasions Bernard had shown traces of drink, but Mallaby had never before seen him so much affected. Yet he was by no means drunk. He might need careful handling, but Mallaby was not afraid of that. While at sea he had seen plenty of drunkenness.

'Sit here, won't you?' he invited, pushing a deep easy-chair up to the fire and putting a box of cigarettes on the table beside it. 'Called about Ainsworth,' Bernard said suddenly. 'Heard of his accident before dinner. Is he badly hurt?'

It was not Mallaby's habit to discuss his patients, but this, he felt, was a special case. He knew Bernard pretty well by this time and he was aware that he was a close friend of the injured man's. He therefore answered his question. For a time they talked of the case and then Bernard relapsed into silence. 'A pleasant gathering we had last night,' Mallaby said conversationally when the pause threatened to grow too long. 'I enjoyed it.'

Bernard grunted. 'Not too bad,' he admitted slowly. 'The Old Devil can be all right when he wants to.'

Mallaby laughed. 'Is that your name for Mr Winnington? He surely scarcely deserves it?'

Bernard was fumbling with the matches. Mallaby struck one and held it out. With some difficulty Bernard got his cigarette alight.

'That's what he is,' he muttered; 'an old devil. Fact is, he's a dam' bad lot. I—I wish he was dead.'

'Not a very wise thing to say in public, Winnington,' Mallaby said, still smiling. 'Apt to be misunderstood, don't you think?'

''Course I wish he was dead,' Bernard repeated argumentatively. 'Who wouldn't in my place? Rolling, and grudges a pound or two to a fellow who's hard up.'

'You want some money?'

'And it's not as if he needed it for himself,' Bernard went on aggressively. 'I get it when he dies. At least he's said so. So why can't I get an advance? What difference will it make if I have a spot of it now? Tell me that.'

'I shouldn't have thought it would have made any,' Mallaby said pacifically, 'but of course I'm not in a position to judge. I suppose you've asked him?'

'Asked him!' he leered. 'Well, what do you think? Just been asking him. Turned it down.'

'Hard luck. Did you want much?'

'Nothing to him. Only a hundred.'

'A hundred's a good deal to some people.'

'Not to him. With sixty thousand coming to us three after death duties are paid? A hundred! He'd miss it as you or I would a penny.'

As Mallaby heard this he felt the bottom slowly dropping out of his world. He stared.

'Do you mean,' he asked in a hoarse voice, 'that Miss Winnington's an heiress?'

'An even division: Bellissa, Christina and me; so he's told us often enough. Twenty thousand apiece.' Then, as if an idea had struck him, he concentrated his gaze on Mallaby. 'And what is it to you anyway?'

Mallaby hesitated, but only for a moment. 'Just that last night I asked Miss Winnington to be my wife. I didn't know about the money. I shall have to take back what I said.'

Then Bernard gave Mallaby his third surprise of the evening. 'Thought you were a bit gone on Christina,' he said. 'Don't take a word of it back. You'd suit her down to the ground and I hope you pull it off. What did she say?'

'She was kind enough to say she would consider it.'

'Kind enough be damned. That was only to keep you in your place. She knows dam' well what she'll do. Huh, I'm glad about that. We must celebrate. What about a spot of whisky?'

Again Mallaby hesitated. 'It's very handsome of you, but you know you've had a spot already.'

'Think I've had too much? Not on your life. I know what I can carry. Come along; fetch it out.'

Rather unwillingly Mallaby did so, but he felt that one more glass would make little difference in Bernard's condition and he did not wish to antagonise a possible future brother-in-law.

'By the way,' he went on, wondering whether he was not being a fool, 'I'm not a rich man, but if you're in difficulties for a hundred pounds I could just manage it.'

Bernard set down his glass and stared at him. 'By heck, old man, that's generous. But I wouldn't really touch you for a penny: between ourselves, you'd never see it again. Don't worry, I'll be all right. A man I know called Montgomery will put it up. But I'll tell you what I'll do, I'll take another glass of your whisky. Dam' good.'

'No,' said Mallaby, 'you've had enough. Doctor's orders.'

Bernard laughed loud. 'Doctor's orders be damned,' and before Mallaby could make a move, he had snatched the decanter, poured out a third of a glass, dashed in a little soda, and gulped it down.

'Dam' good,' he repeated. He rose slowly to his feet and made for the door. 'I'd better go—ick—while the going's good. Thank you, Mallaby. Dam' decent of you. I'll not forget it.'

He went out, walking steadily enough, though a trifle carefully. Mallaby wondered for a moment whether he should see him home. He suggested it, but, as he expected, Bernard strongly resented the idea. Mallaby could only have carried it out by forcing his company on the man, and for this he felt there was no real need.

As he opened the hall door a figure was approaching. Mallaby recognised him as the local postman, a good fellow with an interest in the works of Charles Dickens, about which he and the doctor had had discussions.

'Good evening, Banks. Do you wish to see me?'

'Yes, sir, if you please.'

'Then just a moment. Well, good night, Winnington. I hope you'll get what you want without difficulty.'

'I'll be all right. 'Night, old man, and thanks. 'Night, Banks.' Bernard moved off in a stately manner.

Relieved to see that he had himself under such control, Mallaby turned to the newcomer. 'Now, Banks, come in and tell me what I can do for you.'

'No need to go in, sir, thank you. It's the missus. She's just had a fall downstairs and is complaining of her ankle. I wonder if you'd come round and have a look at it.'

'Of course I'll come at once. No cuts or bleeding?'

'No, sir, just the ankle. She can't move it and it's painful.'

'All right. Half a minute till I get my bag.'

The house was only a short distance away, and Mallaby

did not trouble to take out his car. The two men walked smartly along while the doctor obtained details of the accident. Just before reaching their destination the church clock struck ten.

'Ten o'clock,' Mallaby said absently, thinking that Bernard had stayed nearly an hour. It had seemed like two.

'That's right, sir,' Banks answered politely. 'I like to hear the old clock at night, though my missus says it keeps her awake.'

Mallaby found the injury was a severe sprain, and a good half-hour was consumed before he had completed his ministrations. While he was working his thoughts were occupied with his job, but when at last he bade the Banks good-night and left for home they reverted immediately to his interview with Bernard.

Certainly Bernard had left him a problem! If Christina were heiress to twenty thousand pounds, what about his proposal?

He had been surprised and intensely gratified by Bernard's reception of his news, and the man's suggestion that Christina would accept had given him a tremendous thrill. But this legacy changed everything. If he had already been doubtful that she was for such as he, no doubts now remained. He was not a fit husband for an heiress. God knew he was not out for Christina's money, but would not everyone think otherwise? In a way it did not matter what outsiders thought, but it mattered intensely what Christina thought, and though he did not believe she would doubt him, he wished to avoid even an appearance of self-seeking.

He saw his duty clearly if unhappily, but he did not see just how he was to carry it out. It would take some courage to tell Christina that he must withdraw his proposal. He could not very well give her his real reason, because in all probability she would not release him: as the owner, she would naturally think the money less important than he would. Altogether it was very puzzling and distressing.

He reached his house about half-past ten, but had scarcely settled down in his chair when the telephone rang.

'Dr Mallaby? This is Josephs, sir, speaking from Hurst Lodge. A terrible thing has happened. Mr Winnington; we've found him, sir; dead, I'm afraid. Will you come up?'

Mallaby could hardly believe his ears. Quickly he seized his bag and hurried out to get his car. As he opened the door he once again saw an approaching caller. This time it was Constable Rice, the Little Wokeham policeman.

'Have you heard about Mr Winnington, sir?' he asked as he jumped off his bicycle.

'Just this moment, Rice. I'm going up. Will you come with me? It'll be quicker than the bicycle.'

'No, sir, thank you, I'll ride on. I might want the machine. I only called to make sure you knew.'

'All right, then I'll see you there.'

Besides being shocked at the news, Mallaby was profoundly mystified. It was true that Winnington suffered from myocarditis, but he was only slightly affected and there had been nothing in his condition to suggest a fatal issue. Perhaps they were mistaken about his death. It was probably only a fainting fit.

Haste at all events was needed, and Mallaby seriously exceeded the speed limit as he drove through the village and turned up to Hurst Lodge. Josephs was waiting for him at the door.

'Well?' asked Mallaby sharply, jumping out of the car. 'How is he?'

Josephs shook his head. 'I'm afraid, sir, you can do nothing. He's dead.' He came close and lowered his voice. '*Murdered*, sir, I fear.'

Mallaby looked at him with a sudden horror. 'Good God!' he ejaculated. He made as if to ask some further questions, then changed his mind. 'Let me see him,' he demanded.

Josephs led the way into the hall. Horne was there and came over.

'Terrible affair, Dr Mallaby,' he remarked with real feeling in his voice. 'If I can do anything, I hope you'll tell me.'

Mallaby nodded. 'Rice is following me up,' he said. 'Perhaps you'd watch for him and send him after us.'

In the meantime Josephs was moving towards the library. He opened the door, Mallaby entered, he followed and drew the door to again.

For a moment Mallaby did not see the figure lying sprawling behind the writing-desk, then it caught his eye and he stepped forward. One glance at the shattered skull was enough. Here was death, and instantaneous death at that, and here also was murder, for such a wound could never have been self-inflicted.

Mallaby's horror grew. It was not the sight of sudden death which affected him, even though the victim was his host of the previous evening. It was the thought of Christina. The affair would be a great shock to her, and the police inquiry which must follow would worry her horribly. How he wished he could do something to shield her from the ordeal. Gladly he would do anything, *anything*, if only it would help her . . .

But this was not the time to think of Christina. With an effort he switched back his attention to the immediate present. Getting up from kneeling beside the body, he turned and faced Josephs.

'You're only too correct,' he declared gravely. 'A terrible affair! Tell me what happened.'

Josephs was silent for a moment as if to marshal his thoughts. Then he began:

'We had dinner at eight, sir, as usual, and after dinner Mr Winnington said he wanted to read a magazine article in connection with something for his book, and that he would come here. Mr Horne asked would he like him to go along and take notes, but Mr Winnington said no, that it would be time enough later, if he thought the article was valuable. I therefore brought Mr Winnington's coffee in here and took the rest to the lounge.'

'When was that?' asked Mallaby.

'Just after nine, sir. Mr Winnington thanked me and said I need not collect the tray till later, as he didn't want to be disturbed. That was the last time I saw him alive.'

'Did he seem normal?'

'Absolutely, sir.'

'Very well. What happened then?'

'Shortly before ten-thirty Sir Malcolm Philpot rang up to speak to Mr Winnington about some matter they had been discussing. I came to call him, but found the door locked. I knocked, but could get no reply, so I told Sir Malcolm that Mr Winnington was engaged for the moment, but that he would ring up presently. I then went out and round the house to try to find Mr Winnington, for I supposed he must have gone out through the french window. The window was closed, but the curtains were not fitting tightly and I looked in. You'll believe me, sir, when I say I got a shock.'

'I don't doubt it. Well?'

'I tried the window, and to my surprise found it open, for I had seen that it was locked earlier in the evening. I went in and opened the door to the hall. Then I called Mr Horne from his room upstairs and he came in and had a look. He said to phone you and the police while he told the ladies.'

'That all?'

'That's all, sir.'

Mallaby nodded and turned back to the body. He was not a police doctor, but he knew enough of such work to realise that until it had been examined by experts and photographed he must not move it. However, one question he thought he could settle: the approximate time of death. This in any case would be wanted by the police. Quickly he made his tests. Alive less than an hour ago, he thought. It was now getting on to eleven. Death had probably occurred shortly after ten.

He was about to get up again when something shining on the floor close under the body caught his eye. He looked more carefully and saw that it was a fountain-pen. It had a broken clip.

Mallaby had seen a pen like that before, and he suddenly felt panic rising in his mind. It could not, oh no, it could not be! Bernard was a good fellow, he would never be guilty of such a crime. At least not when he was normal. But Mallaby could not forget that tonight he was not normal. Those extra glasses of whisky! He had had more than enough before he took them, then he had the drink celebrating the proposal, and after it that other to which he had helped himself. That last was a big drink, at least a third of a tumbler of whisky. With all that spirit a man's judgment would be undermined and his self-control weakened. Moreover, he had just had a dispute with Clarence about money, and had said in Mallaby's hearing that he wished he was dead. Perhaps worst of all, if he had walked straight home he would have arrived about ten past ten. Mallaby felt sick.

He forced himself to consider the implications of the idea. If Bernard were guilty, what about Christina? If Bernard were arrested, were tried, were—Mallaby could scarcely bring himself to frame the thought—if he were *executed*, what about Christina?

Distressing as the mere fact of a murder in the household would be for her, it would be absolutely nothing in comparison. Her personal innocence would not save her. She would suffer horribly. It would be no exaggeration to say that her entire life would be ruined.

Then a further idea shot into his mind. Could he not save her from all this? At a cost certainly, the cost of his integrity, of his professional honour of which he thought even more, perhaps even of his liberty itself. But what mattered the cost to him, if only Christina were saved pain?

Mallaby writhed in the anguish of the decision. The worst of it was that he had no time to think it over, no opportunity really to weigh the pros and cons. He must make up his mind now, immediately. Rice would be here at any moment.

As the thought crossed his mind he heard the man's voice in the hall. Josephs turned away to show him in. For the tenth of a second Mallaby hesitated. Then quickly he slipped the pen out from under the body and put it in his pocket.

But was this enough? Even without the pen would not Bernard still be in danger? Could he not do something more to help Christina's brother? Like a flash he saw how he could save him.

Rice had been noting Joseph's story, but now he came over and Mallaby heard the words he had been dreading: 'About what time would you say that death took place, doctor?'

An agony took hold of Mallaby's mind, but he crushed it down and answered as coolly as he could. 'A couple of hours, I should say. I can't tell exactly, of course, but I should say roughly between nine and half-past.'

It was done! He could not go back on it now. He had lost his honour, he had lied on a matter in which truth was of supreme importance, he had made himself an accessory to murder after the fact. Please God it would not be in vain. Please God Christina would be spared suffering.

9

Christina Winnington

On looking backwards over that fateful Sunday following the birthday party, Christina felt that every detail of its happenings was seared for ever into her consciousness.

It had opened promisingly enough. Though breakfast was a movable feast with dishes kept warm on a hotplate, everyone had turned up at approximately the same time. The day was fine and spirits generally were good. After the meal they had all drifted away on their lawful occasions. Lunch had been equally pleasant and so had tea. It was after tea that the discussion about the battle of Blenheim had taken place and Bernard had heard of his friend's accident. Shortly after, Guy had gone home to attend to some work.

By dinner-time the atmosphere had changed. Indeed, the meal was somewhat of an ordeal, for the tempers of both Clarence and Bernard had markedly deteriorated. Clarence was in one of his bad moods, more biting and sarcastic than ever, and Bernard was excited and ill at ease and smelt strongly of whisky. Though he took his share of the conversation, he ate with a heavy frown and addressed as few remarks to his uncle as possible. Christina was shocked to see how much whisky he drank, and decided that on some more auspicious occasion she would remonstrate with him. It was a relief when immediately after the meal the men left the lounge. Clarence remarked that he was going to the library to read an article in a magazine which had been sent him, Horne betook himself upstairs to work, and Bernard disappeared without comment.

Christina and Bellissa sat on in the lounge for perhaps an hour, chatting desultorily. Then Bellissa went to her room to match some silk for her needlework. She was away for an interminable time, insomuch that when she came back Christina remonstrated.

'I could have matched enough silk in the time to reach from here to Guildford,' she complained. 'You've been half an hour.'

Bellissa laughed. 'You've got a touch of Uncle Clarence's complaint,' she retorted. 'But I admit I do potter.'

'Sorry,' Christina smiled. 'I somehow feel a bit east-windy tonight, I don't know why. Reaction from the dissipation of last night, I suppose.'

Bellissa laughingly agreed and they went on chatting.

It was just after half-past ten when there occurred the first scene of that drama which was to change the lives of all of them more fundamentally than anything which they had yet undergone. Josephs suddenly appeared and asked for Horne.

'He went upstairs,' explained Christina, staring at him in surprise, while her heart sank and a premonition of disaster crept into her mind. The man's face was grey and there was a look of horror in his eyes. His manner was furtive and his words a trifle breathless.

'Josephs looks as if he was about to pass out,' she said. 'Something's surely pretty badly wrong.'

'Having my back to him, I didn't notice, but if there's any trouble we'll soon hear it.'

'Mr Horne will deal with it, whatever it is.'

Bellissa looked over with more interest in her face. 'What's happened to our mutual friend? I've met him off and on for a year now, and never before has he come out of his shell as he did this weekend. He's always been polite, you know, but about as genial as an iceberg in a fog.'

'I don't know, but one night he suddenly thawed and told me all about his life. It's his secret, so don't repeat it, but he came here for leisure to write a book. He's not a rotter as we thought, but a thinker and a worker.'

'You don't say so. If he was always like tonight, he'd be a good sort.'

'I think he is a good sort. He seems to be afraid of having his ideals laughed at. That's why he was so close.'

Before Bellissa could reply, the subject of the conversation entered. He was looking not ill or frightened like Josephs, but very grave.

'I'm afraid you must prepare for some dreadful news,' he began, and gently and kindly he told them of the discovery of Clarence's body, going on to explain the apparent impossibility of accident or suicide. 'There's nothing for you to do,' he continued. 'It was obvious that we must have the doctor and the police, and we've rung them up.'

For a moment both women were stunned by the suddenness of the shock. Christina felt numb, and beyond a few exclamations was unable immediately to discuss the affair. Bellissa seemed less affected and talked calmly enough to Horne.

Then suddenly, in spite of herself, the same dreadful idea which had occurred to Mallaby forced its way into Christina's consciousness. Fortunately for her peace of mind she knew nothing of the pen; the circumstances in general were disquieting enough.

'It's good of you to do everything and we're very grateful,' she said rather tremulously, 'but it's Bernard's job. Where is he?'

'Gone out, Josephs says. His coat and hat are gone at all events. That's something I wanted to ask you: have you any idea where we might find him?'

Christina shook her head. 'Not the slightest, I'm afraid. He might have gone to inquire for Mr Ainsworth. I suggest that Josephs ring up them and the Montgomerys and the Arbuthnots and perhaps the Three Swallows. Tell him to use his own discretion. He'll know.'

'And of course Guy should be told,' added Bellissa.

Horne got up. 'I'll speak to Josephs. Then I'll wait to hear what Dr Mallaby says. I'll come and tell you directly I know myself.'

'Oh my God, Christina, what a ghastly affair!' Bellissa moaned when Horne had gone. 'Uncle Clarence! Murdered!'

'I can't believe it. His death perhaps, dreadful as that is. But the other! Oh no, it's simply not possible!'

'Mr Horne's not likely to have made a mistake. No one would say that unless he was sure.'

'But who could have done such a thing? No one hated him to that extent.' Christina spoke confidently, yet that hideous idea was there eating insidiously into her mind.

'One shouldn't think so.' Bellissa did not sound so convinced. 'It's a dreadful shock, Christina, but I don't suppose either of us can pretend a great deal of sorrow. None of us were actually fond of him. He didn't allow us to be.'

'Oh, I *am* sorry. He had his faults, as we all know, but he was straight. He kept his bargain to us for one thing.'

'He will have if he's left us the money.'

The money! In the first shock of the tragedy Christina had forgotten it, but now in spite of herself she could not prevent her thoughts from dwelling on it. If Clarence had left it as he said he would, and she had no reason to doubt him, what a change had come over her prospects! Instead of being a poor relation, a sort of upper servant, she would from now on be her own mistress! With five or six hundred a year added to her existing pittance, she would be well-to-do. She could live as she liked, travel, see life, do anything!

Then she chided herself for thinking such thoughts when her uncle was not yet cold. She was really more mercenary than she could have believed. Let her think of the poor old man lying dead in the next room, instead of her own prospects. Bringing herself back with an effort to the present, she heard Bellissa's voice.

'It won't be very pleasant here,' she was saying. 'In fact, it will be horrible, with police about and inquiries and perhaps an arrest and trial and all that. You must come away, Christina. You must come back with me. You won't be wanted here in any case. Bernard can do everything.'

To Christina the affair continued to open vistas. 'It's going to make tremendous changes,' she answered. 'I suppose this place will be sold. We'll have to get rid of the staff. There'll be a lot to think about.'

They continued talking while the minutes slipped slowly by. Then Horne came back with Mallaby. The doctor somehow looked older; anxious and careworn.

'I'm terribly distressed about this,' he said. 'It will be a heavy blow to you all. I can only say for your comfort that there was no suffering.'

'A mercy!'

'Something to be thankful for at all events.'

'It's only fair to tell you that there must be an inquest and a police inquiry. But you won't be unduly troubled. The police in these cases are always as considerate as possible to the relatives.'

'Thank you, Dr Mallaby. Tell us what you can.'

About the murder he could tell them little more than had Horne. He simply added that in his opinion the affair had taken place about nine or shortly after and that death had been instantaneous. 'Rice had to report to his superiors, of course,' he went on, 'and an officer is coming from Guildford.'

As he spoke, Horne sprang from his chair with a gesture.

'Oh, Mrs Plant,' he said, 'you'll never forgive me, but in the search for Bernard I omitted to phone your husband. I'm terribly sorry and I'll do it now.'

Bellissa took the news calmly. 'Don't worry,' she answered. 'It will make no difference. He couldn't have done anything more than you have if he had been here.'

'That's very generous,' said Horne as he went out.

'We're wondering where Bernard is,' Christina remarked after some further talk. 'He should be here, but we can't find him.'

'He was with me earlier,' answered Mallaby. 'He looked in to ask about Mr Ainsworth. We chatted, I suppose, for nearly an hour.'

"Oh? What time was that?'

'He left just a minute or two before ten; I know that, because I was called out just at that hour. He must have come a few minutes after nine.'

At these words a great flood of relief surged over Christina's mind. The murder, then, had taken place while Bernard was with the doctor! Instantly and intensely she felt ashamed of her earlier thoughts.

'What possible explanation of it can there be?' she asked. 'Who could have done such a thing?'

'I was just coming to a point which may have something to do with that,' Mallaby returned. 'We find that Mr Winnington's keys are hanging in his safe. Horne and Josephs were wondering were your jewels there?'

'Yes, of course!' Christina retorted, suddenly exasperated by his obtuseness. Her voice rose sharply. 'Do you mean the jewels are gone?'

'We don't know. We haven't opened the safe.'

'Don't know!' Christina could have screamed at him, and even Bellissa seemed roused from her accustomed complacency. 'But, my goodness, can't you look? There was over ten thousand pounds' worth of jewellery in it last night!'

Mallaby looked appalled. Horne, who had just re-entered, whistled. 'That's the whole thing,' he muttered, while the doctor nodded his agreement.

'Christina sprang to her feet. 'But are they there now?' she almost shouted. 'What's the matter with you both? If you don't know, go and look! Don't stand there so helplessly.'

Mallaby glanced at Horne. 'We're dreadfully sorry, Miss Winnington,' he said apologetically, 'but it's impossible. The policeman won't allow anyone to touch the safe till it's been tested for fingerprints. We might have insisted, but of course we know, and you must know too, that he's in the right.'

'When's the test to be made?'

'Directly the expert arrives with the apparatus. He's been sent for and should be here any moment now.'

They were right, of course, but it was difficult to sit still and wait for such vital information. Christina was not more fond of money than most people, but the jewels were to be divided equally between her and Bellissa, and apart from her love of the stones for their own sake, five thousand pounds' worth was an amount which few women could consider unmoved.

As they were discussing the matter they heard steps and strange voices in the hall. The two men went out, Horne returning almost immediately.

'Those are police officers and a doctor from Guildford,' he explained, 'and the Chief Constable has come with them. We'll know in a few moments about the jewels.'

as they wanted to get statements from everyone first.

It proved an optimistic estimate. Slowly the minutes passed, but no sign came from the library.

'I wonder where Bernard is?' Christina remarked anxiously, as they tried to keep up a semblance of conversation. 'He should certainly be here when all this is going on.'

'He couldn't know it was going to take place,' Horne pointed out, and his dogmatic certainty comforted Christina unreasonably.

'Guy ought to be here also,' Bellissa remarked. 'Let's see, how long is it since you rang him up?'

'It's five minutes to twelve now. About three-quarters of an hour.'

'He should be here. What's keeping him, I wonder?'

As she spoke there was a movement in the hall and a man's voice sounded.

'There's Bernard,' cried Christina, jumping up. She hurried to the door. Bernard was standing with Josephs, evidently hearing the story.

'Oh, Bernard, isn't this *awful*!' Christina went over.

'My God, yes, it's pretty bad! And Josephs says the jewels are gone.'

'Oh!' Christina felt a bitter pang of disappointment. 'We feared it, but we didn't know.'

'I just heard it this moment from the officer, madam,' put in Josephs.

'What are they doing?' went on Christina. 'When shall we hear the details?'

'They're all in the library, madam; three police officers and Dr Mallaby and another doctor and Colonel Lester. An officer came out just now and mentioned about the jewels, and said no one was to leave the house or to go to bed for the present, I was just coming to tell you when Mr Bernard came in.'

With every moment that passed Christina was growing easier in her mind on at least one point. Bernard was all right! He was certainly smelling a little of drink, but thank God he was completely sober. Also he was showing no traces of uneasiness or fear.

How foolish, how wicked indeed, she had been to allow doubts of him to enter her mind! Bernard was far from perfect, and he had been to blame for giving way to such an extent to his love for gambling, but at heart he was good and true. He would never do anything mean or really evil. Of course she had never doubted him: it was only the drink he had taken that had frightened her. All the same, it was an overwhelming relief to be sure that her fears were groundless.

'Where were you?' she asked, while Josephs discreetly withdrew to the end of the hall. 'I thought you ought to be here with all this going on.'

'My dear, I didn't know it was going on,' he pointed out with a rueful smile. 'As a matter of fact, I felt restless after dinner and went out. I dropped in to see Mallaby to inquire for Ainsworth, and stayed chatting for about an hour. He told me what he had asked you and I insisted on celebrating, with the result that I took a drop too much. I decided to walk it off, so as not to disgrace the house by arriving home drunk. Incidentally, best congrats. I told him I hoped he'd pull it off and he was bucked no end.'

'I can't think of that now. This ghastly business has put everything else out of my head.'

'Of course, and we'll think still more about it before we're through. But we can't pretend sorrow that we don't feel.'

As he spoke, the library door opened and the Chief Constable, Colonel Lester, came out, followed by a plain-clothes officer.

'Good evening, Miss Winnington. Good evening, Winnington,' he said, coming forward. 'May I say how very distressed I am about this affair, and for the unpleasantness that I'm afraid we shall have to cause you? I can only promise that we shall keep our demands down to a minimum.'

Christina held out her hand. 'Thank you, Colonel Lester. We understand, of course, that you have to do your duty, and you'll find us only anxious to help,' while Bernard added: 'Yes, of course, that's understood.'

'Won't you tell us what has happened?' went on Christina. 'We've not had any details yet. Come into the lounge and sit down.'

'We've only just discovered the facts for ourselves,' answered Lester, following her and greeting Bellissa and Horne. 'Mr Winnington, I'm sorry to say, was struck on the head by some heavy object and instantly killed. You'll be glad to know that there was no suffering. But I'm afraid I must add that your jewels appear to have been stolen. At least, the empty cases are there, but no stones.'

'They were locked in the safe last night,' Christina put in.

'So I am informed, and I shall want to get all particulars about them from you.'

'How did the murderer get in?' Bernard asked.

'Through the window at the back of Mr Winnington's desk. He cut out a pane, put in his hand, and opened the window. He seems to have hidden behind the curtains and waited for Mr Winnington's entrance, and when Mr Winnington sat down at his desk he stepped forward and delivered the blow. Then he took his keys and opened the safe.'

'But how could he have known that the jewels were there?' Christina said wonderingly.

'Ah!' Colonel Lester returned. 'There you put your finger on the chief problem in the affair. That's just what we want to find out. And now perhaps you'll help us by answering a few questions? I think I'll leave you; but Inspector Nelson will ask what he wants to know.'

In the middle of the interrogation Guy Plant arrived. He apologised for his late appearance and explained that he had had a little trouble with the car. He seemed unexpectedly upset about the tragedy, though Christina uncharitably suspected that it was the loss of the jewels which had really affected him.

Christina thought the statements taken by Nelson extraordinarily dull and unilluminating, though he appeared satisfied enough with them. After they had been transcribed and signed he withdrew again to the library, leaving the others free to follow their various inclinations. As it was now between two and three, these took the form of an immediate retirement to bed.

10

Joseph French

At five o'clock on that same Monday morning the telephone at the head of Chief Inspector French's bed trilled sharply. Sleepily he switched on the light and put out his hand for the receiver.

'Sorry to knock you up, sir,' came a voice which he recognised as that of one of the men on duty at the Yard, 'but an urgent job has come in. Murder and jewel robbery at Little Wokeham near Guildford. Influential man and all that. We've spoken to the Super and he would like you to take over. The murder was in a house, but they think there may be outside traces and they suggest starting early in case of rain. The Super thought it might be well if you left here at six. That okay?'

French was now wide awake. 'Six will do,' he answered. 'I take it you'll arrange for Carter and the car? Who else shall we want? Hudson and Leech, I suppose. Will you fix it up?'

'Right, sir. They'll be ready.'

French had been anticipating a rather boring day setting

out the evidence against two men who were shortly to be charged at the Old Bailey with large-scale fraud and arson. He was not sorry to think that this work would now be delegated to a subordinate while he tackled a new job away from the Yard. Office work was not his forté, and he preferred investigating a case on the ground to the subsequent desk routine of its development and preparation for the Crown Prosecutor.

'Where is it this time?' Mrs French grumbled. She always grumbled when his rest was curtailed, but already she was up and filling the electric kettle.

'Near Guildford. Place called Little Wokeham. Can't say I know it.'

'Guildford? Then you may get home at night?'

'I hope so. You may be sure I will if I can.'

'I'd better pack your bag?'

'Yes, please. I might have to stay.'

As he dressed, French mused on the difference between the male and the female mind. If Em had been a man she would have asked about the case, not where he was going to sleep. She took no interest in the details of crime, not even whether he was going out to investigate murder or petty larceny. Then he saw that he was wrong; their minds were alike after all. Both were interested in their own jobs.

A few minutes later he told himself it was lucky that this was so, as otherwise that appetising breakfast of eggs and bacon and coffee would not have materialised with such astounding speed. It was due, he realised, to his wife's professional competence that when he left for the Yard he felt on the top of his form and ready for anything which might eventualise.

A large car was waiting, the back stacked with bags and

apparatus, and with it were his three companions to be: Sergeant Carter, his immediate assistant, Hudson the photographer, and Leech, who did the fingerprint work. At one time French had taken his own photographs and prints, but now he delegated this work to specialists, partly because they theoretically did it better—though this he would never allow—but principally because it left him free to go on more quickly with other parts of the investigation.

It was still dusk as they drove out of the gates and turned west past the Houses of Parliament and along the river bank to Putney Bridge. Here they crossed the Thames, working south-west to Putney Heath. Carter, who was driving, made good speed along the Kingston Bypass, but slowed down again on reaching the Portsmouth Road at Esher. As they ran through the charmingly wooded country between Cobham and Ripley the sun was well above the eastern horizon. A beautiful morning, clear and fresh and fragrant, with the promise of a perfect day to follow. French, thinking of his somewhat moth-eaten desk, congratulated himself.

At the Surrey County Constabulary headquarters in Guildford, where they had been instructed to call, Inspector Nelson was waiting for them. He had really little more than returned from Hurst Lodge, but had managed to snatch time for a shave and breakfast.

'It's not an easy place to find unless you know the way,' he said to French, 'so I thought I'd go ahead in my car. Perhaps, sir, you might care to come in with me, and I could tell you something of the case as we go?'

'Good idea, inspector,' French returned cheerily. 'I know Guildford and the Hog's Back well, but I don't think I was ever in Little Wokeham.'

'You were on that Earle case on the Hog's Back, sir? I remember hearing of it. But it was before my time here. I was transferred recently.'

'Yes, I was back and forward between this and Farnham a good many times. A delightful country: I enjoyed it. Now, inspector, I suppose we haven't very far to go, so perhaps you would let me have an idea of things?'

'Certainly, sir.' He swung the car into Quarry Street from the sloping High Street. 'First, I should say that Colonel Lester, our C.C., wants to see you. He said he'd come along to Hurst Lodge later; that's where the affair took place. He was out there with me last night.'

'I'll be glad to see him.'

'He's personally interested in the case, sir. He knew the deceased and the family in a social way. Apart from that, it's an important case. The dead man is a retired colonial governor, and over ten thousand pounds' worth of jewellery has been stolen. The thief—we could only find traces of one man—cut a pane out of one of the library windows, opened the catch and stepped in. He hid behind the curtain, and when the deceased came into the room and sat down at his desk he hit him on the head and stove in his skull. Then he took his keys, got the jewels out of the safe, and walked out of the french window.'

'One of those simple problems that often turn out so difficult?'

'Just what the C.C. said, sir. The thief had made deep footprints on a flower-bed outside the window he entered by but these were too blurred to be useful. The C.C. thought it would be worth looking for clear prints further away, and that's the idea of the early start. He was afraid if rain came we might lose them.'

'Very wise too.' They had been going south, but now they turned east, and passing up a hill along one of the charming sunk Surrey lanes, reached Little Wokeham. The tiny village lay sprawled along the lane; it could scarcely be called a street. Half-way through it was a crossroads, and turning here, they came out on open heath. Soon they reached a large house standing alone and above the others. At the door was a police officer.

'This is Hurst Lodge, sir, and this is Constable Rice, the local man, who was called in when the affair was discovered. Don't go off duty, Rice, until Chief Inspector French has finished with you.'

'If he's been out all night I don't think I need keep him,' French said, with his ready consideration for others. He turned to Rice. 'Tell me what happened before Inspector Nelson arrived.'

Rice consulted his notebook, presumably to indicate the compleat constable, for it was unlikely there was anything he could not have remembered. 'I was rung up, sir, at ten-thirty-five last night by Mr Josephs, the butler, who stated that Mr Winnington, his employer, had just been found dead under suspicious circumstances. I came up at once on my bicycle, only calling on Dr Mallaby to make sure he had heard. That's the local doctor, sir. He was just starting in his car and reached here before me. I saw at once it was a case of murder, in which Dr Mallaby agreed. The deceased's keys were in his safe, and I asked if anything valuable was kept there. Mr Josephs and Mr Horne, that's the deceased's secretary, said valuable jewellery was believed to be in the house and was probably kept there. I didn't want to open the safe in case I should spoil fingerprints, so I rang up headquarters in Guildford and reported.'

'That seems clear,' said French. 'You didn't ring up Guildford directly you heard something was wrong?'

'I got on to him about that, sir,' put in Nelson. 'He should have.'

'I didn't wait to do it, sir,' Rice explained. 'I thought something urgent might be required, and besides I wanted to be sure what to report.'

'I don't think we can grumble about his actions, inspector. And you were very right not to touch the safe. No, constable, you needn't wait. If any point arises I'll see you later.'

Rice, saluting with evident gratitude, withdrew, and the others entered the house. Nelson led the way to the library.

'The body's been taken upstairs, sir, where you can see it when you wish to. The photographs weren't quite ready when we left Guildford, but they'll be sent after us shortly. In the meantime I can describe how things were when we arrived.'

'That'll do splendidly, inspector.'

Nelson told his story, pointing in turn to the broken pane, the footmarks across the flower-bed and behind the curtain, the keys hanging in the safe, and the other objects illustrating the tale. 'Seeing that the man was dead,' he went on, 'the C.C. thought we should first inquire about the jewels, so we got the handle of the safe tested for prints. There were some portions of prints, which were afterwards identified as the deceased's, but there were also smudges, suggesting that the thief had worn gloves.'

'Only to be expected, I suppose.'

'Yes, sir. In the safe were a number of jewel-cases, most of them open and all empty. You can see them there.'

'What about prints? Did you test?'

'Yes, sir, the same thing obtained. There were a number of prints on them, and these have not yet been identified, but over them were the same print-shaped smudges. It was clear again that the last person to handle them had worn gloves.'

'Did you get a note of what was missing?'

'Yes, sir, I took preliminary statements from the members of the household, as well as listing the jewels. I brought carbons of all for your file.'

'Thanks. Let's have a look at the list.'

Nelson ran through the papers in his despatch-case and handed one across. French glanced down it.

'This is a good amateur's description,' he remarked, 'but I'm afraid not much help in identifying the stuff. The emphasis is laid on the setting, you see. For instance: "Brooch, large opal surrounded by seven small diamonds in chased gold setting." When the gold is melted down and the stones are sold separately that description won't be very useful. Was the stuff kept here or in Town, do you know?'

'In Town, sir.'

'Where?'

Nelson looked crestfallen. 'I'm afraid we didn't get that, sir.'

'Well, it seems to me it's about the first thing we want. If it's been in the charge of a jeweller he'll have a proper specification, but if it's been stored in a bank or a safe deposit there mayn't be any. Of course, if we can't get the information in London we probably can in the West Indies.'

'The deceased must have employed a jeweller somewhere.'

'That's it. Now, let's see, this is urgent because we must get a description circulated before the thief can dispose of the stuff, but this footprint business is urgent also. Have you done anything about that?'

'Yes, sir. Directly it became light I put three men on to search the grounds and approaches.'

'That's good. Then, seeing it's a fine morning, we'll deal with the description first. When did the jewels come here?'

'On Saturday. But I'd better get Josephs. He knows more about it than I.'

He left the room, returning in a moment with the butler. French, avoiding Clarence's desk, cleared a table in a corner of the room and drew up a chair. As he sat down Carter took the opposite place, with his notebook ready.

'Good morning, Josephs,' said French. 'I'll not keep you long. I expect you're busy over breakfast?'

'That's all right, sir. It's not ready yet.'

'It's about these jewels. I'm told they were kept in Town. Do you know where?'

'No, sir.'

'When did they come down?'

'On Saturday morning. They were brought by a young man. Looked like an assistant in a good shop or perhaps a bank clerk. He asked for Mr Winnington and I showed him in here. He stayed perhaps twenty minutes, and then Mr Winnington rang and I showed him out.'

'How did he come?'

'By car.'

'Alone?'

'No, sir, there was another man driving the car. He didn't get out.'

'Are the family up yet?'

'No, sir. They were up very late last night. They'll not come down for some time.'

'I want to know where those two men came from. We'll have a look through Mr Winnington's papers, but if we can't find it I'm afraid you'll have to ask the ladies. However, I'll let you know. That'll do for the present.'

French got up. 'I didn't want to tackle the papers yet, but I suppose we must. Inspector, will you and Carter lift the desk drawers out and take them right away. Then go through them for a jeweller's address. I'll take the safe.'

It was soon evident that whatever failings the deceased might have had, untidiness was not one of them. The contents of the safe were methodically arranged and obviously had not been disturbed by the thief. On the top shelf were the empty jewel-cases with all kinds of current matter, bank-books, recent cheque-blocks, income-tax vouchers and such like, together with letters, the latter in folders labelled by subject. Below was old stuff, mostly relating to the period of Winnington's colonial governorship. Glancing over the folders, French selected one labelled 'Personal Property'. With a grunt of satisfaction he picked out a folded paper on which was written in what he presumed was Winnington's hand, 'My Wife's Jewels'.

It was a priced inventory by Messrs Windthorpe & Margesson of Bond Street, made when undertaking the custody of the jewellery some two years earlier. The various items, while no doubt described more accurately than on Nelson's list, were still not sufficiently specific to identify the stones. However, the firm would probably have further information.

'Don't worry with those drawers,' French said. 'I've got what I want. Nelson, just come and check your list over with this.'

The two were practically identical, though Windthorpe

& Margesson's inventory contained two or three small items which the ladies had omitted.

'Forgot them in the upset, I expect,' French commented, glancing at his watch. It was just half-past eight. 'Too early to ring these folk up, so we'll have a look at what your men have done outside. You'd better lock this door to the hall. We'll go out by the french window and you might put one of your men in charge here. You've tested the door-handles for prints, I suppose?'

'Yes, we've got photographs of all. There are prints on the door to the hall, Josephs' probably, though we didn't have time to test that. The same prints occur on the outside handle of the french window, which is also what you'd expect. On the inside handle the smudges of the gloves were over everything.'

'Right, then we may go.' French opened the french window, carefully avoiding damaging the marks. Then he stood in the opening, taking in the view.

It was certainly a pleasant prospect to which this east side of the house faced. To the left the grounds were bounded by a plantation of pines and birches, the former in the rear, standing up dark and tall and austere, the latter lower but thicker and forming an impenetrable screen against the road which ran behind them. To the right the ground sloped down to a tiny valley, across which was a fine extended view of rich agricultural country stretching away to a line of distant hills. In the valley, part of which was inside the grounds, was the small stream which had been dammed to form the pond. A path left the french window and ran down across the lawn to the pond, then sweeping to the right it made a complete circuit of the water. Returning to near the house, it crossed itself at right angles like an inverted alpha, and led on into the fruit and vegetable garden on the left. The flower-garden and tennis-court were at the right side of the house, balancing the garage, which was hidden in the trees near the road.

Stretching along the wall of the house at either side of the walk was a rose-bed, and it was across this, in front of a second window, that the marks of the murderer had been found. French moved over and examined them. There were several prints, superimposed where the man had stood while cutting out the pane, but the soil was sandy, and, as Nelson had said, none of them was clear enough to be of value.

The path was of fine gravel, tramped smooth in the centre and showing no impressions. A branch passed round the house and joined the drive in front.

'Why did you expect to find prints?' French asked. 'It seems to me that the murderer could have walked round the house and down the drive keeping on the hard all the way.'

'That's right, sir, he could. It was just an idea of the C.C.'s. He thought that between nine and half-past he might have hesitated to go on the drive in case of meeting someone. If he didn't go on the drive he must have walked over soft ground somewhere.'

'On the grass perhaps?'

'Yes, sir, the C.C. admitted that. All the same, he thought there was just a chance. He suggested that if we went round the boundaries of the place we might find where he had got in or out.'

'I agree with him; it's well worth while searching. What about seeing what your men have done?'

As Nelson led the way round the house towards the

flower-gardens on the right, French felt his old satisfaction in getting to grips with a job. For some time at least he was going to have plenty of work. He was not afraid of work; what he did hate and fear was coming to the end of his resources with his problem still unsolved. So far as he could see, such a condition would not obtain in this case for a long time to come.

11

Joseph French

Constable Fleming met them as they turned the corner of the house. In reply to Nelson's question he explained that he had been over the whole of the east of the little estate, covering the tennis-ground, the flower-garden and a large area of shrubs and lawn, and he was certain that there were no traces in that direction. Sending him in to take charge of the library, the others found the second man. He had done the front of the house and down to the road, and was working round to the west. He also had seen nothing.

As they moved north towards the pond they saw the third man approaching. He saluted.

'I've found some prints in the lane adjoining the property, sir,' he reported to Nelson. 'They show only here and there, but they seem to lead from the road to and from a gap in the hedge bounding the grounds.'

'That's interesting,' said French. 'Let's see 'em.'

They walked down the path along the tiny lake, passing the spur which led to the boat-house and slip. Where the path approached the boundary the constable pointed to a thin spot in the hedge.

'Someone has squeezed through there, sir,' he asserted. 'If you look you'll see broken twigs.'

'That's right,' French approved, 'and the grass below has been trampled. Take a note, Carter, to search this place thoroughly. You might find a scrap of wool on one of those thorns.'

'You can get out here, sir.'

The constable pointed to another gap and they all squeezed through. The lane was narrow, with a gravel surface in some places washed by rain and in others muddy.

'Not bad for prints,' French observed. 'Let's see what you've found, constable.'

The man led the way towards the road. At the point where they were walking there were smooth grass edges, but a little further some bushes on either side had restricted the width to the actual cartway. Here at odd intervals were footprints and parts of prints pointing in both directions. They suggested that a previous passer-by had been forced off the grass. What marks were visible were admirably clear.

French whistled when he saw them. 'A bit of luck, this,' he declared.

'It looks promising,' Nelson admitted. 'A man's tracks, and made by the same person in each direction.'

'That's right,' French agreed. 'And he went first towards and then away from the gap. You notice that this step pointing towards the road is superimposed on that going the other way?'

'One for the C.C., sir.'

'It certainly is. Did you look along the lane above the gap in the hedge, constable?'

'Yes, sir. I could find nothing beyond the gap.'

'What about the other direction?'

'I've been down to the road, but I lost the prints on the hard.'

'We'll look again. Man might have got into a car and there may be traces of where it was parked.'

They walked to the last print, which was within about fifty yards of the road, and then began a systematic search of the grass and bushes at the sides. Presently Nelson gave a call.

'Something here. There's a print on that soft place between those shrubs.'

French, who had been examining the other side, crossed over. The print was not clear, but it looked the same size and shape as the others. French stared at the place and then pointed to the ground. Between the bushes was the faint trace of a bicycle tyre.

'So that's how he came,' he observed. 'Parked it between the bushes and walked up. Pity that print of the tyre isn't clearer.'

'No good for identification, I'm afraid.'

'No. And no other traces between here and the road. Well, we can't have everything. Carter, you might go and tell Leech I want a couple of casts of these footprints. That one and that,' he scraped crosses beside particularly clear right and left impressions. 'Tell him I'll be back here before he's finished. Also get Hudson to do some photos of the lane and prints and the gap and where the bike was left. He'll know if you explain things to him. Meantime, Nelson, I want this man of yours to stay here and keep passers-by off the prints.' He glanced at his watch. 'I'll go back to the house and try if I can get Windthorpe & Margesson on the phone.'

Neither of the jeweller principals had come in when French got through, but the assistant who replied knew all about the jewels. After expressing his concern at the theft, he said the jewels were normally kept by his firm in their strong-room, and sent down to Hurst Lodge on Mr Winnington's request. Usually they remained away for one night only, but owing to Sunday intervening, in this instance the rule had been broken. Arrangements had been made, however, for their collection that morning. He did not know at first hand whether there was an inventory of the actual stones, but he would speak to Mr Margesson directly he came in and ring Mr French up.

'Thank you, I'd be glad to know,' French answered, 'but I think I'll send someone round to you from the Yard, so that the necessary steps to trace them may be taken without delay.'

The assistant agreed that this would be wise, and French rang up his department and asked that suitable arrangements be made.

All this took time, and when he returned to the lane he found that Leech had completed two admirable prints. Hudson had also taken a number of photographs, which French thought covered everything.

This seemed to complete the matter of the prints, but before passing to the next item of the investigation French knelt down and closely examined a couple of the impressions. They were of men's shoes with rubber soles, well worn. On this French congratulated himself, as worn rubber soles are practically as distinctive as fingerprints. The shoes were size eights, a narrow fitting with rather pointed toes. If only he could find such shoes, there would be no trouble in making a convincing identification.

As he gazed, he noticed an unusual distribution of the wear. Most persons throw a greater weight on the outer and rear portions of the heel and sole, but here the greater wear was on the inner and forward portions. He had read up the matter on more than one occasion, and while he could not remember the exact percentage of each class, he knew that that causing inside wear was very small indeed. Here then was an additional and valuable clue to the murderer's identity.

As he continued looking at the impressions, he gradually became conscious of some kind of inconsistency in this wear. For some time the explanation eluded him, then suddenly he saw what it was. The outer and rear edges of the prints were the more deeply sunk.

He stared, wondering if he were not mistaken. Then he moved along the lane examining the remainder of the prints. No, he was correct. The outsides of all of them were the deepest.

Here was a direct contradiction. The man walked on the outer edges of his feet while the shoes were worn on the inner. This was unusual. More than that. It was simply incredible.

Then French grasped the only possible explanation. The walker was wearing someone else's shoes!

French swore mentally. He was evidently up against brains. If the shoes could be found, he must now look, not for their owner, but for someone who could have stolen or 'borrowed' them. Or it might be that the murderer had bought them second-hand. In such a case it was most unlikely that the purchase could be traced, and if the murderer had got rid of them skilfully, as he was pretty certain to have done, this whole clue would become valueless.

Incidentally, French was not very pleased with Leech. Prints of all kinds were the man's speciality and he ought to have spotted the point. A bit self-satisfied, was Leech. Well, he would take him down over this.

Then Leech's competence or otherwise faded into the background. What a fool he was himself! He was just about to overlook his obvious next step. He was not by any means at the end of his tether.

'Leech,' he called, 'this chap has been wearing someone else's shoes. You should have seen it and it's up to you to find out how I know. But leave that for the moment. I'm wondering whether we have enough prints to do a trace?'

'I think we might manage it, though they're a bit fragmentary to be very reliable. I'll try if you like. I'm sorry I missed the other, sir.'

He took out a ball of fine cord and a couple of iron pins, and with Hudson's help pinned a length of cord down along what looked like the centre of the trace. There were not enough prints to be sure that the walker had actually passed over this straight line, but it was probable that he had, as in such as appeared the inside edge of the heel just touched the cord.

'Looks all right, sir.'

'Yes. Get your measurements.'

It was not possible to measure the length of any one step, as consecutive right and left prints nowhere occurred, but by noting where the centres of all the heelmarks came in, Leech was able to calculate the stride.

'A normal step,' he reported. 'It spaces out regularly at twenty-nine inches.'

'A bit short for that size of shoe, surely?'

'Perhaps a shade, sir, yes. But I don't think enough to build anything on.'

'Very well; now the footline.'

Leech now laid down on the first print an umbrella rib, moving it about till it lay as nearly as possible along its centreline. Then, taking a square with sides graduated in inches, he placed it with its longer leg along the cord, so that both legs crossed the rib. Having noted the scale readings at the intersections, he repeated the operation with the remaining prints.

'Normal again, sir; the same angle every time as near as doesn't matter.'

'What is it?'

Leech began figuring in his book. 'Perpendicular, 9 inches, divided by base, 15 inches, gives a tangent of point six.' He looked up a reference table. 'That's almost exactly 31 degrees.'

'A 31-degree foot angle,' French repeated. 'Can we learn anything from that?'

'It's an average size, sir; I don't think we can. I know it has been stated that so big an angle usually means a person of the upper classes, but I don't think that's reliable.'

'It's what I meant; but you're quite right, it's a probability rather than a definite indication. A working man usually walks with a smaller angle because in this way he uses less energy and time in getting along. The upper classes have plenty of both for their walks and don't carry weights. So the chances are in favour of our man being well-to-do.'

French stood looking down, trying to memorise the trace. What a pity there weren't some consecutive prints! The wide spacings between them largely invalidated what might have been a useful clue. Yet on second thoughts he was not so sure of its value. All the items, the heels just touching the centreline, the evenly spaced 29-inch steps, and the feet turned out to right and left at an angle of 31 degrees, made a combination so normal and usual that it would be common to a very large number of people. However, it might at least be useful as negative evidence. If a suspect made a similar trace it would not be a proof of his guilt, but if he did not, it might establish his innocence. French glanced round and turned on his heel.

'That's all we can do here, I think,' he decided. 'You may withdraw your man, Nelson, and we'll go back to the house.'

As they reached the library French was called to the telephone. It was Mr Margesson of Messrs Windthorpe & Margesson, and from his voice he was evidently very perturbed about what had occurred. He besought French to express his shock and horror to the members of the household, and it was not till French had promised this that he condescended to explain that Inspector Cleaver from the Yard was waiting to speak.

'I'm afraid we can't do much on this job,' Cleaver announced. 'Mr Margesson has no detailed specification of the stones which would enable them to be identified apart from their setting.'

'I'm surprised at that,' French returned. 'I shouldn't have thought he would have taken charge of them without it.'

'He has explained the reason. The deceased brought the jewels to the firm when he returned to England about two years ago, asking them to undertake their care. Mr Margesson agreed and made the best inventory he could. What you found is obviously a copy. He could not describe the stones individually. For instance, a vital particular is their weight, and this could not be ascertained unless they were taken out of their setting for the purpose. Mr Margesson discussed doing this with the deceased and it was decided that it was unnecessary.'

'But there must be a proper specification somewhere. Large stones like these wouldn't be handled without it.'

'No doubt; Mr Margesson agrees to that. He says the firm who made them up will have it. Question is, can you find out who it was from the deceased's papers?'

'I'll have a look,' said French. 'Where will you be?'

'At the Yard. I'm going back to circulate descriptions of the stuff.'

'Right. I'll ring you up if I find anything.'

French added the search to the list he had already made of the things he wished to do. Of these the first was to check the footprints at the house. A few seconds at the rose-bed told him that the impressions upon it were of the same size and shape as those on the lane, and he passed into the library to examine the traces there.

This took much longer, as every time the murderer had set down his foot the impression was fainter. The marks, however, were clear enough to confirm Nelson's view of what had taken place. The murderer had undoubtedly crossed the flower-bed, opened the window, climbed in, stood for some time behind the curtain, stepped forward to the desk, walked from there to the safe and from the safe to the french window. These traces could only be accounted for by assuming he had waited till Winnington had seated himself at his desk, murdered him, taken his keys, opened the safe, removed the jewels and left with them through the french window. French next checked over the fingerprints on the various door-handles, finding that they amply confirmed this conclusion.

As he finished this part of his work a constable arrived from Guildford with the photographs Nelson had taken. They were so good that French felt he did not require any more, and he told Hudson he might go back to the Yard. Then he saw the body, from which he obtained no further information.

Having set Leech to look for fingerprints in the library, he settled down in the easiest chair to study the preliminary statements Nelson had taken and to fix in his mind the subsidiary actors in the drama. From the statements it appeared that dinner on the previous evening had been at the usual hour of eight, and that five persons had been present: the deceased his two nieces, Christina Winnington and Bellissa Plant; his nephew, Bernard Winnington; and his secretary, Richard Horne. All were normal in manner and appearance. The deceased was in a rather sarcastic mood, but this was not uncommon. Both Mrs Plant and Horne had thought that Bernard Winnington seemed a little depressed, though here again not more so than on many previous occasions. Nothing of the slightest significance had happened during dinner. After the meal the deceased had returned to the library. This was not usual, though he had done it occasionally. He had explained that he had just received a magazine containing references to his family history. With the help of Horne he was writing a book on the subject and he wanted to examine the article as soon as possible in case it referred to the chapter on which he was then engaged. Horne had offered his help, but the deceased had declined it. It was known that he had gone direct to the library, as Josephs had followed him within two or three minutes with his coffee. The deceased had told Josephs that he had some work to do and did not want to be disturbed, and that he need not therefore come back for the tray.

Shortly before ten-thirty Sir Malcolm Philpot had rung up from Guildford, wishing to speak to the deceased. Josephs, finding the library door locked and being unable to obtain any response to his knock, had gone round to the french window. Through a chink in the curtains he had seen the deceased lying on the floor. He had tried the window. To his surprise he had found it open, as he had himself locked it before dinner. He had gone in, let himself out to the hall and given the alarm. During the period between taking the deceased his coffee and the telephone call he had been engaged in his duties about the house, and had noticed nothing unusual.

Of the others, Miss Winnington and Mrs Plant had been in the lounge during the entire time from dinner till Josephs came looking for Horne to tell him of the tragedy, with the exception of about half an hour from approximately ten to ten-thirty, when Mrs Plant had gone to her room in connection with some sewing. Richard Horne had spent the time writing in his room. Bernard Winnington had gone out. He had walked straight to Dr Mallaby's, where he had sat for almost an hour. Then, having taken a little too much whisky, he had gone for a tramp to walk off the effects. This was confirmed during the critical period by Mallaby.

The doctors' reports French took together. They were agreed that the deceased had died from shock following the fracture of the right parietal. The injury was severe, the broken bone being driven down into the brain. Death was instantaneous. The injury appeared to have been caused by a round instrument such as a jemmy or tommy bar, which had been wielded with great force. The position of the fracture was consistent with the suggestion that it had been inflicted by a right-handed person standing behind the deceased's chair.

With regard to the time of the occurrence, the two practitioners held slightly varying opinions. Dr Mallaby believed death had occurred shortly after nine or at least before half-past nine, but in Dr Henry's view it might have been later than this, though as to how much later he would not commit himself. French thought there was little in the discrepancy. The point was notoriously difficult. No doctor under such circumstances could be dogmatic, but as Mallaby was on the scene nearly an hour before Henry, his view was more likely to be correct.

With an uneasy feeling that he was not making the progress that was desirable, he knocked off for a snack lunch in the car.

12

Joseph French

French had not long returned to work after lunch when the Chief Constable was announced.

Colonel Lester was a heavily built, thick-set man, dark and swarthy like a native of a more southerly clime. Determination showed in his strong jaw and square chin, and a balanced judgment in his steady eye. His quiet self-contained manner suggested reserves of latent strength, and French felt sure he would be wanting in neither energy nor resource should the occasion demand these qualities. He greeted French pleasantly though without any waste of words, then, seating himself at the table at which French had been working, went at once to business.

'I have very little to say to you, Chief Inspector, because by this time you must know as much about the case as I do, and probably a lot more. I suppose Nelson has told you what we did last night?'

'Yes, sir, he gave me very complete details.'

'I think I ought first to explain my reasons for calling in the Yard, though, as they are fairly obvious, I expect you have seen them for yourself. Here, I thought, we had two crimes, murder and burglary; could we say which was fundamental and which incidental? I believed we could. It seemed to me on the face of it, and Nelson agreed with me all through, that the essential crime was the theft of the jewels, and that the murder was an incident in that theft.'

He paused interrogatively, and French expressed his agreement.

'If so, the obvious question followed: Who was likely to commit a crime showing such high technical skill both in planning and execution? Not, I thought, a native of Little Wokeham, nor even of Guildford. It seemed evident that this was a professional burglar's job; and a professional burglar would almost certainly have come from Town.'

'Seems very probable, sir.'

'The rest follows. If he came from Town we couldn't handle it. Therefore we applied to Scotland Yard.'

'We certainly can get more easily in touch with London criminals than you can.'

'Quite. These conclusions may of course be completely wrong; they are only what struck me at the first glance. But even if so, we still have made no mistake in applying to you people: it may not have been necessary, but it was not wrong. And now, perhaps it's too soon to ask, but have you formed any opinions or made any discoveries since you arrived?'

'No opinions, sir; I've been trying to get hold of the facts. One discovery: the murderer came on a push bicycle. He entered the estate from the north side, walking up the lane separating this property from the next, and then along the path across the lawn. It was just as you suggested, sir. We got some excellent footprints in the lane.'

'The direction in which anyone from London would approach?'

'That's correct, sir, though whether anyone would cycle the sixty miles here and back is another matter.'

'It's a long way, but well within the powers of an active man. I think for the sake of ten thousand pounds' worth of jewels a good many would try it.'

'I expect you're right, sir. One other point we're having a bit of difficulty with. So far we haven't succeeded in getting a proper description of the separate stones: only of the finished jewels.'

'What have you done?'

French told him.

'It seems all that is possible for the moment. You'll go into the deceased's history, of course?'

'Directly I've got all the perishable data: prints and so on.'

'Quite. Then I suppose your fundamental question will be: Who knew the stuff was here? Seems to me that if you, answer that you're half-way to your man.'

French smiled ruefully. 'I appreciate that very fully, sir. I'm afraid a good many people might have known, but there hasn't been time to go into it yet.'

'Quite. Now what can we do for you, Chief Inspector? Would you like Nelson to stay with you, or can you manage better with your own staff?'

French realised the answer required tact. 'I should like him for the rest of today, if he can spare the time. Probably after that I can work without local help. Perhaps we might leave it till we see how we stand tonight?'

The Chief Constable thought this a good idea, and after a few more remarks he got up, somewhat more genially wished French good luck, and took his departure.

French was pleased with the interview. Colonel Lester's attitude had been very correct. His ideas also seemed sound, and French determined to give them full consideration at the earliest opportunity. In the meantime he rang up the Yard, gave the details of the crime and asked that two matters of routine in such cases be carried out: first, that the Crime Index be consulted, and second, that the whereabouts of known burglars between eight and twelve on the Sunday evening be ascertained.

The Crime Index, as is well known, is a compilation founded upon the fact of man's innate conservatism. History teaches that if an evil-doer brings off a successful coup he will usually, if he decides to repeat his attempt, adopt a similar method. In the Index the various peculiarities of criminals are tabulated, with lists of the 'practitioners' who follow each. In the present instance, if the same name appeared under such classifications as, for example, 'Cuts hole in pane and reaches in hand to open snib or handle of sash', 'Uses bicycle to reach site', and 'Wears other person's shoes', the chances of having found the Hurst Lodge thief would be rosy.

French next got Nelson to ring up Guildford and ask whether a cyclist was noticed approaching or leaving the district about the hours in question, and Constable Rice was instructed to make similar inquiries in Little Wokeham.

The list of those who knew the jewels were in the safe was French's next care. While he realised the need for making the attempt, he was not sanguine about results. Few who had mentioned the affair would be conscious of having done so, and those who remembered would be unlikely to admit their indiscretion.

The matter was made more complicated by the fact that

this party was the second to have been held at Hurst Lodge. It was inconceivable that on the first occasion no comment about the jewels should have been made outside the household. The servants must surely have mentioned them to their friends. If so, the information might have become widely dispersed. A birthday party, moreover, suggested a recurrence in twelve months' time, and through indirect inquiries the actual date could easily have been learnt. There was therefore no doubt that a professional burglar might be guilty.

Having telephoned to Inspector Cleaver at the Yard, asking him to make inquiries on the subject from Messrs Windthorpe & Margesson and their staff, French called the members of the household one by one into the library and discreetly questioned them. All denied having mentioned the jewels to any other person, just as he expected they would. The three members of the family and Mr Plant said that they knew beforehand that the jewels were to be worn, and also had watched the deceased locking them in his safe after the party. Horne knew neither that they were coming her where they were kept. Josephs declared that while he expected that they would be worn, he did not know this definitely till the arrival of the Windthorpe & Margesson messenger, whom he had seen on a previous occasion. He also protested that he was not aware that they had been placed in the safe.

French questioned only this last statement. Where did Josephs think they would be put, if not in the safe?

'The safe was a very obvious place, sir,' the man answered. 'I thought it would be more like Mr Winnington to have provided some more secret hiding-place. I did not know whether he had done so or not.'

Horne made a similar answer to the same question, and French thought he might accept it as true. The other servants declared they knew nothing about the affair.

At the conclusion of each person's statement French made him or her a little speech. 'We have found a number of fingerprints in various places,' he told them, 'and we are anxious to know whether these belong to members of the household or an outsider, that is, whether they're there legitimately or otherwise. To settle this we must obviously get the prints of everyone in the house. I can't demand it, but would you have any objection to my taking yours?' No one seemed to mind, and he soon added a complete collection to the file.

His thoughts reverting to the original source of the jewels, it suddenly occurred to him that some light on the point might be ascertained by studying the deceased's book. Such a matter would probably be mentioned in the earlier chapters, which he understood from Horne had already been written. He called Horne back to the library and put the question.

'Oh yes,' answered Horne, 'the jewels are mentioned, but it does not say where they were originally obtained. They belonged to Mr Winnington's mother.'

'I'd like to see the references, if you could turn them up.'

'Easily. To prevent Mr Winnington repeating himself I had to keep an elaborate index. Here it is, if you're interested.'

He turned to a nest of drawers and withdrew a card labelled 'Jewellery'. It bore a number of page references with a word or two of descriptive matter opposite each. Then from a cupboard he took a thick typewritten volume bound in a loose-leaf cover.

'This is the first eleven chapters of the *magnum opus*,' he explained, 'We were just working at the twelfth. I don't suppose it will ever be finished now.'

The references conveyed a little more information than Horne had given. Clarence Winnington's father, a Yorkshire man, had been the managing director of the Paris works of a large Anglo-French engineering company. He was a man of wealth and position and had married a Frenchwoman, the youngest daughter of an old but impoverished family. He had evidently been infatuated with her, his greatest delight having been to gratify her whims.

'I wonder if that doesn't give us what we want,' said French. 'The reference on page 60 tells us that the jewels belonged to his wife: where did she get them? It doesn't say, but if she was the youngest daughter of an impoverished family, it's not likely she inherited them. Probably they were one of the whims her husband delighted to gratify. What does that suggest? The shops of Paris, surely. What about dates? Can you turn up anything that might help?'

'Yes, here's the family tree. Tallard Winnington, that's the deceased's father, married Berthe Auclair-Descottes in March 1860. She died in December 1869.'

'There should be records of such valuable sales. An inquiry from the Sûreté seems indicated. Thank you, Mr Horne; that may be quite useful.'

When the secretary had gone, French decided that, for the sake of a couple of hours' delay, he would not approach the French police until he had gone through the deceased's papers. With Nelson and Carter he settled down to the job.

He obtained some interesting information, though not

about his immediate quest. First he found that Clarence had been financially in a very strong position. Most of his money was invested in gilt-edged securities, and while he evidently spent lavishly, his income considerably exceeded his outgo and he was continually increasing his capital. Next, papers about his governorship showed that he had been quite an important man even as governors go. He had rendered good service to the nation and had received official thanks and a C.M.G. Lastly French came across his will. Save for a few small legacies, Clarence had left his money to be divided equally between his nephew and nieces, and as far as French could work out, this meant that each would receive about £20,000 after death duties had been paid. In addition, Hurst Lodge was to be Bernard's and the jewels were to be divided between the nieces—by agreement if possible; if not, by sale and division of the proceeds.

French had just brought his researches to a close when he was rung up by Inspector Cleaver. In accordance with their invariable practice, all persons connected with the Windthorpe & Margesson firm had been most careful to avoid mention of the transport of the jewels to Hurst Lodge.

By the time French had acknowledged the message and arranged for inquiries to be made in Paris, he found it was after seven. As far as Hurst Lodge was concerned he decided to call it a day. Nelson went home, having arranged to return in the morning, while French and Carter put up at the Three Swallows.

At this time of year few visitors stayed at Little Wokeham and they were the only guests. After dinner French chose an easy-chair, lit his pipe, and settled down to take stock of the case as far as it had gone.

He considered first the Chief Constable's question: Was

the theft of the jewels the essential crime and the murder incidental to it, or did the murderer go to Hurst Lodge with the object of killing Winnington and take the jewels as an afterthought?

On the information so far available, either view was possible. The burglar might well have broken into the library with the intention of cutting open the safe, believing that on a Sunday evening the room would be deserted. After he had entered, but before starting on the safe, he might have been disturbed by Winnington and taken refuge behind the curtain. He would hear Winnington's order to Josephs about the coffee-tray and realise that he was in for a long wait. In such a case he must have known that discovery was inevitable, if only because he could not remain still indefinitely. The temptation to knock Winnington out would undoubtedly grow overwhelming. Such a course would not only enable him to escape from his impossible situation, but by obtaining the keys of the safe he could get the jewels and clear out before further untoward events occurred.

But the ascertained facts would equally justify a quite different conclusion. The unknown might have visited Hurst Lodge with the object of murdering Winnington. In this case he would have done what the local police suggested: entered through the window and waited behind the curtain for his victim to appear. Winnington had obliged not only by doing so, but by ensuring there would be no further interruptions. Having taken advantage of these admirable arrangements, the murderer would have seen the safe and realised that the keys were within his reach. Probably he had no idea that the jewellery was there, and its discovery was a lucky accident.

The broad view thus proving inconclusive, French wondered how the details fitted in with these theories. Again the Chief Constable had pointed the way; the question might be settled if only the criminal's knowledge or ignorance could be deduced. If he had not known that the jewels were in the safe, his object could not have been to steal them, and only deliberate murder was possible. On the other hand, if he had not known that Winnington would come to the library, his object could not have been to murder him, and only burglary was possible.

Here French thought the facts were swinging towards the professional burglar theory. As he had previously seen, talk about the earlier party might have given away the necessary information about the jewels. On the other hand, it was surely impossible that anyone could have known that Clarence Winnington would visit the library. It was not his habit to do so at that time, and no one knew that he was going to break through his rule till he actually did it. Deliberate murder seemed therefore out of the question.

All this was extremely unsatisfactory. French felt that he was still far from the right road.

His thoughts turned to Clarence's actions on that Sunday night. Were they not, to say the least of it, a trifle peculiar? Why the extreme hurry to read the magazine? It was part of his work—or hobby, if the word be preferred—and a man whose hobby has become work to such an extent as Winnington's usually confines it to fixed hours. Was that magazine about his family history or some other and more urgent matter? He must get it and have a look.

Then French sat up suddenly. He had seen no magazine at Hurst Lodge.

He turned up in the file Nelson's description of the scene of the crime. No, there was no reference to a magazine.

'I say, Carter,' he directed, 'just slip over to Hurst Lodge, will you, and fetch that magazine the deceased went off to read. If you can't find it, get them to have a look round. Mr Horne could probably help you.'

It was as he had expected. When Carter returned it was to say that no such magazine could be found.

Then was the story of the magazine false, and had the deceased gone to the library for some other purpose? Or had the murderer removed the magazine perhaps because it contained some clue?

It was when French was considering this that another point occurred to him. Why had Winnington given Josephs that strange order about the coffee-tray? Why would so routine an operation as removing the soiled cup be an 'interruption'?

French could see only one answer to the question. Winnington had been expecting a visitor, a visitor coming surreptitiously on some secret mission. This idea, moreover, met the problem of how the caller knew that Winnington would be there. For the first time French felt that he had taken a step forward. Then he found himself up against a snag. If Clarence had had an appointment, he would have let his visitor in. Did the fact that the burglar had broken the window not prove that he was an uninvited guest?

It certainly seemed so, and yet French was not satisfied. He slowly knocked out the ashes of his pipe and refilled it as he thought over the point.

Could there, he wondered, have been two visitors: the first, who had broken in with the object of stealing the

149

jewels, had been disturbed by Winnington, and had murdered him; the second, the expected caller, who had seen through the curtains what had happened, and who had fled, fearful of being suspected?

Though this seemed possible, French thought the coincidence of the burglar coming on the very evening the other secret guest had been arranged for was too far-fetched for acceptance.

Then he saw that he was wrong: the cutting out of the pane by no means proved that Winnington had not expected his visitor. Suppose the caller had been admitted through the french window and that, whether by previous intention or as the result of a quarrel, he had murdered his host. He would naturally have seen the safe and realised that the key would be in the dead man's pocket. Why not then have staged a burglary to direct attention away from the private quarrel? Having found and taken the jewels, he could have gone outside and removed the pane, re-entering by the window.

Then once again French saw that he was wrong. The burglary could scarcely have been an improvisation. The window had been broken skilfully. No sound of the splintering glass had been heard and no glass had been found on the floor. That meant preparation, and preparation involved premeditation.

French felt completely up against it. He was getting stale and he decided to drop that point for the time being and turn, to another. If Winnington had an appointment, who could his visitor have been? Obviously he was known to Winnington, and to have agreed to a secret meeting, Winnington must have considered either him or his alleged business important.

Someone whom Winnington knew in the West Indies? A criminal whom he had helped to bring to justice? The friend of a murderer whom he had refused to reprieve? Someone whom in some way he had ruined?

It might well be. And yet would Winnington have arranged a private meeting with such a person? It was extremely doubtful.

All the same, it might be well to find out from the West Indian police whether any such episode had taken place. Or perhaps Horne could turn up a useful reference from the book.

Then French started. Horne! Was Horne merely the harmless secretary he represented himself to be?

Horne had the knowledge, and unless French was a pretty poor judge of character, he had the ability to carry out the crime. He knew of the existence of the jewels from the book, and probably that they would be at Hurst Lodge for the birthday party. He might easily have looked into the library and seen them being locked up in the safe. He could have followed Winnington to the library and, on the excuse of showing him some paper, have got behind him as he sat at his desk. He could then have killed him, faked the breaking and entering, and stolen and hidden the jewels. Having made the tracks in the lane, he could have destroyed the traces of his adventure and returned to his room. His services would naturally be dispensed with on his employer's death, and when he left Hurst Lodge he would take the equivalent of ten thousand pounds with him.

Against this view there was the track of the bicycle. Horne could scarcely have managed to produce and dispose of the necessary machine.

French was far from satisfied with his conclusions as he knocked out his pipe preliminary to turning in. All the same, he decided that next day he would find out a good deal more about Mr Richard Horne, formerly of Fleet Street in the City of London.

13

Joseph French

Next morning French found that his ideas on the Winnington tragedy had become clarified. It was not the first time that such a thing had happened, so much so that he frequently invoked the help of whatever mysterious nocturnal powers there might be by 'sleeping on' his problems. Ignorant of modern psychology, he attributed the phenomenon to the automatic action of his mind during unconsciousness.

The point which seemed now to cry out for recognition was one to which he had paid little attention on the previous evening: the powerful motive which the members of the family had for encompassing their uncle's death. The breaking into the library, the footsteps in the room and in the lane, and the disappearance of the jewels had seemed at first sight to postulate an outsider, but since he had seen how Horne might have produced these, it was obvious that any member of the household could have done the same.

He began with an attempt to check the motive. Ringing

up Cleaver, he asked him to call on Monkton, Amery & Monkton of Lincoln's Inn Fields, the deceased's solicitors, and find out if there was a later will than that he had discovered. Half an hour later, while French was still checking over his notes, there was a reply; Cleaver had seen Mr Amery, the present head of the firm, and so far as they knew, there was no second will. That found by French had been drawn up after Clarence Winnington's return to England, when he had made his arrangement with his brother's family before joining forces at Sheffield. Mr Amery admitted that French's estimate of the amount of the legacies was approximately correct.

By this time Nelson had arrived, and he and French went up to Hurst Lodge and saw Horne.

The secretary did not seem to have grasped the fact that he could possibly be suspected, and he answered French's questions with the utmost readiness. His life-history was simple. His parents, who were now dead, had lived near Matlock, and he had been educated at a local school and gone on to Cambridge. He had worked on the staff of two London papers, and had applied for his present position with the object of writing his novel.

The more French saw of him, the more unlikely it seemed that the man was a criminal. French could not imagine him committing murder for his private gain, but many persons who would not commit a crime for their personal benefit might do so for a cause. Horne, however, did not appear fanatical. Besides his general bearing, his manner was carefree and untroubled to an extent which French believed was incompatible with his having a murder on his conscience.

Though not completely ruling him out, French noted

him as an improbable and turned to the next name on his list, that of Bernard Winnington.

Bernard's manner when he came to the library was not so assured as Horne's. He was nervous and uneasy and obviously realised that he was, or might be, suspected. Though he recounted his movements on the Sunday evening with readiness, his statement carried less conviction than the secretary's.

He said that after dinner on Sunday night he had felt restless and could not contemplate an evening in the lounge. It had occurred to him that he might walk down to Dr Mallaby's and inquire for his friend Archie Ainsworth, who had met with an accident that afternoon. He had remained with the doctor till about ten; then, feeling he really would like a good tramp, he had gone for a six-mile round.

French suggested that there was surely some reason for that?

Well, yes, there was. He had unfortunately drunk too much all day; first at lunch, then in the afternoon and then at dinner. He had felt he wanted more, and when Mallaby had told him the interesting news that he had proposed to his sister on the previous evening he had insisted on celebrating. Those last drinks had been a little too much for him, and as he had not wished to return to Hurst Lodge fuddled, he had decided to walk till the effects wore off.

French realised that owing to the medical evidence Bernard could not be guilty after he had left Mallaby's, so proof or otherwise of his innocence hinged on the hours at which he had left Hurst Lodge and arrived at the doctor's. As he thanked him and asked him to send Christina in, he noted that these times must be checked.

Directly he began to talk to Christina, French became impressed by her transparent honesty and kindliness. Irrespective of her story, he could not believe her guilty of a serious crime, nor did he think, had she been so, that she could have spoken of it with so untroubled an air. When in addition her statement was supported on every point, minor and unessential as well as major, by Bellissa's, he thought he might dismiss her from suspicion.

He quickly reached the same conclusion about Bellissa. He was satisfied that the two women were alike in their innocence, though otherwise their characters contrasted. While Christina appeared to him the embodiment of active goodness, Bellissa represented the passive virtues. Their names he marked off with Horne's as possibles though highly improbables.

Very different was the impression he received when Guy Plant came into the room. Here was a tight-lipped, shrewd-eyed man with a hard unpleasant expression and a streak of furtiveness in his manner; a watchful man who obviously considered carefully the implications of his answers before making them. He would be, French imagined, what is often called a 'good' business man, i.e. one who had a heart like a flint and would allow no considerations of decency or honour to stand between him and whatever money he could legally filch from his competitors. In short, he would be just the type of man to commit a murder, provided the profit was big enough and his safety could be assured.

French of course was well aware that impressions are not evidence, and he merely noted that he must not accept any of Plant's statements without adequate corroboration. He was careful that his manner should not betray his ideas, and was just as suave and pleasant to him as he had been to the sisters.

Plant's story, however, proved to be perfectly reasonable and consistent. He had spent Saturday night and Sunday at Hurst Lodge, but had returned home in time for supper, as he had some professional work which he wished to complete before Monday. He had been horrified when Horne rang him up with the news of Mr Winnington's death, and had replied that he would come down at once. He had set off shortly, but owing to having trouble with the car, he had arrived rather later than he had intended.

'Thank you, Mr Plant, I think that's all I want to know.' French glanced at his notebook and went on: 'Perhaps for completeness I ought to ask just what you did to the car?'

'Speck of dirt in one of the jets. I cleaned it out.'

French nodded. 'Quite.' He scribbled a word and closing his book, leant back in his chair.

'That of course is entirely satisfactory, but you must understand, sir, that in murder cases we are not allowed to accept any statement without corroboration. I merely mention that so that if you hear I have been making inquiries you need not think it means doubt of what you have said.'

A somewhat more unpleasant look crept into the accountant's eyes, but he replied civilly enough: 'I understand that you have to do your business in your own way. I suppose I can go back to Town when I want to?'

'Of course, sir. You could have done so at any time after giving your preliminary statement to Nelson.'

'I went yesterday for a couple of hours, but now I want to stay at Weybridge.'

'Perfectly all right, sir.'

There was nothing, French thought as he went over the story, even remotely suspicious in it. Moreover, so much of it could be checked that the man would scarcely have told it unless it were true. All the same, he could take no risks: he would investigate every point. Most of the work would have to be done at Weybridge, but there was one minor item which could be checked immediately.

'Come out to the garage, Nelson,' he said.

The building was hidden in the trees to the west of the house. French opened the door with Clarence's key. Beside the two Hurst Lodge cars was Plant's Vauxhall twelve.

French raised the bonnet. 'Carburettor,' he muttered. 'Let's see, how do you get at those jets? Are you a mechanic?'

Nelson pointed to the joint which must be opened and to the bolts holding it down. With his lens French examined them. Over all the surfaces was a dried film of oil and dust. Neither had been recently disturbed.

'Got him in a lie first shot,' French commented. 'Those jets haven't been cleaned for long enough.'

'Not on Sunday night at all events,' Nelson agreed. 'Some time since a spanner was on any of those nuts.'

French was puzzled. The matter seemed entirely unimportant; why then had Plant troubled to lie? Was there more in the affair than appeared on the surface?

'We'll have him in the library again,' French decided, as he closed the bonnet and locked the garage.

As they passed behind some shrubs on their way to the library window French happened to glance back. Plant was approaching the garage from another direction. Clearly he had not seen them. There was something furtive in his movements which appealed to French's suspicious instincts.

'Steady!' he breathed. 'Keep still a moment.'

Plant opened the garage door and disappeared inside. The others went back softly and glanced in. He had raised the bonnet of his car and was taking a spanner from the tool-box.

French waited till he had begun work on a nut and then stepped forward.

'You're too late, Mr Plant,' he observed casually. 'We've just been looking at those nuts. You should have seen to them earlier.'

Plant was horribly taken aback. His face became drained of colour and a look of absolute terror showed in his eyes. Why? French wondered again.

'I think this requires an explanation,' French went on, 'but it's my duty to tell you that you need not make it if you do not wish to. What would you like to do?'

Plant, now a ghastly green, muttered incoherently. French waited in silence. Then, with a gesture suggesting a sudden burst of candour, Plant went on.

'I've made a mistake, Chief Inspector; I've told you a lie. It was foolish and I shouldn't have done it. I can now only tell you the truth.'

'It's usually the wiser policy,' French said mildly.

'The fact is that I had no trouble with the car at all. I got the message about ten minutes past eleven, as I told you, but I didn't start till just on twelve and I drove down without any halts or delays.'

'So I gathered from the look of your carburettor. But that's scarcely an explanation.'

Plant's colour was returning. 'Well, it's really quite simple,' he answered with more assurance. 'It sounds callous, but I didn't like the late Mr Winnington, and when

I heard of his death I wasn't particularly upset. In fact,' he hesitated, then added, 'I didn't care two hoots whether he was dead or alive. But I wanted to finish my work. It was nearly done and it was easier to finish it then, when everything was arranged about me, than to start all over again later. I decided to wait till it was done. But I couldn't let my wife know I thought so little of her uncle. Hence the story of the breakdown.'

'Why were you so upset when I discovered the—er—evasion?'

'Well, I think you might guess that for yourself.' The man was now almost himself again. 'I was naturally afraid that if you thought I had been—er—evasive, you might suspect me of the murder. Surely you've discovered by this time that Mrs Plant will come in for a lot of money, from which of course I'll benefit?'

The explanation certainly covered the facts and French could see no reason why it should not be true. It might be argued that Plant's anxiety was greater than his story accounted for, but of course to be suspected of murder was a terrible thing, nerve-racking in the extreme to the suspect. French's reason told him that the incident had been cleared up satisfactorily, but his intuition warned him to be careful. He was interested to find that Nelson had precisely the same feeling.

'It sounds all right,' was the inspector's comment, 'but the chap seems to me a twister. I take it we'll check up pretty closely on that alibi.'

'You bet we'll check up on it,' French returned grimly, 'but I want to see the rest of these people first. A bit of not very promising routine, but we must carry it through.'

So far as his own actions were concerned, Josephs had

little to add to his preliminary statement to Nelson, but when French asked of matters mentioned by the other members of the household, he confirmed all of which he could reasonably be aware. The maids, Somerville the gardener and Deanes the chauffeur had nothing helpful to report.

Having made an after-lunch appointment with Mallaby, French and Nelson walked across from the Three Swallows to Green Gables. French felt an immediate liking for this middle-aged man with his elderly air and slightly deprecating manner. He could not believe that he was criminally inclined, and yet he realised that he also was extremely uneasy. Why? French did not know, but he saw that his interrogation must be exhaustive.

It was obvious that Mallaby might have had a motive for the murder. He had proposed to Christina Winnington; was he after her money? According to Bernard's statement he had not at the time known she was an heiress, but was Bernard deceived? If Mallaby had only learnt the fact from Bernard, this motive could not have operated, as there would not have been time to devise and carry out such a murder. On the other hand, could he have been on intimate terms with the family for so many months without discovering it?

Mallaby, however, said nothing more than he had told Nelson. French listened to him with care, trying to gauge at what point, if any, his uneasiness reached a crescendo. In this he had no success: the doctor seemed equally embarrassed throughout the interview. All the same, French's careful questioning merely, confirmed the man's statement.

They called next on the postman, John Banks, who stated the time at which Mallaby had reached and left his cottage, as well as that at which Bernard Winnington had patted from the doctor at the moment of his call.

The tales certainly seemed to hang together. French could find no discrepancy anywhere. But there still remained the Guildford doctor. He turned to Nelson.

'I think we should call on Henry next. Ring him up, will you, and find out if he can see us in half an hour. We might go on from there to Weybridge and do Plant's alibi.'

Nelson had come out that morning by bus, so they went in the Yard car, he and French in the rear and Carter driving. Like the others they had interviewed, Dr Henry had little to add to his statement to Nelson. With his colleague, Dr Mallaby, he had carried out a post-mortem on Clarence Winnington's remains, and had satisfied himself that there had been no drugging or natural cause of death. Had he alone examined the deceased he would probably have put the time of death slightly later than Dr Mallaby, but by this admission he by no means wished to contradict his colleague. As French must know, accurate timings in such cases are impossible, and Mallaby was more likely to be right, as he had seen the remains earlier.

French was disappointed, though he knew this was unreasonable. The reply was as informative as he could have expected. It did at least prove that the coffee had not been drugged, a contingency which he had been bearing in mind. With regard to the hour of death, it was unlikely that Henry would contradict a brother practitioner, even in the event of feeling himself in a position to do so.

French was a silent companion as they drove to Weybridge. Supposing that at the coming interview he learnt, as he was sure he would, that Plant's story was true, what should he do next? Would confirmation of the tale mean the end of that line of inquiry—in fact, of every line except that of the professional burglar?

Suddenly it occurred to French that he had evidence as to the truth or falsity of the burglar theory which up till now he had overlooked. The magazine! Did Clarence Winnington's remark about the magazine not preclude the existence of a professional burglar? Now it seemed to him that it did.

First, suppose the statement were true and that the magazine had been there. It was not there now. Someone had removed it, and the only possibles were Josephs and the murderer. It was unlikely that Josephs had done it, therefore the murderer must have. But if so, he had not been a professional burglar, but a caller interested in something in the magazine.

On the other hand, suppose Winnington had lied and there was no magazine. Why should he do this if it were not to explain his desire to be undisturbed? And how could such a desire be accounted for otherwise than on the theory of an expected visitor, again ruling out the burglar. To French this view was almost proved by Winnington's direction to Josephs not to come back for his coffee-cup.

Whether this were so or not, French felt that an early move must be to check up on the magazine. Did it come by post or messenger, or had Winnington visited any place from which he could have obtained it? If the point could be settled, it would at least be progress.

14

Joseph French

Ivy Cottage was the last house in The Broad, a suburban road leading from Weybridge in the direction of the river. A picturesque little building, it stood in its own small but neatly kept grounds. It was isolated to be so close to a town. Its nearest neighbour was fifty yards away and well screened by trees, and it was clear that, barring some unlucky chance, Plant could have reached or left it unobserved. The drive ran back along one side of the house to the garage, a separate brick building. In front and at the other side was a tiny grass lawn, cut up into formal flower-beds and fringed by the screening shrubs. French and Nelson walked to the door, leaving Carter in the car.

The door was opened by an elderly woman of highly respectable though not very intelligent appearance.

'Mrs Miggs, I think?' said French politely, raising his hat.

'Yes, sir, but I don't—'

'It was Mr Plant who gave me your name. Mine is French,' and he told her who he was. 'This is my friend, Mr Nelson, and I may say that Mr Plant knows we're calling. We're making some inquiries in connection with a matter which does not concern you personally, but you may be able to help us with information. May we come in?'

'Certainly, gentlemen.' She led the way to a sitting-room on the ground floor. 'Won't you sit down?'

French chatted about his interview with Plant, which became strangely sublimated in the process, about how pleasant Mrs Plant had been to him, about the charming neighbourhood and like topics. It was only when confidence had been established in the housekeeper's mind that he turned to business.

'It's about the death of Mr Winnington, Mrs Plant's uncle. A sad affair.'

Mrs Miggs considered it was not only sad, but dreadful.

'Dreadful indeed,' French agreed dutifully. 'Now, Mrs Miggs, you will understand that we have to make a report on everything that happened. Among other things, we want to get the time Mr Plant arrived at Hurst Lodge. He cannot quite remember. Perhaps you can help us?'

She shook her head. 'I'm afraid I don't know.'

'Of course not, but if we could find out the time that he left here, we might be able to work it out.'

'Oh, I can tell you that. It was just getting on to twelve, about five minutes to. I had sat up writing to my son in America. Mr Plant rang for me when I was on my way to bed, and I happened to look at the clock.'

'About five minutes to twelve. That's very helpful.' French glanced at his notebook, then went on as if from a new idea. 'Perhaps we should check up the events of that evening when we're about it. You were alone in the house, I understand?'

165

She looked puzzled. 'Oh no; you must have misunder-stood Mr Plant. He was here himself all the evening.'

'I meant that no maid was in?'

'Well, yes and no. Ellen was out for the evening, but she came in about ten. She sat in the kitchen for a little, then went up to bed.'

'I follow. Mr Plant came in and had supper. What happened after supper?'

'He said he had some work to do and went up to his study; that's on the back landing. He switched the telephone through and told me, if anyone called, to say he was out, as he did not want to be disturbed.'

'And did anyone call?'

'No, sir.'

'Did the telephone ring?'

'Yes, but he answered it himself.'

'About what time was that?'

'A few minutes after eleven, I should think, but I'm not exactly sure.'

'That's near enough. Were you not lonely, by yourself all the evening?'

She smiled a trifle ruefully. 'Writing to my son keeps me busy. But in any case I couldn't be really lonely with Mr Plant in the house.'

'You had the knowledge, of course, that he was there, but that's not the same as actually seeing or hearing him.'

'Oh, but I heard him all right, practically all the time.'

'Ah, that's not so bad.' French smiled genially. 'But I should scarcely have thought it possible. He tells me he was writing. You couldn't hear that, surely?'

'He typed what he wrote, sir. I mean, he would type for three or four minutes and then there'd be a silence and he'd type some more. He did that off and on the whole evening, except at nine, when he turned on the news. Besides, I heard him poking the fire and walking about.'

French nodded. 'All that would certainly be company.' He leant forward and spoke gravely. 'Now, Mrs Miggs, I have to tell you that this matter is more serious than appears at first sight. If it became necessary, would you be prepared to swear in court to all that you've told me?'

Her eyes grew round, but indignation soon followed surprise on her expressive features and she drew herself up.

'Are you suggesting that what I said wasn't true?'

French smilingly made a gesture of negation. 'Of course not. It's merely that we must be sure that no slightest error has crept into your statement. Now, you're ready to swear that you heard Mr Plant in the study during the whole evening?'

'At intervals. Yes, I am. I said so, and I'm not in the habit of telling lies.'

'Please don't think I'm doubting you, Mrs Miggs. Evidence for court has always to be prepared in this way. Now I wonder if We might see the study? It makes everything so much clearer, you understand.'

'Of course, gentlemen. Come this way.'

The house was mid-nineteenth-century in plan, what used to be called a double house: a hall with a somewhat similar layout of rooms on either side. From the hall the stairs went up, with a back wing at the top of the first flight. In this the principal room was the study. It was small, but comfortably furnished, with a long low window giving on the lawn at the side of the house. French looked sharply about him, but could see nothing of special interest.

'Where were you sitting that evening, Mrs Miggs?'

'In the kitchen, sir. It's downstairs.'

'Perhaps we might see it too?'

The kitchen was immediately below the study, an identically similar room except that the window was on the opposite side, looking towards the garage. It was fitted up as a part sitting-room, with two basket-chairs drawn up to the combination grate.

'Go up, Nelson; let's hear you walk about, rattle the fire-irons, speak as if to the telephone and so on.'

It was soon evident that the housekeeper could not have been mistaken as to what she heard. The sounds carried clearly.

An idea suddenly seemed to occur to the lady. 'Are you trying to find out whether Mr Plant was really there?' she asked in a scandalised tone. 'You can't possibly mean—?'

'We don't mean anything,' French interposed, thinking she was not such a fool as she looked. 'Just trying to get all the circumstances complete.'

Though French did not himself know just what this signified, she seemed to find it satisfactory.

'That's all right,' she admitted graciously. 'But if it had been that, I could have told you he was there, even if I hadn't heard a sound.'

'Oh?' said French conversationally. 'That sounds like black magic. How could you have known?'

'Because of the smoke. Mr Plant's a heavy smoker, and that evening the room was clear, for I'd had the windows open all day. But when I looked in after he had gone to see that everything was right in the study, the room was absolutely thick.'

French smiled. 'You're a fine detective, madam. We shall

have to get you to help us at the Yard. Well, I'm sure we're much obliged to you. Now could we have a word with Ellen?'

The maid was a pretty, if somewhat muddle-headed girl, but her evidence was crystal clear. She had come in about ten, and from then till she had gone to sleep she had heard her employer in the study. With compliments and a little extremely sublimated chaff the two men took their leave.

'Any possible loophole there?' French remarked when they were once more in the car.

They agreed that there was none. Mrs Miggs was not nearly clever enough to have invented her statement, even if she had not been so transparently honest. There could be no possible doubt as to its truth, and if so, it constituted a complete corroboration of Plant's alibi.

'It's always a bit disappointing when a likely line peters out,' French went on, 'but I always tell myself I ought to be glad.'

'Why's that, Mr French?'

'Well, if it peters out it isn't the truth, and to continue on it would only be wasting time. *Any* certainty is a step forward, even if it seems to leave you completely stranded.'

'That's what this has done,' Nelson returned. 'As far as I can see, there's nothing but the professional burglar left, and we know how likely that is.'

'Plant's out of it,' said French thoughtfully, 'and I can't seriously suspect either Mrs Plant or Miss Winnington. But I confess Bernard Winnington struck me as a probable, at least as far as character is concerned. I think, Nelson, we'll have to concentrate a bit further on Bernard.'

'I should have said his alibi was as good as Plant's.'

'So should I. But perhaps we're wrong.'

'If he was at Dr Mallaby's at the time the murder was committed, I don't see how we could be wrong.' French thought so long over this that Nelson looked at him in surprise. 'Unquestionably,' he agreed at last, 'but let us for the sake of argument reverse the statement. If he's guilty he was not at Dr Mallaby's at the time the murder was committed. Where does that lead us?'

'It brings us up against all the statements we've had: his own, Josephs', Mallaby's and that postman's.'

'Ah,' said French, 'but steady a moment; does it? Consider this first: Could Bernard have committed the murder before he went to Mallaby's?'

Nelson paused in his turn, then answered slowly: 'Utterly impossible, I should say. Remember, he would have had to go to that lane to make the footprints.'

'Let's try and estimate. The deceased went to his library at nine, as nearly as doesn't matter. Every single person agrees to that, so we must take it as true. Now suppose, instead of going out, Bernard followed the old man to the library and knocked him out. That would only take a minute or two.'

'Joseph said he went out.'

'Suppose he came in again?'

'There was the breaking of the window and the stealing of the jewels.'

'How long would that have taken? Ten minutes?'

'I don't think he could have done it in the time.'

'Then say ten minutes. Then he had to go to the lane, another three, make the footsteps, perhaps two, and walk to Mallaby's: say five more. That's another ten; twenty altogether.'

'He had to change his shoes twice and get rid of those he made the trail with.'

'You mean he couldn't have done it in twenty? I agree: say twenty-five. Now both Mallaby and Mrs Hepworth declare that he was at Green Gables by five minutes past. That does seem to rule out murder before the visit.'

'It's quite certain, sir.'

'Very well. If Bernard went direct to Green Gables and stayed there till ten, as we agree he did, he could only be guilty If the murder took place after ten. Why could not that have happened?'

'Dr Mallaby's evidence.'

'Ah, now we're coming to it. This is getting interesting, Nelson. Dr Henry didn't agree with Mallaby's evidence; he put the time later.'

'He was doubtful about it.'

'Quite; the medical trade union. He would give Mallaby the benefit of the doubt. Besides, he said, and we know, that it's a matter you can't be sure of. Suppose Mallaby was the one to make the mistake?'

'He'd be more likely than Henry, certainly,' Nelson considered. 'It's Henry's job as police surgeon to judge things like that. It's outside Mallaby's line.'

'There you are. Let's carry on. If Bernard had gone straight back to Hurst Lodge, he would have been there at five or six minutes past ten. The body wasn't found by Josephs till ten-thirty, if I remember right.'

'That's correct, sir.'

'Then Bernard would have had ample time to commit the murder, say about ten past ten. What about it, Nelson? It's looking promising to me.'

Nelson agreed with restraint. 'I suppose it means going into the matter of that walk?' He paused a moment, then continued: 'I wonder if that's right, sir, after all? Do you think Mallaby could have made such a mistake? I mean, it was a very big mistake.'

'He said the murder took place between nine and nine-thirty, whereas if we're right it really happened between ten and ten-thirty. You mean an hour's too large an error?'

'I think so, if you take into account the time at which he examined the body, which was about ten-forty. I mean, if it was the difference between nine hours and ten it might easily be a mistake, but between thirty minutes and ninety it's not so likely. I don't believe any doctor would go so far wrong. Do you, sir?'

'It's a point,' French agreed, 'and a good one. I shouldn't wonder if you're right, Nelson. Then Bernard's alibi holds?'

'I think so.'

Once again silence descended between the two men. French was thinking hard. Was their idea that Mallaby might be wrong really supported by Henry's evidence? Was Henry surer of his ground than he had made out? It was likely. Where possible one doctor will support another, and rightly of course.

'Let's go and see Henry again,' said French.

They were by this time near Guildford, and Nelson turned into Epsom Road. Luckily Dr Henry had returned from his afternoon round.

'Very sorry to trouble you again, doctor,' French began, 'but since our call the point about the hour of the murder has taken on fresh importance. We'd be grateful if you could give us a little more detailed information about it.'

'Just what do you want to know?'

'I recognise no one can be dogmatic, but in your opinion, apart from Dr Mallaby's, could the death have taken place as late as ten past ten?'

'You mean apart from Dr Mallaby's report of the conditions he found?'

'If you please.'

Henry looked at him searchingly. 'I think I perceive the trend of that,' he answered. 'Well, I'm not interested in your suspicions, but only in the medical evidence. That's right, I suppose?'

French smiled. 'Since you say so, sir, I would not presume to contradict you.'

'Diplomatic, aren't you? Then, since you put the direct question, I would not presume to mislead you. I think the death might have occurred as late as ten past ten.'

'I'd like to ask another question, but I'm afraid it wouldn't be tactful. Do you think it could have occurred as early as nine-thirty?'

'Oh yes, I think it's possible. You understand that I did not see the remains till eleven-forty, an hour later than Mallaby. As you say yourself, one can't be, dogmatic.'

French glanced speculatively at the shrewd but kindly face. 'I see, sir, that we shall have to put our cards on the table if we want your help. We fear that Dr Mallaby, with the best will in the world, has made a mistake. We should like to know the exact evidence for the death having taken place after ten. I can assure you it's important.'

Henry shrugged. 'Seeing that you people pay me for my work, I, suppose I shall have to agree, though it goes against the grain to criticise a fellow-practitioner, particularly so able and so likeable a man as Mallaby.'

'We may all make a mistake, sir.'

'Quite. As you doubtless know, under normal circumstances the cooling of a body takes place fairly regularly; its curve approximates to a straight line. It doesn't always do so, of course: for example, with certain diseases the temperature rises slightly after death, and other circumstances may influence the rate of cooling.'

'In this case were there any special circumstances which might have done so?'

'I didn't find any.'

French nodded and Henry went on: 'Dr Mallaby gave me the temperature reading he had taken when he arrived at ten-forty, and if it was correct it certainly suggested that well over an hour had elapsed since death. My reading, taken at eleven-forty, was lower, but only very slightly. This puzzled me because it showed that, even if the death be assumed at the earliest hour it could have taken place, the drop between it and ten-forty was much more rapid than between ten-forty and eleven-forty. I took other readings at one and two, and these showed a steady fall, about half-way between the other two rates. Do you follow me?'

'Very clearly. The readings showed, first, a short rapid fall; second, a short slow fall; and third, a longer moderate fall?'

'That's correct.'

French was impressed. 'Could we actually plot the curve, sir?'

'Of course.' Dr Henry took a block of squared paper from a drawer and busied himself with a pencil and ruler. 'There,' he passed over his work, 'you can see the hollow at ten-forty and the hump an hour later.'

'Quite,' said French, 'and the practically straight line from eleven-forty till two. Now, sir, will you project that straight line back till it reaches blood-heat?'

Henry, smiling slightly, did so. 'I thought you would ask

that, Chief Inspector. It strikes the blood-heat line at five past ten.'

'Is that not reliable?'

Henry shrugged. 'Nothing in this matter is reliable. As an approximate indication I should say yes, but it's certainly not proof.'

French rose. 'We're extremely grateful to you, Dr Henry. You've given us exactly the information we required.'

Then the medical evidence did not constitute an alibi for Bernard Winnington. French saw with crystal clearness where lay the next part of his investigation.

'It seems to me that we've got to follow up two lines,' he said to Nelson. 'I'll go up to Town tonight and see what they've done about tracing the jewels and possible burglars. I admit it's unlikely it was a burglar, but we've got to be sure. Tomorrow you might get your local man and inquire into Bernard's walk. If you go over the route you may find some confirmation or otherwise. Suppose we meet in Guildford in the afternoon?'

Having telephoned his plans to the Yard, French left the car with Nelson and went up by train to Waterloo.

15

Joseph French

French was pleased to have the night at home. For once Mrs French seemed interested in his case, and as he told her of it his own ideas became sharper and more clarified. Then, it being too late to take her to the pictures, he forgot business and lost himself in a novel.

Next morning he found Inspector Cleaver waiting for him at the Yard.

'Glad you were able to come up, sir. I've got one or two things to report—mostly negative, I'm afraid.'

'I've been telling Nelson down at Guildford that negative information, if true, is progress. I'm not so sure that I believe it myself. However, go ahead.'

'I'm not so sure I do either, sir,' Cleaver grinned. 'What I have to tell you doesn't sound like progress. There are three points in particular. The first is that we can't get anything from the Crime Index. There are a good many burglars who break panes to open the window-catches, but we've been able to check up on all of them; as a matter of fact, most of them are inside at the moment. We couldn't find anyone who wore other people's shoes, or did any of the other things you mentioned.'

'It was only a chance at best.'

'Quite. Then with regard to professional burglars, as you know, sir, there are few who handle such big jewellery jobs. We were lucky about this, or unlucky, as you look at it: we were able to check up on these men also. All accounted for themselves on Sunday evening.'

'Another chance only.'

'Of course, sir. I don't know whether you'd like anything more done on those two lines?'

'Not at present. Anything else?'

'Yes, there's been a reply from the Sûreté. They've found the jewellers who supplied the stuff to Winnington; Messrs Pouchot Fils of the Rue de Rivoli. They've got a detailed specification of all the stones and they're sending it over by air this morning.'

'That's better,' French approved; 'a step forward at last. Well, you know what to do with it when you get it.'

'Yes, I'll see that the information's properly circulated.'

'Right. Now there are a few other things that I want you to do, Cleaver. We have a journalist down there, secretary to the deceased: name of Horne. States he was with the *Daily Standard* and the *Evening Mail*, and took this job for leisure to write a book. You might drift round and pick up what you can about him.'

Cleaver made a note and looked up inquiringly.

'Then go round to the Yellow Star offices in Queen Victoria Street. The accountant, Guy Plant, is the deceased's nephew by marriage, and Mrs Plant benefits considerably through the death. Do the same about him. Particularly find out if he did any work during that weekend: some statement required for their Chairman today. I told him inquiries would be made, so you may go about it openly. Also, if you can do it without his getting to know, find out if he was hard up; in fact, any general information.'

Cleaver made further notes.

'What were those solicitors like?'

'Very sticky, sir, till I told them you had the will. Then, seeing the mischief was done, they told me all I wanted to know.'

French got up. 'Right. I think that's all I want. I expect I'll be at the Three Swallows at Little Wokeham tonight. Ring up if you get anything.'

Having had a report-progress interview with Sir Mortimer Ellison, French settled down for a couple of hours' work on routine matters which had been held up by his absence, returning after lunch to Guildford. Inspector Nelson had just come in, and they went to his room for a discussion.

'We got a bit of information this morning, Mr French. It's not absolutely conclusive, but I think myself it's okay.'

French expressed his interest.

'As you suggested, Constable Rice and I went over the route Bernard Winnington said he walked. We had a bit of luck. We inquired at all the houses we passed, and about a mile from Little Wokeham we came on a labourer's cottage with a big hedge and some shrubs round the gate. The wife was away and we saw a daughter, a girl of about twenty. When we asked her where she was at ten-fifteen on Sunday night she said she was at home, but she looked upset and I guessed there was something behind it. So I told her she had nothing to fear and all that, and at last we got the truth from her. It seems she'd been out with her young man, Jacob Shields, and about ten-fifteen they were standing talking at the gate, pretty well hidden from the road by the hedge and shrubs. As they stood there a man passed. Shields told her it was Bernard. They stopped talking till he passed, and she didn't think he saw them.'

'A bit of luck certainly.'

'We went on, of course, and saw Shields. He corroborated the statement and said he knew Bernard well and was certain it was he. It was too dark to see his features, but he knew him from his size and walk. Also he was carrying a stick under his arm as Bernard does. He was walking a bit unsteadily, and Shields thought he'd had a drop too much. As Bernard would have just passed the place at the time if his statement was true, I took it this was good enough.'

'No possibility of a put-up story, I suppose?'

'Oh no, sir, not a chance. Besides, Rice gives both Shields and the girl very good characters.'

'That's fine, Nelson. I agree with you it must have been Bernard. It would be a strange coincidence if someone else, like him in build and walk, a little tipsy and carrying a stick as he did, should have been there at the very place and time he mentioned.'

'Too strange for real life.'

'It's convincing, because Bernard could scarcely have arranged it. Very well, assume he was there. That means he's got a complete alibi?'

'It certainly does. It covers all his time not already accounted for between dinner and the discovery of the body.'

'Quite: something definite for a change. Unless we get some further information we'll rule Bernard out.'

'That's what I thought. But if Plant's innocent and

Bernard's innocent and there are no other suspects, it doesn't make the affair much easier.'

'It doesn't, Nelson. It looks as if you and I are going to have headaches in the near future. Just let's see where this gets us.'

'The inside-job theory's not looking so happy, sir. Any hope in the professional burglar line?'

French told him of his interview with Cleaver. 'I've been thinking, Nelson, of what you said yesterday about Mallaby's mistake,' he went on more gravely, 'for I believe we may take it his reading of that thermometer was wrong. You said, if you remember, that it was an almost impossibly big mistake because of Mallaby's being there so soon after the death.'

'I think so still, Mr French, though I admit I don't understand it.'

'Well, coming down in the train I thought of an explanation.'

'That's good news. We could do with it.'

'Suppose,' French said, leaning forward, 'he made no mistake.'

Nelson stared, then shook his head. 'I don't follow. You mean that the reading was correct?'

'No,' French said slowly, 'I don't.'

Nelson whistled. 'That he faked it? Not like him, sir, I shouldn't think.'

'No, an abnormal act. But the circumstances were abnormal.' French paused impressively. 'Has it occurred to you that he might have had a particularly good reason for it?'

Nelson stared. 'You're not suggesting he's guilty, I suppose?'

'Well,' French returned, 'I agree it seems unlikely, and yet you can make quite a case for it.'

'You mean that he wanted to be sure his future wife would inherit before he married her?'

'That's putting it a bit crudely. If Miss Winnington married Mallaby she would probably break up her uncle's home, for it was unlikely that he'd get anyone so suitable to take her place. The legacy was the real payment for carrying on. What if Mallaby believed that if the house was broken up the deceased would cut Miss Winnington out of his will?'

'It's possible enough,' Nelson admitted.

'I'm not suggesting that Mallaby wanted the money for himself. I'm not suggesting that he ever thought of himself except to sacrifice himself for her. He would argue that if Miss Winnington married him without the money he could not give her what she was accustomed to, that in spite of herself she would become discontented and their happiness would be ruined. Quite a strong motive.'

'You've made a case for it all right, Mr French.'

'He could have done it in the time. On returning from the postman's he could have gone up to Hurst Lodge, knocked at the library french window, gone in, killed Winnington, faked the break-in, made the footprints and been back at his house before Josephs rang him up.'

'His housekeeper didn't hear him go.'

'She wouldn't if he had moved quietly.'

'That's true.' Nelson paused, then an idea appeared to strike him and he went on. 'I wonder, sir, if you've not got it? How would this work? Suppose Mallaby was worried, wondering whether Miss Winnington was an heiress and whether he ought to ask her to marry him. Suppose he decided to take the bull by the horns and find out from the only man who knew for certain. That's not impossible.'

'Go on.'

'Suppose he made an appointment with Winnington for that evening. That would account for Winnington going to the library and the tale of the magazine.'

'Go on.'

'Mallaby would have gone up earlier, but he was prevented, first by Bernard and next by the postman. He went as quickly as he could.'

French nodded. 'Then perhaps the old man was so offensive when he told him that Mallaby saw red, picked up the poker and bashed in his head.'

'Scarcely seems in his character.'

'Not if Winnington was merely offensive to him. But if he said some-thing foul about Miss Winnington, Mallaby might do anything. A moment's passion and it would be done. Then of course he'd be sorry, but it would be too late and he'd fake the burglary to avoid suspicion.'

'Do you suppose he could have thought all that out in the time?'

Nelson nodded sagaciously. 'A man will do a lot if his neck's in danger. But look how it goes on, sir. He'd see the faked burglary mightn't be enough, but if he could prove the murder took place when he was at his home, that would do the trick. Nothing easier than to say it happened just after nine instead of just after ten.'

''Pon my soul, Nelson, that's not bad. But I'm not convinced. I can't but think the thing was premeditated. For instance, if it wasn't, how could Mallaby have got those shoes?'

Nelson seemed slightly dashed. 'A snag there right

enough. What about getting Mallaby's walking trace? That might settle the matter.'

'We'll do that, of course, though somehow I'm not hoping for much. Murder seems out of the picture with Mallaby. However, we can't tell till we try.' French paused. 'But steady a minute, Nelson.' A rising excitement showed in his manner. 'Isn't there another explanation? Something we've overlooked?'

'What's that, sir?'

'Your theory has just suggested it to me. Let's follow Mallaby's actions, assuming him innocent for the moment. He's rung up by Josephs, goes up to Hurst Lodge, finds Winnington dead and sees he has only just been killed. What does he think? What must he think?'

Nelson, staring, shook his head.

'Why, Bernard of course! He knows Bernard's motive, what he'll land when his uncle dies. He knows Bernard has had too much to drink and is therefore abnormal. He sees Bernard would have had plenty of time to do the old man in while he himself was visiting Mrs Banks: at the very time, mark you, that we believe the death actually occurred. During this critical time Bernard can't be found: he would know that, or Bernard would have met him at Hurst Lodge. I'd bet you ten to one in sovereigns—if there were any—the first thing Mallaby thinks is that Bernard is guilty.'

'But Bernard is innocent.'

'We know that, yes. But Mallaby wouldn't have known it.'

'It's a fact.'

'If Mallaby doubted Bernard, everything else follows. Police suspicion of Bernard, not to mention his arrest or execution, would mean ghastly trouble for Miss Winnington. Mallaby sees how he can save her all this. A little false evidence will do the trick. Besides, it's pretty safe, for doctors notoriously can't be dogmatic on the point.'

Nelson was obviously impressed. 'That's the best so far,' he approved. 'It pretty well covers Mallaby and it's just what he'd do. But have you thought, sir, that it leaves us no further on with the murder? If Mallaby's innocent, who's guilty?'

'I know, confound it. I said we were going to have headaches. But one thing at a time. How can we be sure about Mallaby?'

'Not so easy. He'll deny it, and proof won't be had just for the picking up.'

'I believe I can get it,' said French, rising. 'Come along out to Little Wokeham and we'll see what he has to say.'

They called at Green Gables, only to find that Mallaby had gone to Town and would not be back till eleven.

'In that case, Mr French,' Nelson decided, 'unless you want anything else, I'll get back to Guildford. I have to look into one or two things before going home.' French went on with Carter to the Three Swallows, dined, and then was called to the telephone. It was Cleaver, speaking from Weybridge. He had completed his inquiries, but would prefer not to report over the telephone, and if French could see him, he would come right down now. French told him he would be welcome. He turned up just as French had finished listening to the nine o'clock news.

'I got a bit of information, sir, that I thought you ought to hear without delay,' he explained. 'The easiest way seemed to run down and tell you.'

'Very glad to see you,' said French. 'Come and have a drink.'

He had made friends with a number of the bar regulars, and when they entered they were at once included in the circle present. For a few minutes they chatted, then, on the plea of work, withdrew. French led the way to his room.

'Friendly crowd of people in this village,' he said, 'but if you're going to get home before tomorrow we'd better get to business. I gather you've had a successful day?'

'Not too bad, sir. I'd better tell you what I did from the beginning, though I expect only the last item of my report will interest you.'

'Let's have it all.'

'I began with the Green Lion in Fleet Street, and as I expected, met some of the men from the *Daily Standard* and *Evening Mail*. A drink or two and we got talking, and I had no trouble picking up a bit about Richard Horne. His statement to you seems to have been okay. He wasn't exactly what you'd call popular, but, he was respected and well enough liked. They said he was decent and straight, but too much of an idealist for the Street. When I said I'd heard he was writing a novel on social subjects there was a laugh all round. They said it was just what he would do and that it would be so full of propaganda that it wouldn't sell. They clearly didn't think him the type for murder.'

'I didn't really suspect him, but I'm glad to have that confirmation of his story.'

'Then I went on to the Yellow Star Line offices. Plant was at a conference and I saw his confidential secretary, Miss Beamish. She wasn't exactly communicative, but I managed to pick up most of what I wanted. More by what she didn't say, I gathered that Plant's a bitter pill. He's

185

certainly neither respected nor liked, and I got the same impression from one or two others. But he's all right at his job. They hold no one can pull the wool over him and not much goes on that he doesn't know. As for the report, he told Miss Beamish to send the necessary figures to his house on Saturday, and he brought his roughly typed draft for retyping when he came in on Monday. So there's no doubt he did do the work on Sunday evening as he said.'

'I imagined that too, but again I'm glad to have confirmation.'

'I could find out nothing about his private life nor finances at the office, so I asked when he left for home and went down to Weybridge and called at his house about an hour before he was due. Mrs Plant was still at Hurst Lodge and the cook, Mrs Miggs, was in charge. I gave her my correct address and said you had sent me and asked for Plant. When she said he hadn't come home I said I thought I ought to wait and see him. As I had hoped, she showed me into his study. I took a bit of risk then, but I thought it was worth it. I managed to shoot back the lock of his desk and had a look through his papers.'

'Without a search warrant!' French's voice sounded outraged. 'I'm ashamed of you, Cleaver, and deeply pained. I've always been ashamed of myself and deeply pained when I've done the same thing. I hope you had luck?'

Cleaver grinned. 'Not more, I think, sir, than I deserved, though I have to say it for myself.' He grew more serious. 'I found that Plant was desperately hard up.'

French stared. He had not expected this.

'There was first of all a letter from his bank manager, calling his attention to his overdraft and saying that the directors had instructed him to require an early and drastic reduction. Then I ran through his other papers and I saw what the trouble was. He's been gambling on the Stock Exchange. Going on for a long time too. I should have liked to get particulars of his deals, but it was getting late and I didn't want to be caught. I relocked the desk and told Mrs Miggs I was sorry I couldn't wait longer and that I'd call back. I got out just in time. He drove past as I was going to the car.'

'That's certainly news, Cleaver. Excellent. You came on nothing else: women, second establishment, or anything of that kind?'

'Nothing to suggest it, sir.'

'Well, that's something for me to think about. But you know he's got an alibi?'

'It doesn't follow that because he's hard up he's guilty of murder.'

French absently agreed, and after some further talk Cleaver drove off. When he had gone French remained sitting motionless on his bed, wondering if by any chance there could be a flaw in the alibi. He did not think it possible: Mrs Miggs would go into the box and swear the man was there all Sunday evening, and no jury would fail to believe her. And her evidence would probably be true. Yet here was a quite adequate motive emerging. French swore as he realised that what he had dismissed as a certainty was still open to doubt.

Having rung up Green Gables and made an appointment with Mallaby for the following morning, French went upstairs again and turned in.

16

Anthony Mallaby

Anthony Mallaby returned home on that Sunday night of the murder in a condition bordering on despair. While at Hurst Lodge he had been too much occupied to appreciate the full horror of the calamity which had befallen all of them. Now for the first time he was free to weigh its implications, and particularly those of his own appalling contribution to it.

With the reaction which comes from the taking of a difficult decision, he saw more clearly the drawbacks of his choice. He had smirched his professional honour, destroyed his happiness, and risked his freedom, if not his life. Tampering with evidence in an attempt to shield the guilty man made him an accessory after the fact; and he was liable to the penalties. Any policeman could arrest him at sight. Though at the moment he did not see how what he had done could be discovered, he knew the police did find things out in a quite uncanny way.

Then as his thoughts passed on to Christina he felt some comfort. If he had done wrong, it was for her. If he had to suffer, it would be for her. And if it was for her, he could take what might be coming to him with resignation; even with thankfulness.

Unhappily she would suffer too. God, how she would suffer if the truth became known! Believing Bernard guilty, he saw her the sister of a murderer! If her brother were executed, what would life contain for Christina?

Then a fresh and agonising thought pierced his consciousness. He himself could not give her the help and support he would like! Now, whether he were suspected or not, he dare not marry her. He could not risk her finding her husband share the same fate as her brother.

His anguish grew almost unbearable. Caught in a ghastly trap, he had acted for the best. As a result, the worst had happened. Whatever horrors might or might not happen to Christina, happiness was no longer for him.

He scarcely expected to sleep, but his weariness was so great that he dropped off almost as soon as his head touched the pillow. As a result, he woke feeling much more his own man, and when after breakfast he went up to see how things were going at Hurst Lodge, he showed no more signs of distress than were natural.

As he reached the door Bernard was just seeing his brother-in-law off to Town. Mallaby stared at him with repulsion, which speedily became mingled with astonishment. How could a man with the weight of murder on his conscience look so carefree? Bernard's face was clear, his glance straightforward, his manner natural. Was it possible, Mallaby wondered, that he could be mistaken? Or was it merely that Bernard was a better actor than he had believed?

As Plant's car passed down the drive Bernard took Mallaby's arm and led him aside.

'Just a word with you, old man, before you go in,' he said in a low voice. 'I want to ask a favour. We had some conversation last night at your house. I don't want you to repeat it.'

All Mallaby's suspicions raced back. In spite of himself he disengaged his arm. 'You mean?' he said, anxious to gain time.

'Well,' Bernard answered uneasily, 'look at it like this. I don't know whether it has occurred to you, but this ghastly affair has put me in a pretty awkward position. I wasn't on good terms with Clarence and I stand to gain fairly considerably by his death. See what I mean?'

'It had occurred to me,' Mallaby admitted.

'I told you last night that I had just asked him for an advance and he had turned me down. It wouldn't help me much if that were to come out. No one knows about it but you and me.'

Mallaby did not reply. In considering the evidence of the pen he had overlooked that of the quarrel, for it obviously had been a quarrel. Certainly Bernard's fears were not misplaced.

'You really can't report it to the police,' the man went on with a note of entreaty in his voice. 'I needn't remind you that people can only testify of what they know of their own knowledge. What I said was only hearsay evidence to you.'

'I'm just thinking about it,' said Mallaby.

This was not strictly true. Of course he would not mention the conversation: when he had kept silent about the pen, why should he? It was the pen which filled his thoughts. Should he tell Bernard he had found it and put the implications fairly before him? He felt that he should have it out with Bernard and know where he stood, yet he felt an extraordinary shrinking from doing so. His whole being fought against risking the possible confirmation of his suspicions. He did not know what was best, but—

'Well?' Bernard's anxious voice broke into his thoughts. 'Surely you don't have to think over it like that?'

Still Mallaby hesitated. Bernard glanced at him more sharply and his expression changed.

'Mallaby, you don't—You couldn't possibly suspect that I—killed him? You don't believe I'd do such a thing?'

'No,' Mallaby answered slowly, 'of course not. Normally I know you wouldn't. But, Bernard, what frightens me is that last night—you were drunk.'

Bernard shook himself as if to dispel an evil dream. 'I swear to you that I'm innocent,' he declared earnestly. 'When I left you I walked round exactly as I told you. I walked myself sober. I didn't get back here till just on to midnight. Don't you believe me, Mallaby?'

Mallaby felt his manner was convincing, and not only his manner: his appearance and speech were also those of an innocent man. More than that. He had never imagined that Bernard would murder in cold blood. As he had said, it was only because of his condition that he had doubted him. But surely this crime was not one of drunken passion? Did not all that business of breaking the window and stealing the jewels mean careful preparation? The others must be correct when they said it was the work of a professional burglar.

'Yes, I believe you,' he answered, and he meant it.

'And you won't mention the conversation?'

'I won't mention it.'

Some of the tension went out of Bernard's manner. 'You're a good fellow, Mallaby,' he said unsteadily. 'I've felt in a trap. Your evidence would have been the lid. You don't know what it's like to feel in a trap. But your promise is an ease to my mind.'

As Mallaby thought over the little scene, thankfulness grew in his mind. He believed his action had been justified. It had prevented an unjust suspicion from falling on Bernard. It had saved Christina from pain. He was only sorry he had not mentioned the pen. It would have been better to have had it out with Bernard. He decided he would take an early opportunity of doing so.

All the same, Mallaby remained profoundly unhappy. Even in Christina's company he could not forget his worries. If Bernard were innocent, who was guilty? Was his sacrifice going to help Christina, or had he thrown away his peace of mind for nothing? So distressed was he that he could not hide the fact, and, fearful of acting abnormally, he avoided Hurst Lodge. As a result, no opportunity of speaking to Bernard about the pen presented itself, and though he felt he was being weak, he did not seek one.

So things continued till on the Thursday morning he received another and infinitely ruder shock. On the previous evening Chief Inspector French had rung up making an appointment, and after breakfast he and Inspector Nelson called.

'Come in, gentlemen,' Mallaby greeted them. 'Sit down. Won't you smoke?' He held out cigarettes.

'Thank you, sir, but we don't when we're on duty,' French returned, taking the chair to which Mallaby waved.

They were polite, and yet Mallaby sensed a chill in the

atmosphere. He had talked on previous occasions to both officers, and French at least had seemed more than polite, actually friendly. Now this friendliness had vanished.

'What can I do for you?' Mallaby asked more formally.

'We want a little help, sir. We should like you to clear up a point in your evidence. To be quite candid, we're not entirely satisfied about the time of Mr Winnington's death. Do you think you could explain more fully how you reached your conclusions?'

Mallaby's heart gave a leap. They *couldn't* have discovered! What must be his line? He thought rapidly, gaining time by slowly lighting and puffing at his cigarette. Suddenly he saw that directness was his cue.

'Do you mean that you think the time I stated was wrong?' he asked.

'I do not say that,' French answered. 'What I'd like is to be absolutely sure it's correct. Would you have any objection to discussing the observations you made?'

A show of reluctance seemed indicated. 'It's a rather unusual request, isn't it? I don't know how many of my colleagues would agree, but personally I haven't the slightest objection. What exactly do you want to know?'

'Just what led you to your opinion. You know, of course, that Dr Henry didn't entirely agree with you, and when doctors differ—' French shrugged and gave a wry smile.

'I see your difficulty.' Mallaby fought down his fears. 'But I should like to call your attention to two points: first, that I saw the deceased about an hour before Dr Henry, and second, that Dr Henry did not say that he considered my opinion incorrect.'

'I recognise both facts. All the same, the matter has become so important that we must be as sure of it as we can. I may say that Dr Henry has given us his actual observations and we hope that you will do the same.'

Mallaby saw that there was nothing for it but to stick to his lie. 'Oh yes, certainly. Let me look up my notes.' He took some papers from a drawer. 'But you must have seen my figures,' he went on; 'I gave them in my report. I found,' and he repeated the temperature statement French had already considered.

'I did see those, sir. But do they really prove your conclusion? I don't mean to be offensive: I ask because the issues depending on it are so serious.'

Attack was often the best defence. 'May I ask what those are?'

French hesitated. 'Like you just now, we don't usually answer that sort of question, but as you've met us, I'll meet you. You must have seen for yourself that several considerations suggest that the murder was an inside job. How, for instance, could an outsider have known that the jewels were in the safe, or alternatively, that the late Mr Winnington would be in the library? You must have realised that several other facts point in the same direction?'

'I'm afraid I didn't think of it.'

'No, sir? Well, the facts were as available to you as to us. At all events we thought so, and we therefore naturally considered the members of the household. There were four men, and we took them one by one. Josephs, we were satisfied, had no motive; in fact, he had a strong motive for keeping the deceased alive, to hold his job: it wasn't Josephs. Precisely the same arguments apply to Mr Horne: it wasn't he. Mr Plant was definitely in his house all the evening; his housekeeper can swear to it and it is proved by all sorts of other facts: it wasn't he. Lastly, Mr Bernard's time is fully accounted for between the end of dinner and the finding of the body; first, he was with you and then he took a walk: it wasn't he.'

'It was absurd to suspect any one of the four,' Mallaby said more sharply. 'You didn't know them, of course, but I could have told you.'

'You would have been quite correct if you had,' French returned disarmingly. 'But now you see where the facts are pointing? The only other members of the household were the ladies.'

Mallaby's mouth suddenly went dry. He had not foreseen what was coming.

'But, my God!' he gasped, 'you don't suspect them?'

French made a gesture of regret. 'Well, you see, sir, it's this way. If Mr Winnington died between nine and nine-thirty the question could not arise, for the ladies were together in the lounge till ten. But if he died after ten the circumstances are quite different. Then the ladies were alone. Mrs Plant went to her room in connection with some sewing she was doing, while Miss Winnington remained in the lounge. I'm not, of course, making any accusations, but I tell you this to show the importance of accurately fixing the time of death.'

Mallaby was speechless. He gazed at French with an expression of growing horror. For some seconds silence reigned, then an idea occurred to him and he muttered: 'Does all this mean that you think I did it?'

'It means what I say, Dr Mallaby, and neither more nor less,' and French's voice was sharper. 'It means that unless we're sure when Mr Winnington died we may suspect the wrong person. The question is: Can you help us to greater certainty?'

Mallaby felt absolutely up against it as he found his original problem presented once again, and in a more acute form. On what he said now might depend Christina's whole future life, as well as his own. Then a sixth sense warned him. This was a trap! French had not said he suspected Christina. He couldn't suspect Christina. No one could! Mallaby should therefore think of himself. Admission would be asking for arrest: madness! He steeled himself to speak calmly.

'I'm afraid I cannot alter the facts. You have the details of temperature and so on which I noted. You can interpret them in any way you choose. I don't claim that mine is infallible.'

French leant forward, and his intense gaze seemed charged with menace.

'We have reason to believe, Dr Mallaby, that the deceased did not die till after ten and that you deliberately recorded an incorrect temperature. You are not bound to answer me, but you'll be asked the question in court and then you'll have to answer. You should consider whether it wouldn't be easier for you to do so now.'

It was like a blow in Mallaby's face. Instantly he felt that he must tell the truth, but once again he feared the possible repercussions. Oh, if he could only have five minutes to think it over! But he hadn't five seconds. French was waiting.

In the end he denied the accusation. On the spur of the moment it seemed the only thing to do. If on consideration it should appear wiser to tell the truth, he could go to French and explain.

French seemed disappointed. He went on asking questions, but the urgency had gone from his manner and presently, with Nelson, he took his departure.

When Mallaby was alone he found himself shivering like a man with ague. French suspected what he had done! Had he been wise in sticking to his statement? He had been either very wise or very foolish: which? He felt completely in the dark and correspondingly baffled and frustrated.

All through the morning he continued worrying over the problem, and as the day dragged slowly on the burden grew heavier. Increasingly he felt he must share it. The urge for confession drove him on. He must put the case to some sympathetic friend and get his advice.

To whom could he turn? It must be someone interested, someone who would give the matter real attention. Bernard? No, even if, as he now believed, Bernard were innocent, his counsel would be biased. Christina? He could not bring himself to disclose either his own weakness or his doubts of Bernard. Bellissa? Her opinion would be of little use. Guy Plant?

As Mallaby thought it over it seemed to him that Plant was his man. Admittedly he did not personally care for him. Plant was too much a man of the world, too hard-headed, too cynical, too—well—selfish. But he was shrewd, and these very qualities were just those which would make his advice worth having. Besides, there was no one else. Mallaby could only think of his solicitor, and he did not wish to consult his solicitor on the best way of escaping the consequences of a crime.

Then he was halted by a fresh consideration. Was there a chance that Plant might himself be guilty? He soon saw that quite a case could be made for it. Clarence's money supplied an obvious motive: Plant would undoubtedly use what came to Bellissa. Generally speaking, too, Plant was not a man who would allow moral restraints to stand between him and his goal. Of course, Plant's guilt would not explain the pen, but to Mallaby the pen was beyond understanding in any case.

Then Mallaby breathed more freely. He remembered that French had been satisfied as to Plant's innocence: it was proved by all sorts of facts, he had said. He rang up Plant and asked could he see him privately. The reply was an invitation to dine that evening in Town.

Plant had engaged a room at a small Soho restaurant, and there, after pledging him to silence, Mallaby told his whole story, from his proposal to Christina with his subsequent misgivings when he learnt of her expectations, to his finding of the pen and his falsification of the evidence. He certainly could not complain of the reception of the tale.

'I suppose,' Plant said grimly when it came to an end, 'you realise what you've done? You've made yourself accessory after the fact to a murder. I suppose you know what that means if it's discovered?'

'Yes, of course I know,' Mallaby returned irritably. 'What happens to me isn't the point. I did it for Christina, and it's of Christina I'm still thinking. If Bernard is clear of suspicion and if my false evidence is going to make French suspect her, then I must tell him the truth.'

Plant nodded. He looked old and careworn, but extremely wary. 'I see your point,' he said slowly, 'and I appreciate your attitude.'

'Then you think I did right to try, as I thought, to screen Bernard?'

Plant smiled, again a little grimly. 'Whether you did right or not I'm not prepared to judge. But if you don't mind

my saying so, I think it was rather splendid. You deliberately sacrificed yourself for your friends. That appeals to
me, though I'm afraid it's more than I'd have done myself.'

'Then what do you think I should do?'

'Have you mentioned the affair to anyone?'

'No: only you and I know it.'

For a very long time Plant considered. 'You must do
what you think right, of course,' he said at last, 'but since
you have asked my opinion I'll give it to you for what it's
worth. First of all, while I admire you for your good
intentions, I don't think myself your action was necessary.
It seems obvious that Bernard had dropped the pen and
the burglar found it and thought he could divert suspicion
by planting it.'

'I thought of that since,' Mallaby said, discouraged. 'The
clip holding it in the pocket was broken.'

'There you are: I think that explains it. Now let us face
the thing. You've made this statement and altered and held
back your facts, and on a second interrogation you've
stuck to your story. French may doubt it, but he can't
disprove it. He can prove nothing about the pen, and about
the cooling at worst he can only accuse you of having
made a mistake in your reading. If you tell the truth now,
you will not only convict yourself of participation in
Clarence's murder, but it will do no good. French won't
believe you. He'll say you simply alter your story according
to what you think will best help Christina.'

'Then you think I should say nothing?'

'I can only answer that in your place I should say
nothing.'

Mallaby nodded thankfully. 'I'll take your advice,' he
declared.

'Only if you feel it's right,' Plant insisted. 'In any case, let me know what you finally decide. I'm interested now.'

'I have decided: I'll take your advice, of course with the limitation that if I find Christina is seriously suspected I'll tell. Whether French believes me or not, I must do that. But otherwise I'll keep silence.'

Plant nodded.

'I'm greatly relieved by what you've said, Plant, and I'm ashamed of having suspected Bernard. You know,' and Mallaby's inherent love of truth drove him on, 'I even suspected you: and I'm ashamed of that too.'

'Me?' Plant returned. 'Tell me about it. That's interesting.'

Mallaby outlined his ideas, explaining that they had entered his mind only to be rejected. Plant seemed impressed, but wished him good-night cheerily enough.

As Mallaby returned to Little Wokeham he felt strangely comforted. Plant had approved his conduct. Moreover, he had had no doubt as to his best course, and the very moderation of his advice had made it more telling. Yes, certainly he would take it.

17

Guy Plant

Before Mallaby's visit Plant's fear that the episode of the pen should become known to the police had almost died down. He had naturally said nothing about the matter, but on the Monday Bernard had brought it up. 'By the way,' he had said, 'I think you have my pen. I didn't get it back from you last night.'

Plant had foreseen a remark of the kind and had prepared himself for it. 'Oh,' he answered with a gesture, 'that reminds me. I'm terribly sorry, Bernard, but I seem to have mislaid it. When I was undressing last night I remembered about it, but I couldn't find it in my pockets.'

'Did you put it in your pocket when you had finished your sketch?'

'I don't remember anything about it, so I think I must have; automatically, you know. I suppose Josephs hasn't found it?'

'He'd have mentioned it if he had, I imagine.'

'Of course he would. I'm sorry. I needn't say that if it doesn't turn up I'll send you one to replace it.'

Bernard had half-heartedly demurred, but Plant had insisted, and had actually bought and taken down a new pen on his next visit to Hurst Lodge. Beyond an acknowledgment from Bernard, nothing further had been said about it; indeed, Plant believed that no one else knew anything of the transaction.

Of course, the settlement with Bernard was only half the affair, and the small half at that. What really mattered was whether the police had found the pen. As the days passed and French said nothing about it, Plant grew more and more satisfied on the point; believing that he must have dropped it when he was throwing the ladder and other things into the Wey.

Mallaby's story, therefore, came to him with all the greater shock. Though he managed to hide the fact from the doctor, he listened to it with consternation.

Indeed, as he continued to turn over its implications in his mind, his feelings approached absolute panic. Here, he told himself, might be the wreck of all his plans, the loss of his money, of his liberty, of his life itself. The hideous danger that he had at first feared, but which increasingly he had hoped to avoid, was now upon him. If French were to learn what Mallaby had to tell, his fate was sealed.

When first faced by this fear, Plant had argued that a resolute insistence that he had left the pen for Bernard on the hall table would clear him of suspicion. Now he saw that this had been mere wishful thinking. French would ask why he had not mentioned the matter to Josephs, who had been there when he was leaving, and later to Bernard when they were discussing the affair. To these questions there would be no real answer. No; once French's active suspicion was aroused, he would never let the thing drop till he reached the truth. He would probe and pry and ferret and worm till he discovered the fake in the alibi. Plant's panic grew as he visualised the result of this. Nothing could then save him. Why, the alibi alone, the alibi in which he had put his trust, would seal his doom. How could he explain it—otherwise than by the truth.

He felt actually sick as he faced up to the prospect. Often he had read of the conviction of murderers, but seldom had he felt sympathy for them. Their downfall, he had thought, had been their own fault; they had been careless. Now he began to see differently. Here he was threatened and he had not been careless. He had had a stroke of bad luck and his safety was hanging by a thread. As this simile passed through his mind, Plant shuddered.

Then he rallied himself. Though Crippen and Mahon and Smith and the rest of them might bungle and allow themselves to be taken, he was of sterner stuff. At least he would not go down without a struggle. If his life were threatened, he would fight for it. That was the way things were in this world: if you wanted anything you had to fight for it or you would not get it. And a mere passive defence would avail him nothing. The best way to defend was to attack: how often had he heard that? So here he must attack. He must attack . . .

Attack! What did attack mean? Once again he grew sick as he saw what attack meant.

Attack meant action to prevent that fatal information from reaching French's ears. As it was, he was safe. French had accepted the alibi. There was no reason why he should not, because there was nothing to make him suspicious. But if he knew of the pen . . .

French must not know! At all costs he must not know. *At all costs . . . !*

Plant wiped the sweat off his forehead as his active brain leaped to the challenge. Another murder? God, how ghastly! Then he saw that another murder would not do. Another murder so soon and in the same surroundings would certainly be connected by French with the first. It would rule out a burglar: it would show that the murderer was one of the party. No, another murder was out of the question.

An accident? An accident would be no better. An accident would constitute too strange a coincidence. French would question it, and if French seriously questioned it, he would ferret out the truth.

Suicide? Plant gave a deep breath as he thought of suicide. If Mallaby were to commit suicide it would be regrettable, but not incompatible with the other facts. Everyone had noticed how worried he had seemed since the murder. Plant had heard Christina and Bellissa discussing it. Bernard had also mentioned it. French must have noticed it. Suicide would be not expected, of course, but entirely consistent with the circumstances.

Again Plant wiped his wet forehead. He had, he believed, a little time. After their interview he felt sure Mallaby would say nothing at the moment to French. But if he became satisfied that Bernard was innocent, and particularly if he thought Christina was in danger, he would speak. So, though Plant had a little time, he might not have very much. The preparation of his plans would take it all. He must act at once.

How would a doctor commit suicide? As he thought of his own father and of all he had learnt when a boy, of a doctor's life, Plant felt there was little doubt. With dope, he was sure. A medical man would take an overdose of veronal or some other drug and simply go to sleep and not wake up. It should be easy to administer a fatal dose to Mallaby.

But would it? A little further thought and Plant saw that, so far from being easy, it would be practically impossible. He could not get the stuff. He knew something about the law now controlling the sale of drugs, for a couple of years earlier he had been troubled with sleeplessness and had gone to his doctor for some draughts. He had not obtained them easily. It was only after watching the case for some time that his doctor had given him a prescription, and then merely for six powders. It happened that his health had improved more rapidly than either he or the doctor expected and he had only taken four of the six. The remaining two he had kept, and he had them still. But these would be no use for his purpose. They would cause sleep, but they would not kill. He began to consider other methods.

Plant was ingenious at all times, but now under the stimulus of danger his mind became positively sparkling. Scheme after scheme was evolved, considered, modified and finally rejected. But these schemes showed a continual improvement, and at last he reached one which he believed would meet the case. It seemed certain and it seemed safe. So far as he could see, it could not be wrecked by other people's mistakes or by anything less than quite phenomenal bad luck.

He worked at the details during most of that Thursday night. His previous venture had functioned smoothly in certain particulars, such as the alibi and the journeys to and from Little Wokeham. These he decided to repeat. The actual murder would, of course, be carried out quite differently.

Early next morning he rang up Mallaby from a street call-box. 'I want to speak to you privately. I don't mean to talk of it on the phone, but I've found out something important about that pen. I think you'll have to take action, but don't do so till I see you. We must discuss it and settle what's best to be done. But it would be better if our meeting was not known. I'll drop in whatever evening you're alone.'

Mallaby was immediately interested. 'I'll come up and see you if you'd prefer it,' he answered.

'No, you might have to explain why you did so. No one will know if I go down. When will you be alone?'

'Let's see: this is Friday. It happens that on Sunday evening Mrs Hepworth is going to see some friends. She'll be out till about eleven.'

'I'll be with you before ten.'

Next he had to enlist Crossley's aid. On the evening after the Clarence affair he had met Crossley secretly and shown him the newspaper report of the crime, explaining that that was what he had assisted in. 'I tell you this,' he had added grimly, 'so that you may understand that if the thing becomes known you will hang as well as I. So don't let it become known.' Crossley had been deeply moved, and before they parted Plant had so terrified him that he was satisfied the secret would be safe.

'You fixed up your alibi that you were at the pictures?' Plant had gone on.

'Yes, I told my landlady I was going and I described the picture to her after I came back. I had seen it before at another house.'

'Very well,' Plant had answered. 'Don't refer to it again unless she does.'

That was on the Monday. Now on, the Friday he had another secret interview with Crossley, after dark and at the far end of one of the Victoria platforms. 'I'm sorry there's some more trouble,' he told him. 'Dr Mallaby at Little Wokeham has made a discovery. He has found a small article I dropped that night. He doesn't know what it involves, but if he were to show it to French, French would know. He mustn't show it. I'll tell you what I propose.'

Actually this was the last thing which Plant intended. He felt that Crossley, however terrified, would not stand for a second murder. He therefore judiciously modified his statement.

'On Sunday evening,' he went on, 'the doctor's house-keeper is going out and he will be alone in the house. I shall go down to Little Wokeham, ring him up from a neighbouring call-box, and make a faked sick call. As soon as he leaves his house I shall burgle it, get hold of the article and bring it away. That'll remove the danger.'

When Crossley understood that he must assist in the affair he went nearly crazy. Plant became alarmed lest he should collapse completely, and he set to work—partly to frighten and partly to encourage him.

'You silly fool! You'll either do it or risk your neck! Don't you see that if Mallaby acts you'll hang? Pull your-self together, man, and don't be so spineless. Now we're both in danger, but if I pull this second job off we'll both be safe. You'll have nothing to do with the breaking in, but only with the alibi: nothing more than before. Well? Would you rather hang?'

Crossley had moaned and all but wept, but between his own terror and Plant's stronger personality he had no chance of disagreement. He promised to do everything he was told.

'Then look here: these are your instructions. On Sunday evening you will make another alibi of going to the pictures. You'll ride down to my house, climb up to the study and impersonate me for two or three hours: exactly as before, except that this time there's to be no typing. See?'

Crossley saw only too clearly.

'There'll be another modification on our previous programme: listen to it carefully. During the evening I'll ring you up. That's to let you know I've reached Little Wokeham. I'll say: "This is Plant speaking. Is that Mr Hemingway?" You will answer in my voice, "Wrong number, I'm afraid," and ring off. Do you follow?'

Crossley nodded.

'You will then count thirty seconds and ring up Dr Mallaby. I'll give you his number. As soon as he replies—you must get Mallaby himself—say nothing more, but ring off. That's all. Now repeat.'

Crossley having been thoroughly coached, Plant paid another disguised visit to the East End, carrying out a new set of purchases very similar to the last. He obtained the materials for the rope ladder, the shoes, the hat and coat, in addition buying two second-hand books on anatomy and elementary surgery. This time he omitted the cloth, birdlime and length of lead pipe.

On returning home he made up the ladder. He also dissolved his two sleeping-powders in the minimum quantity of whisky he found necessary, putting the result in a small bottle.

All Sunday Plant studied his medical books till he felt

sure he could carry out his plan. Bellissa was still at Hurst Lodge, so that precisely the same arrangements could be made at Ivy Cottage. On this occasion Plant said nothing to Mrs Miggs about work, merely remarking: 'I'm expecting a call, so I'll switch the phone through to the study.'

When Crossley appeared, at the agreed hour of eight, Plant whispered to him: 'I daren't tell Mrs Miggs a second time not to show up visitors. No one will come, but if anyone does, hide in the bedroom. Then slip away by the ladder and pencil on the bottom rung the hour you go. I'll enter by the hall door and say I was out posting a letter or somewhere that would fill the time.'

Once again Plant, suitably disguised, found the bicycle and rode off, and once again he kept to the by-roads and met no policeman. Shortly before 9.30 he reached Little Wokeham. Leaving his bicycle in a wood at the back of the house, he reached Green Gables unseen. Under the bushes in the garden he reverted to his normal appearance, knocked, and was admitted by Mallaby.

'Now this is very interesting and mysterious,' Mallaby greeted him. 'Come in. How did you come down?'

'I left my car along the road,' Plant lied. 'But this is all very confidential. I hope we won't be overheard. Are you alone?'

'Oh yes, Mrs Hepworth has gone to her friends and it's unlikely I'll be called out at this hour. What's your news?'

'It's a long story. Let's sit down and I'll tell you.'

'Of course. And you'll have a drink after your drive?'

'Well,' Plant said, 'thanks; I never refuse a good offer. It's quite chilly tonight. Your fire's very pleasant.'

Mallaby replied vaguely as he brought whisky, a siphon and two glasses.

Plant sighed with relief. This drink was an essential feature of his scheme, and as Mallaby drank little, he might have had to ask for it and to urge Mallaby to join him. So far things were going well.

He was careful to continue his chatting while Mallaby settled down, then before the subject of his visit could again be mentioned, he suddenly slapped his thigh.

'Bless my soul, I've forgotten to give a message about tomorrow! Hang it all, I must do it at once. May I use your phone, old man?'

'Of course.'

Plant went to the hall, dialled his own number and said: 'Hullo. This is Plant speaking. Is that Mr Hemingway?'

To his satisfaction he heard an unrecognisable voice saying: 'Wrong number, I'm afraid,' and the telephone went dead. He mumbled some business instructions, which if Mallaby chanced to overhear them would sound natural. Then he returned to the sitting-room and again picked up his glass.

He had no sooner done so when the telephone rang again. Bravo, Crossley! With a word of apology Mallaby went out.

This gave Plant his opportunity. He had his dissolved sleeping-powders ready, and he quickly emptied the bottle into Mallaby's glass, shook it round, wiped his prints off, and when Mallaby returned, was leaning back at his case, his own glass in his hand.

Mallaby seemed indignant. 'Some funny people in this world,' he grumbled as he sat down. 'Some chap asked for me—there was no mistake, he mentioned my name— and directly I replied, he rang off!'

'Probably not his fault,' Plant said smoothly. 'He's been cut off. You'll have another ring in a moment.'

'I suppose that's it. Now, Plant, what's your news?'

'Well,' Plant smiled, 'we haven't had our drinks yet. Here's to you.'

Plant was the first to put down his glass. 'I see you've got that foreign rye whisky,' he remarked before the doctor could speak. 'You get it now a lot. Some people don't like it, but I do.'

Mallaby was looking with a puzzled expression at his glass. 'I never tasted it before,' he said. 'It's strange, because it's not a new bottle.'

'It's the rye,' Plant repeated firmly. 'It goes like that. A man I know in the trade told me. It's perfectly good, only that slight taste. Now, Mallaby, about the pen. Did you know that Christina, innocently of course, was the culprit?'

As Plant had expected, the mention of Christina drove all thoughts of the taste of the whisky—and of everything else—out of Mallaby's head. He reacted with the intense interest Plant had expected.

'Christina?' He spoke as if unable to say more.

'Christina,' Plant nodded. 'I'll tell you. On Sunday between tea and dinner she wanted to write a letter and couldn't find her own pen. She had simply mislaid it, because it turned up afterwards. But at the moment she couldn't get it, and knowing that Bernard wouldn't mind, she went up to his room and took his from his coat pocket. So that's the explanation.'

'Explanation?' Mallaby gasped. 'That's no explanation! If Christina took it, what did she do with it? How did it get under the body?'

'Perfectly simply. When Christina had finished her letter she found she was out of envelopes. So she took the letter and the pen to the library and got one out of Clarence's desk. She sat down at the desk and addressed it there. In getting a stamp she believes she left the pen lying on the desk.'

'Good God!' Mallaby exclaimed helplessly. 'And that's where the burglar found it!'

'Well,' Plant returned, 'it's a question if he ever did find it. It's much more likely that it was knocked off the desk accidentally when the body fell. We may have been building a mountain out of a molehill about the pen.'

Mallaby doubted if this was so, which was just what Plant wanted. It enabled him to prolong the discussion, and this he did ingeniously and with plausibility. He even achieved an air of philosophic calm, though all the time he was on tenterhooks. Would the drug never act? A delay now would imperil the success of the entire undertaking.

At last, to his immense relief, he saw the doctor's eyes grow heavy and his head begin to nod. He talked on, and presently the eyes closed and the head sank back against the chair. The breathing grew regular. Mallaby was asleep.

It was just ten o'clock: ten minutes later than he had reckoned on. Plant cursed beneath his breath. He must hurry. A lot had to be done before Mrs Hepworth's return.

Quickly he put on his rubber gloves, and moving stealthily, though no one was in the house, he went into the surgery. The doctor's handbag stood on a table. He opened it, and searching through it, found a case of instruments. From this he abstracted a small deadly-looking knife, the one which from his book he thought most suitable for his purpose. He had handled everything as little as possible, and now he carried bag, case and knife to the sitting-room and put them on the table beside the doctor, as if the latter had used them.

The recollection of his father's practice, refreshed by the books he had just studied, told him that Mallaby would have a special bag for midwifery cases, and that this would contain chloroform and a mask for administering it. He now went back to the surgery and after a short search found it. He carried it to the sitting-room, and taking out the mask, poured a few drops of the chloroform on the lint and held the apparatus over Mallaby's mouth. This he repeated at intervals, till after about five minutes the man's stertorous breathing told him that the required result had been achieved.

Now came the hideous part of the evening and Plant had to steel himself to continue. First he tested Mallaby's conjunctival reflex as described in his book, thus satisfying himself that the man was completely unconscious. Then, having covered his own arm with a cloth, he took the small knife, and picking up the man's left wrist, he made a quick deep cut in the direction in which diagrams had indicated that the artery ran. Spurting blood showed that he had successfully found and severed it. The flow was much less strong than he had expected, and he congratulated himself that the cloth had completely protected his clothes from stain.

The worst was now over. Gingerly holding the knife by the blade, he pressed Mallaby's fingers against it in the same positions as his own had occupied. Then he dropped it on the floor. Mallaby's right hand and arm he held in the blood till they were marked like his own. Next he went to the kitchen and washed his gloved hands.

Returning to the sitting-room, he switched off the light and opened both windows fully. This would dispel the faint smell of chloroform which lingered. Working with his torch, he repacked the mask in the midwifery bag and replaced it in the surgery. He found where the glasses were kept in the dining-room and washed his own and put it away, leaving Mallaby's beside him with the dregs of the sleeping draught. Then, closing the windows—the smell had now disappeared—he switched on the light again and looked carefully round to see that nothing had been forgotten. Leaving the light on—he congratulated himself on remembering this—he let himself out into the night. He had been longer than he had expected, and his relief to be gone before Mrs Hepworth's return was great. He walked swiftly away from the house, found his bicycle and rode back to Weybridge.

In silence he climbed to the study. Crossley was still there, no one having called. In silence also Crossley departed, and Plant turned to complete the single matter which still required attention. Calling to Mrs Miggs that he was going out to the post, he hurried down to the river and threw in at separate points his two books, his rubber gloves, and the bottle which had contained the drug.

Thankful that he was now safe, but a little sick from the horror of the evening, he went up to bed, though not to sleep.

18

Joseph French

After a week's intensive work on the Little Wokeham case French had taken that Sunday afternoon as a half-holiday and had gone home to enjoy it. It was not only that he wanted a little free time. He really did feel stale and he believed a short rest and a change of thought would help him later.

He was a good deal worried as to his progress. He had done a lot of work, he had amassed a multitude of facts, he had tested a number of theories. In fact, he could think of no inquiry which he had omitted and no source of information which he had left untapped. But all this was mere routine. He had not made any real advance towards the solution of his problem. He had not found any trace of the magazine, he did not know what had brought Clarence Winnington to the library on that fatal Sunday night, he could not state with certainty what had taken place there, and he had failed to discover either the location of the jewels or the identity of the murderer. A poor result for that week of ceaseless labour!

It was in vain he told himself that most cases were baffling during their first period: that of the collection of evidence. During this period their difficulties did not matter: explanations were not required. Explanations were for the second stage, the difficult stage, the stage of evolving a theory to cover the facts. That was the stage that tested a man. It took insight and imagination: work for a finer brain. For a dozen who could collect the facts, perhaps one could find their significance. French had always secretly believed that in this part of his job lay his strength, and it was now disconcerting to find himself failing in it.

He spent a satisfying evening of slippered ease over the fire and went up early to bed with a novel. Presently he grew drowsy, put down his book and switched off the light. He had just fallen into a dreamless sleep when his telephone sounded.

'Phone from Inspector Nelson, Guildford, sir. He reports another tragedy at Little Wokeham. Dr Mallaby has just attempted to commit suicide. He's not dead, but he's unlikely to recover. Nelson did not think you would be interested, but he advised us in case you might wish to go down.'

The news gave French rather a jar. It was at least unfortunate, however one looked at it. If Mallaby were guilty he had tried to cheat the law, which would not redound to French's credit. If he were innocent, it might be worse still. French wondered whether in this case he himself could have been responsible. Was it his accusation and threat, for it had been a threat, which had driven the doctor to attempt his life? Though French believed that every word he had used was justified, he would be terribly distressed if an error of judgment on his part had led to such a tragedy. Under the circumstances he thought he would like to know more about it.

'Thank Nelson,' he said, 'and tell him I'll go at once. You needn't trouble Carter: I'll work with Nelson.'

A couple of hours later he called at police headquarters at Guildford, to learn, as he expected, that Nelson was at Green Gables. He drove on.

Constable Rice was at the door. He saluted and said his inspector was inside. Nelson hurried out.

'Come in, sir, to the sitting-room. I hope I did right in ringing you up? I did it from Guildford on Rice's report. Of course there's always a chance of murder in these cases, but now that I've had a look round I think it was attempted suicide all right.'

French followed him in. A sergeant was sitting in a corner making notes. French wished him good-evening and turned back to Nelson.

'How is he?'

'Very low, I understand. Only just alive.'

'I wondered if what I said to him could have had anything to do with it.'

'I wondered that too. Also if the man was deeper in the thing than we had believed.'

'You mean deliberately screening the Winnington murderer?'

'That, yes, or even if he'd done it himself. It must have been something pretty serious, for I shouldn't have said Mallaby was of the suicide type.'

'Nor I. Well, tell me about it.'

'I have only Mrs Hepworth's statement for most of it, but I think she's reliable enough. It seems she was out with some friends in the village during the evening and she got back rather earlier than she expected, about half-past ten. On arrival she went to the sitting-room in accordance with her usual custom, to make sure the doctor was there before locking the front door and to see if he had any instructions for the morning. She found him lying slumped back in that chair with a face like parchment, and the knife and that pool of blood on the floor as you see them. A slight spurt of blood was still coming from his wrist. She has her head screwed on, has Mrs Hepworth, and she knows something of first aid. She put a tourniquet on his arm and stopped the bleeding and phoned for Dr Armstrong from Bramford. He arrived in about ten minutes and treated Mallaby and took him to the hospital in Guildford, where I understand he has had a blood transfusion. He rang up Rice before they started, and Rice rang through to me.'

'A nasty business, particularly coming so soon after the other. This will mean more trouble for the Hurst Lodge folks, however it ends.'

Nelson agreed, and French, standing just inside the door, began slowly and systematically to scrutinise the scene. The armchair where Mallaby had sat, with on the floor beneath it the pool of blood and the surgical knife lying where it had dropped from his nerveless hand. The table with the bag and case of instruments, the decanter and siphon and the dregs in the glass, the dying ashes in the grate.

'Was that light on?' he asked, nodding at the standard lamp beside the chair.

'Yes, just as you see it.'

'Been through the other rooms?'

'Yes, but we could find nothing out of place.'

'Where is Mrs Hepworth?'

'She's gone back to her friends just a bit down the road. You can see her at any time.'

'I'll see her presently. Also I'd like to have a word with that doctor. Armstrong, you said his name was. Ring him up, will you, and ask him to come over. Steady a moment: the telephone's only been used once since the tragedy?'

'Three times. Mrs Hepworth rang up Dr Armstrong and he rang the hospital and Rice.'

'Then it scarcely matters. I was thinking of prints, but go ahead.'

Suicide, French thought. No suggestion whatever of anything else. And yet one point was curious. Would a doctor who had access to any drug he wanted have adopted so comparatively painful a method as to cut open his own wrist? Yes, he supposed he might. He would get Armstrong's view.

Dr Armstrong turned up shortly. He was a small, slightly consequential man, and French felt that careful handling might be necessary if he were to get what he wanted.

'Good evening, doctor,' he said politely. 'I'm sorry to have troubled you and grateful to you for coming up, but as this is the second tragedy in a week in this area, we thought it ought to be carefully looked into. I've come down from London to help Inspector Nelson.'

'That's all right. I know you have to do these things.'

'Well, not to keep you I'll go straight ahead. Perhaps you'd tell me the medical side of the affair?'

'Certainly. I was rung up at ten-forty by Mrs Hepworth, Dr Mallaby's housekeeper. She said it was very urgent, so I came immediately. I found the doctor unconscious and suffering from a deep incised wound in the left wrist, which

219

had bled freely. The bleeding had been arrested by a tourniquet, applied to the upper arm by, Mrs Hepworth
informed me, herself. I telephoned to the Guildford hospital
for the ambulance and it was here in just under fifteen
minutes. I went with Mallaby to the hospital, and they
were going to give him a blood transfusion when I left.'

'Do you think he will live?'

'As a matter of opinion I don't, but it's possible.'

'Did you form any idea as to whether it was an attempt
at suicide?'

Dr Armstrong shrugged. 'It's not my province exactly,
but since you ask the question, I thought so.'

'Where was the cut, sir?'

The doctor marked the position on his own wrist.

'He was going for the artery?'

'Presumably.'

'Did he get it?'

'I couldn't examine. They'll tell you at the hospital.'

French nodded. 'I suppose the affair must have happened
just before Mrs Hepworth came in?'

'That depends on what you mean by "just". To have
produced so large a haemorrhage some little time must
have elapsed. Here again in the absence of a complete
examination it's not possible to say how long.'

'I follow, sir. Now there's one other matter. What do
you think about the method? Would a doctor who wished
to kill himself open an artery in his wrist?'

'That's certainly a point,' Armstrong admitted. 'I imagine
most medical men would take a drug. One of the barbi-
turates occurs to me: difficult for an outsider to get, but
easy for a doctor.'

'Take your dose and go to sleep comfortably and never

wake up, that would be my idea if I wanted to do the job and had the stuff. But you know as well as I do, Dr Armstrong, that human nature is unaccountable in these matters. Many suicides adopt' the most painful methods possible. You remember a case that Taylor gives, one of many, in which a man heated a bar of iron white-hot and managed to force it some inches into his stomach.'

'Yes, I agree. I doubt if any conclusion can be built on it.'

'I don't want either to exaggerate or to minimise its value. Would cutting that artery be very painful?'

'Not very, and the death would be easy: he would simply get weaker and weaker till he faded out.'

'Then may I take it that in your opinion Mallaby might have adopted that method?'

'Oh, definitely. I shouldn't have done it myself, but that's no reason whatever for saying he wouldn't.'

'Thank you, doctor, I'm glad to have had your opinion. All the same, I take it suicide is proved by another point?'

Dr Armstrong looked his question and Nelson's interest grew keener.

'That he didn't struggle,' French added.

'Bless my soul, I never thought of that!' Nelson exclaimed. 'Of course you're right. No one would sit still and allow another person to open up his wrist. That finally settles it.'

'Unless he was knocked out first?'

'He wasn't: there are no marks or bruises.' The doctor stood up. 'Is there anything else you're likely to want? If not, I'll be off home.'

'Just one thing, doctor. Show me how you hold that knife: here on this pencil.' He polished the pencil and passed it over, holding it in his handkerchief.

Freeman Wills Crofts

When Armstrong had left, French stood staring vacantly into space. A likeable chap, Mallaby. Seemed a bit of an old woman at first, but you quickly saw that, though quiet, he was nothing of the kind. He was steadfast and kindly and unselfish. French felt convinced also that he was no coward. He wondered whether there were relatives with whom he should communicate.

'Have you looked over his papers?' he asked Nelson.

'Not yet, Mr French: there hasn't been time.'

'Then suppose you start? I'll join you presently.'

French continued his musings. There could be no doubt as to what had happened. He wondered if he might conclude at once it had been attempted suicide and let the thing go, or whether he should look further into it? After all, though it probably meant nothing, the choice of method was peculiar. He whistled tunelessly as was his wont when undecided, then his gaze fell once more on the glass. Did that suggest anything? A way of preventing a man from struggling? He doubted it, and yet . . . Presently he heard himself telling the sergeant to bring in his bag from the car.

'I'm going to do a few prints,' he told him. 'You might bear a hand.'

Nelson called in from the next room. 'Sorry I didn't bring our man, sir, if you want prints. I didn't realise they'd be necessary.'

'That's all right, Nelson; I don't expect they are. I just thought I'd be happier after a test or two. You carry on with what you're at.'

Working with his usual careful precision, French held the knife where it was bloodstained and blew powder over the clean parts of the handle. Clear impressions came out. These he checked with his collection. Not only were they

222

Mallaby's, but none except Mallaby's were present. Next he developed Dr Armstrong's prints on his pencil and compared them for position with those on the handle of the knife. The latter were correct as to place and number.

This seemed to settle the matter, and once again French was tempted to proceed no further. Then his character and training stepped in. Thoroughness, he admonished himself, was what did it! He mustn't be lazy. A job that was worth starting was worth finishing.

He picked up the case of instruments, holding it by its opposite corners, and having closed it, dusted it for prints. Soon he got them: all over it. Two or three which he examined proved to be Mallaby's. Again everything was okay.

He was about to put down the case when he paused and then suddenly stiffened. Here and there over the mass of prints were clear spaces, oval spaces. He stood looking at these, then very carefully replaced the case on the table.

'Nelson!' he called. 'Come here a moment. See, there's the case that the knife was taken from. Don't touch it, but suppose you were going to open it, where would your fingers press? Take this book and assume it's the case.'

Nelson arranged his fingers on the book so as to open it in the middle. There was a spring catch to the lid of the case and his right thumb fell naturally upon the corresponding position of this on the book, while the fingers gripped the book's spine, representing the back of the lid. The left fingers and thumb fell below those of the right on what represented the body of the case.

'That okay? Now look at the case.'

At every point corresponding to Nelson's fingers there was a clear oval on the case!

Both men stared, while a little wave of excitement titillated French's nerves. The last time that case was opened it was not by Mallaby! Someone else had done it, someone who wore gloves!

Nelson's eyes goggled. 'But, good lord, Mr French, that means—'

'I'm afraid it does,' French nodded, 'and we were just going to miss it. Thank heaven we didn't!'

'But—he didn't struggle! You said it yourself. If it had been—murder, he would have struggled.'

French pointed to the glass. 'We'll have those dregs analysed. I think there's enough for analysis.'

'By heck, yes! It's an ideal But enough dope to knock him out? I'm not so sure, sir. Wouldn't he have tasted it?'

'Might,' French admitted. This was certainly a difficulty, yet the evidence of the clear ovals seemed overwhelming. Then another point occurred to him.

'Look here, Nelson, what do you make of Mallaby's character? Would you call him unselfish and conscientious?'

'Extra, I should say. More than most people.'

'Exactly. And we believe that to save Miss Winnington's brother he monkeyed with the time of Winnington's death, and that he was afraid his action was now going to injure Miss Winnington herself?'

'After what you said he couldn't doubt it.'

'Exactly again. Now do you think that under such circumstances a man of Mallaby's character would have passed out without squaring the thing up?'

Nelson stared. 'You mean leaving a note?'

'That's just what I do mean.'

'Bless my soul, sir, that's pretty cute Nelson was visibly impressed. 'He believed you suspected Miss Winnington

224

because of what he had done? You're dead right! He'd never have left things like that! Certainly he'd have done everything he could to repair his error.'

'So, since there's no note—?'

'Since there's no note, there's no suicide. That's good, Mr French, if I may say so.'

'One thing follows at all events. You may send for your technical people. Whether our suspicion is right or wrong, the job must be done thoroughly now. We'll want photographs and the place to be gone over for prints. And tell someone to call at the hospital and bring along Mallaby's keys. Then suppose you carry on with those papers.'

Left to himself, French sat down to try to reconstruct what might have happened if an attempt had been made to murder Mallaby. In this case there had been a murderer and he had got into the house. How? Though Nelson had looked over the other rooms, French re-examined the doors and windows for himself. All were fastened on the inside, but of course it was not certain that this condition had obtained before the murder. If one had been open he might have entered, fastened it, and left by drawing the front door after him. They would have to be tested for prints, particularly the knob of the hall door.

All the same, two considerations made French doubt that entry had been by a window. First, as none was broken, one would have had to be unlatched, which the murderer could scarcely have foreseen. Second, Mallaby could not have been doped by anyone who had broken and entered, and without doping he would have struggled. It therefore looked as if Mallaby must have admitted his visitor.

As French continued his slow, painstaking attempt at reconstruction, another point struck him. If the murderer doped Mallaby's drink, that drink must have been there on the table during his visit. Knowing Mallaby, French felt he would never have drunk himself without offering a drink to his caller. Had he done so?

Of course the murderer could not leave a second glass on the table. Had he washed it and put it away?

French went to the dining-room and found where the glasses were kept in the sideboard. As he was hesitating about beginning work on them, Nelson's helpers opportunely turned up from Guildford.

'You've come at a good time,' he greeted them. 'I'm just ready for you. I want the position of all those glasses noted, and each to be tested for prints.'

As each glass was removed and dusted with powder, the shelf was marked with chalk. The result gave French another mild thrill. All of them bore prints, unknown prints, except one. And that one was the last to be put in.

'Later on you might take the housekeeper's prints and check up with these,' he directed, though he knew it would prove only a matter of form. All the glasses but the last had unquestionably been washed by her.

He had now no doubt whatever that he was investigating attempted murder masquerading as suicide. All the same, the discovery was only his starting-point. Now must begin that amassing of facts which formed the foundation of every case. But first, could he make any more deductions?

His reconstruction had been successful so far, and sitting down in an easy-chair, he tried to continue it. If the murderer had washed his glass, he had used a sink. Which, he wondered? There were two, one in the surgery and one in the kitchen.

'Try those taps,' he ordered.

On the two in the surgery Mallaby's prints showed distinctly, on the cold tap in the kitchen were the same prints as on the glasses, but on the hot there were none. Once again French felt his thrill of satisfaction.

Then still another idea struck him. Blood had flowed freely from the wound, and its distribution on the knife-handle showed that it had stained the murderer's hand. He turned to the sergeant.

'Got a shifting spanner?'

A search of the tool-bag on Mallaby's car brought one to light.

'Open the plug of that trap beneath the kitchen sink,' French went on, 'and save whatever's in it for testing.'

He did not expect, and did not get, a spectacular result, but the chemists at the Yard would settle the matter. Another mistake the visitor had made, he thought with grim satisfaction. If he had used the surgery basin, the presence of blood in the trap would have proved nothing. Probably he had used the kitchen because he thought it would be less carefully examined, or because the cloth for drying the glass was there.

'Take a sample from the pool of blood also,' he went on. 'I want to know its group.'

As he watched the men carrying out his orders with care and skill, he felt profoundly thankful that he had come down to look into the matter for himself. Though of course he would not say so, he was sure that Nelson would have been deceived. All the same, he must not be complacent. He had learnt that murder had been done, but he had no more idea than the man in the moon who was guilty.

Going into the next room to assist Nelson with the papers, he saw that to discover this might prove as difficult as in the case of Clarence Winnington.

19

Joseph French

During the remainder of that night French supervised the Surrey officers as they carried out the routine investigations inseparable from a case which might prove to be murder. Fingerprints were sought and photographed, exhaustive search was made for some small object which the murderer might have dropped, and the general layout of the crime was studied in the hope that some clue might become revealed. Except that clear oval spaces were found on the hall-door knob, showing that the murderer had drawn the door after him, none of these yielded any helpful results.

French's own researches disclosed one small point only, and that so trifling that he did not at first give it serious consideration. In the corner of the surgery was a small old-fashioned safe. With Mallaby's keys French opened it and systematically went through its contents. These were what naturally might have been expected in such a receptacle; a small cabinet of poisons, a bank-book, a professional ledger, letters, medical certificates and other private papers.

In a drawer was a tiny collection of jewellery which French thought might have belonged to the doctor's mother. With them was a rather incongruous object, an old fountain-pen with a broken clip. It was this incongruity which attracted French's attention. He had noticed a much better pen in Mallaby's waistcoat pocket when last he had seen him, and as this one was of no great intrinsic value, he assumed that it must have had some sentimental associations for the doctor.

Whether from mere idle curiosity or from his ingrained habit of examining *everything*, French picked up the pen and unscrewed the top. The spot of dried ink on the nib looked fresh and he tried the pen on a piece of paper. It wrote perfectly.

This was mildly surprising. Its position in the safe had suggested a history, but Mallaby had evidently been using it recently. Why should such a commonplace object have been locked away with such care?

Again from idle curiosity or ingrained habit French picked up his insufflator, and having screwed on the top, ejected a little cloud of grey powder on to the pen. Except for his own, there were no prints on it. Obviously Mallaby had wiped it clean.

As French considered this discovery his interest grew. Once again, why should Mallaby have done such a thing? Had the doctor recently broken the clip and bought the new pen in his waistcoat pocket? French looked again at the clip. The fracture was worn smooth. This then was not the explanation.

It now occurred to him to wonder whether, when Mallaby had wiped the old pen, he had made a complete job of it. He took the top off again and blew his powder over the part adjoining the nib, which during his first test had been covered. Ah, he was right! Here were prints. Most of them were smudged and indistinct, but one was fairly clear. Calling for his case, he took out his collection of the party's prints and began to compare them.

When he found, as he did a few seconds later, that that on the pen was not Mallaby's, his interest grew still further. It was not Josephs', nor Christina's, nor Bellissa's, but— French stared. Yes, it was Bernard's. This must be Bernard's pen, and Mallaby had evidently found it and locked it away till he could return it. The curve of French's interest declined steeply. Bernard was not concerned in the troubles which had been taking place, so the pen episode was unlikely to prove helpful. However, he might as well ask Bernard about it.

The time dragged slowly by, and then, just as French was beginning to think of breakfast, the Chief Constable turned up. He listened with a grave expression while French and Nelson made their reports, French mentioning everything except the pen, which he scarcely thought was relevant.

'A bad business,' remarked Lester. 'Two tragedies within a week of each other in a little place like this! Are they connected, do you think?'

'It's an attractive theory,' French answered, 'but so far we've found nothing either to support or contradict it. I have to admit, sir, that I don't yet know who killed Mr Winnington. I ought to have asked for a conference before this, but I just wasn't ready for it.'

'Whom have you suspected?' French smiled wryly. 'Everyone in turn. All the members of the family had motives. Mr Bernard I suspected first. He didn't seem to

231

be the man for murder, but he had taken too much drink that night, enough to make him act abnormally. Then I saw that getting drunk would not explain a carefully premeditated murder, and finally I found he had a perfect and unprepared alibi. Then I thought of Mr Plant. He's the most likely of the lot so far as character is concerned, and also he had a strong motive, he was very hard up. But it wasn't he; his alibi is also unshakable. I don't believe that either of the women could have done it.'

'Nor I. What were Bernard's and Plant's alibis?'

French told him.

'I suppose,' Lester went on, 'Mallaby himself couldn't have been guilty?'

'I thought of that,' and French stated the pros and cons of the argument. 'I believe he deliberately faked the time of the death, but I don't think he committed the murder. Of course it might have been a genuine burglary, as it looked at first, though I think that's unlikely. They're working all out at that at the Yard, but so far we have traced neither a possible man nor any of the jewels.'

The Chief Constable grunted. 'Quite a problem. If Mallaby did any faking with the time of the death, it would look as if he had found evidence against someone. What about that someone discovering it and attempting to bump him off to prevent its coming out?'

'I thought of that also, sir, and it's a very attractive theory too. I needn't say that I'll keep it carefully in mind. I'll try, of course, to trace all the letters or messages Dr Mallaby received recently and the persons he met. We may get some light that way.'

'If Mallaby recovers?'

'Ah, sir, then things would be easier.'

The Chief Constable had been pleasant enough, indeed friendly, and yet Nelson seemed a little discouraged by the interview. Presently he voiced his feelings.

'He had expected more progress, Mr French,' he remarked plaintively, 'but I don't see that we could have done more than we have. It's just a bit of bad luck that we haven't got our man.'

'One thing we haven't done that we should do at once,' French returned: 'pay a visit to the Three Swallows. You'll feel better after coffee and ham and eggs.'

After breakfast French took Mrs Hepworth's statement, which contained nothing more than Nelson had reported, and then, while Nelson began work on the recent contacts made by Mallaby, he went up to Hurst Lodge. He asked for Bernard, but was shown into the lounge where he and Horne and Bellissa were seated. French murmured his regrets about the fresh tragedy and his having to intrude on them at such a time.

They were obviously greatly pained and shocked by the occurrence, particularly Bernard, who seemed to think they had somehow been disgraced by it.

'Have you heard how Mallaby is this morning?' he asked. 'Miss Winnington rang up and could get no satisfaction except that he was still alive, so she's gone into Guildford to inquire at the hospital. She's hoping to see him.'

French shook his head. 'From what Dr Armstrong said last night, I question if she'll be allowed to do so. However, no doubt they'll give her all particulars.'

Though nothing actually was said, he gathered that the others had strongly disapproved of Christina's expedition, on the grounds that it was unwise of her to associate herself with a would-be suicide. French wished he could

233

tell them the truth, but felt that in the interests of justice he dared not.

Presently he began his interrogation: When had they last seen the doctor? What was his frame of mind? Did he show signs of worry or distress? and so gradually by suggestion rather than direct questioning to, Where were they between nine and eleven on the previous evening?

He was able to get the information without probing for it or giving anything away. They had a complete joint alibi. All, including Christina, had been together in the lounge for the entire evening, and during the fateful period the rector and his churchwarden had been with them discussing the erection of a memorial to Clarence Winnington, for which he had left a sum in his will. No doubt confirmation from these two gentlemen would be forthcoming, and if so, the quartet might be eliminated from further consideration.

As French reached this conclusion Horne stood up. 'If you've finished with me, Chief Inspector, I'll go. I've got to do some work.'

'I too,' said Bellissa. 'I want to write a letter.'

French saw that Bernard wished he would leave, but there was still the matter of the pen to be dealt with. He therefore sat down again when the door closed behind them.

'With your permission, Mr Winnington, I'll take advantage of this opportunity. I wanted a word with you alone.' He took the pen from his pocket. 'Have you ever seen that before?'

Bernard's eyes goggled. 'My pen!' he exclaimed. 'It was lost. Where did you find it?'

'I'll tell you that in a moment, sir. When did you lose it?'

'I didn't lose it,' Bernard returned; 'at least not personally. I lent it to Guy Plant. It was he who lost it.'

'It's not of much importance,' French declared, 'but will you tell me the circumstances?'

Instead of clearing up the matter, French found that the recital made it more puzzling than ever. He thought for a moment, then spoke casually.

'Oh well, it's pretty clear what has taken place. I found the pen at Green Gables, and it's evident that Mr Plant must have dropped it and Dr Mallaby picked it up.'

Bernard seemed completely puzzled. 'I don't see how that could have happened,' he answered uncertainly.

'What other explanation is there?' French queried. 'Incidentally, I should say that until we see how things turn out I must keep it as having been found in the house. Can you do without it for a day or two longer?'

'I don't want it at all. Guy sent me a new one to replace it.'

French rose. 'Then that's all I want.' He moved towards the door, but paused before teaching it. 'Dr Mallaby was probably looking for the owner. I suppose he couldn't have known that it was yours?'

Bernard thought over this. 'He should have,' he said presently. 'A week or so before my uncle's death we were doing a puzzle and I had it out and Mallaby borrowed it to draw a line. He remarked on the broken clip, so he should have recognised it from that.'

'I expect he was waiting for an opportunity to return it. Well, I'm much obliged for your help.' French hesitated, then went back across the room. 'Just one thing, Mr Winnington, if you please,' he said more gravely. 'I'm going to ask you not to mention this matter of the pen to anyone:

neither Mr Plant nor Miss Winnington not anyone else. It's just for a day or two till I make some further inquiries. Will you oblige me?'

Bernard looked surprised. 'Why, of course, Chief Inspector, if you wish it.'

'Thank you, sir. The less talk there is about the details of a case like this, the better.' With this remark, as cryptic to himself as to Bernard, he nodded himself out.

He was a good deal more interested in this matter of the pen than he had admitted. A phrase used by the Chief Constable had stuck in his memory: 'If Mallaby did any faking with the time of the death, it would look as if he had found evidence against someone.' The same thought had occurred to French himself, and he wondered increasingly if the pen could have been the evidence in question.

If so, where might the doctor have found it? There was one place which might account for the whole episode. Suppose it was in the library or somewhere about the body? At the time he examined the body Mallaby could not have known that Bernard was innocent, and if he faked the time to prove him so, it was obvious that he must also remove the pen, supposing it to have been there.

At this point in his cogitations French reached Green Gables. There he found that Nelson was out searching the grounds for footprints, and he therefore continued with what was in his mind. He sent Carter to inquire from Constable Rice and Mrs Bentham of the Post Office whether Mallaby had made any move through them to find the owner of the pen. He also rang up the Guildford papers with the same object. In both cases the answer was in the negative.

Mallaby, then, had made no move about the pen. If he had known it was Bernard's he had not returned it, and if he had not known, he had taken no steps to find the owner. Why? Had he forgotten about it? Most unlikely when he had taken the trouble to wipe it clean and lock it in his safe. Obviously he had considered it important.

The more French thought over it, the more he felt that only the theory that Mallaby had known the pen was Bernard's and that he had found it near the body would adequately account for the man's actions.

He tried to visualise Mallaby's reactions to the discovery. His first idea would probably be to destroy the pen, but he would be afraid to do so lest later circumstances should make it desirable to prove that he found it. He would, however, do the best he could for Bernard; he would wipe off incriminating prints which might prove Bernard had been the last to handle it. Admittedly most people under the circumstances would have put the matter to Bernard, but French could understand that a man of Mallaby's character would shrink from doing so as long as possible.

Full of his idea, French returned to Hurst Lodge and called Josephs into the library.

'We had the Chief Constable round this morning,' he told him, adding mendaciously: 'He has asked for a more detailed reconstruction of the scene when Mr Winnington's body was found on Sunday week. Just tell me once again, more fully if possible, what happened.'

Josephs was clearly resentful at having to repeat himself, but French insisted on going through the entire happenings, step by step. As a result an interesting fact was revealed. When Rice had arrived Josephs had gone out into the hall to conduct him in. This had left Mallaby alone in the room, and at that time he was kneeling down, stooping over the body.

Mallaby, then, would have had not only a strong motive but an adequate opportunity for abstracting the pen, and French was by this time pretty sure that he had done it. But this by no means cleared up the problem. If it were correct, how did the pen get there?

French's thoughts turned back to Plant. Could Plant be guilty after all? It was an intriguing thought that a pen with a broken clip might well fall out of a waistcoat pocket if the wearer were stooping over a body. Could Plant possibly have faked his alibi? French would like to have thought so, but in the light of Mrs Miggs' evidence he did not see how he could.

Deep in thought he walked back to Green Gables. Nelson greeted him eagerly. He had just made a discovery.

20

Joseph French

Nelson was showing a carefully repressed excitement as he made his report.

'I've been having a search round the house in daylight,' he explained, 'and in that wood at the back I've found the marks of where a bicycle has been parked, and two indistinct footprints beside it. You'd better come out and see them.'

'Good work,' said French, and when he reached the place he thought even better of it. The marks were only just visible and might easily have been overlooked. They showed merely the outlines of the feet without any identifying detail. The bicycle trace also was of the slightest, a faint and smooth depression.

'Not much good but for one thing, and of course that's not conclusive,' Nelson went on. He spoke disparagingly, but French saw that this was a mere concession to convention. 'I mean the angles. There are only two prints, but we've tried to measure the stride and the angles of the trace. They're identical with those in the lane at Hurst Lodge.'

French stared. This was important.

'Fine,' he approved, 'it was a good thought. And of course, now you mention it, there's another thing.'

Nelson looked his question.

'The bicycle,' French pronounced. 'In these days of cars the use of a bicycle is more of a pointer than it was. Not conclusive, of course. And as the angles of the footprints are about the mean of the range, they're not, as you say, conclusive either. But both together. Cumulative evidence! The odds are certainly that the same man was on both jobs. What about the size of the prints?'

'Slightly smaller than before.'

'Last time we thought he wasn't wearing his own shoes, so that may not mean anything. Well, that's good, Nelson. A suggestion that the two crimes were connected and that we've only to look for one man.'

'It's given us nothing to find him by,' Nelson returned, still trying to hide his satisfaction.

'You want too much. Did you expect him to sit here and wait for you?'

French recognised that the evidence was indeed valuable. While it did not constitute technical proof, he felt that its suggestion was strong enough to justify action. He began to pace up and down, trying to square it with what he had previously learnt.

It seemed to fit uncommonly well. If it were true that an attempt had been made to kill Mallaby because he had found a clue to Clarence Winnington's murderer, the same man would naturally be guilty of both crimes. It could not be otherwise.

French was delighted. Not only did the discovery indicate that he was right so far, but it absolutely confirmed

Bernard's innocence, for Bernard could not possibly have attempted Mallaby's murder.

Only Plant therefore seemed to be left, and the immediate problem became crystallised into two questions: Had Mallaby found the pen near the body? and if so, had Plant dropped it there? On the way back to the house French discussed the matter with Nelson.

'If Plant's our man,' he concluded, 'he was here last night. Was he? There's a cut-and-dried issue. Let's get down to it. What about another interview with the charming Mrs Miggs?'

They repeated their proceedings of a few days earlier, Carter driving the others to Ivy Cottage and remaining with the car while they went in. Mrs Miggs greeted them as old friends and once again showed them into the sitting-room.

'Last time we called,' French explained, 'you told us what you did and saw on the previous Sunday evening. Now we want your help again: just the same information, but about yesterday evening instead of a week ago.'

'Do you mean, was Mr Plant here during the evening?' she asked shrewdly.

French laughed. 'The time he went out, please, if he did go out. If he didn't go out, of course you can't give the time.'

'He didn't go out, at least not till about quarter to twelve. He was in the study before that.'

'What? Typing again?'

'No, sir, but I could hear him all the same.'

'Oh? Doing what?'

'Moving about, stirring the fire, turning on the wireless, speaking on the telephone, and there was the smoke too.'

241

'A pretty convincing list. I congratulate you on your observation; I wish all our police officers were as good. Then he went out later?'

'Yes, he called to me that he was going to the post: he often does post his letters late at night.'

'Not meaning to be impertinent, but you sit up pretty late, don't you?'

'On Sunday evenings only. I write to my son in America.'

'Oh yes, you said that, of course. Was Mr Plant out long?'

'About ten minutes: time to walk to the pillar box and back.'

'About what time was the telephoning?'

'I don't know exactly, but I think about half-past nine.'

'I suppose you couldn't hear what was said?'

Mrs Miggs looked shocked. 'I'm not in the habit of listening to other people's conversations,' she said severely.

French declared smoothly that he had not supposed so for a moment, but that sometimes remarks at a telephone were involuntarily overheard. It was soon evident that the good lady had heard nothing, and he expressed his thanks and wished her good-day.

'No shaking that story,' he remarked to Nelson as they got into the car. 'I must admit I believe the woman. At all events, no jury would question her evidence.'

'No, Mr French, and that means that your doubts of Plant were misplaced.'

'I'm afraid it does, Nelson, and the mischief is that we've no other suspect to replace him. All the same, let's be thorough. Let's trace that phone call while we're here. If we can get confirmation from the other end that he really did telephone, that would remove the last doubt.'

They went to police headquarters at Weybridge and enlisted the aid of the local superintendent. He agreed to see the telephone manager immediately. Presently he returned with information which considerably interested French. Plant had rung up Mallaby!

Though he could not obtain evidence from Mallaby, French saw that this was a final corroboration of Plant's innocence. The attempted murder had taken place somewhere about ten: Armstrong had given between 10.00 and 10.15 as the extreme limits of error. If Plant had rung up from his house about 9.30 he could not have reached Little Wokeham in time to commit it. Even with a car it would have been utterly impossible. There would be first the journey, say 25 minutes, the arrival at Green Gables and the doping of Mallaby, at least another 25, and the preparation for opening the wrist, say 10: an hour altogether. French was positive he had not overestimated the time, and his opinion was confirmed by Dr Armstrong, whom he consulted on the point over the telephone. Moreover, it was in the highest degree improbable that Plant had used a car: it would have been too difficult to conceal, and besides, there were the traces of the bicycle in the case of both crimes. With a bicycle, of course, the travelling alone could not have been done in the time. Plant's guilt was therefore out of the question.

'What about asking if our people can check up anything about the call at the other end?' Nelson suggested.

'I don't see how they could,' French answered, 'but there's no harm in trying. Give the Super a ring.'

They lunched while waiting for the reply, and then were again interested. Though the local exchange could not trace incoming calls, there were records of those sent out. Mallaby had rung up Plant that evening.

'Plant's alibi is unshakable, I, agree,' said French, 'though I perhaps have more reason than most to doubt unshakable alibis. But it's a strange thing that at every step in this business we come across the man's trail. We must get the thing squared up: see him and get his explanation of these points. Ring him up and say we'll be at his office in an hour.'

Plant had given instructions for them to be shown in to him on arrival. His manner was civil but dry as he asked what he could do for them. French noticed that he smelt of whisky, but as it was just after lunch this probably had no significance.

'The usual thing, Mr Plant,' French told him; 'just to answer one or two questions. You know, of course, about Dr Mallaby?'

'Yes, a terrible business. My wife rang up. I knew he was worried, but not to that extent. For Miss Winnington's sake I should have gone down, but I had an important meeting this morning. I'm going now, as soon as I can get away.'

'We shall not keep you long, sir, just these one or two questions.' He paused and looked up his notebook, a plan he had always found stressed to his examinee the routine nature of the inquiry. 'The first is about a rather trifling matter, a fountain-pen which I understand you borrowed from Mr Bernard and lost.'

French imagined a sudden gleam appeared in the man's eyes, but it vanished so quickly that he could not be sure. His manner, however, grew more wary. He nodded without answering.

'You did borrow and lose the pen, I suppose?'

'Oh yes.' Plant spoke without hesitation. 'Unfortunately I did.'

'I'm rather anxious to find out where you lost it. Have you any idea?'

Plant smiled crookedly, though no mirth softened his eyes. 'If I knew that, it wouldn't be lost,' he pointed out drily. 'I put it into my pocket when I had finished using it in the Hurst Lodge lounge—I suppose you know the circumstances under which I borrowed it?'

'Yes, Mr Bernard told me.'

Plant nodded. 'I put it into my pocket lest it should get lost, intending to return it to Bernard when he came back. But he was then full of the accident to his friend and we both forgot about it. Then when I was undressing I missed it from my pocket. I have no idea where it fell. How did you know about it, or is that a question I mustn't ask?'

'Not at all, sir; I'll tell you. Dr Mallaby found it.'

Plant's features registered a lively surprise. 'Mallaby?' he retorted. 'But how on earth . . . ? Where did he find it?'

'That unfortunately I don't know. Does the mere fact not give you any hint?'

Plant shook his head and remained silent. He was obviously thinking keenly. French waited with growing interest. He could have sworn that under the man's iron control he was deeply moved.

'One thing does occur to me,' he said at last, speaking with hesitation. 'I don't say that this is the explanation, you understand; I don't know. But in the light of what you tell me, it may be. I brought the car round that night to the hall door and then went back to the lounge to say good-night and so on. As I was getting into the car again I dropped my glove. I groped round but couldn't find it, and I had to open up my overcoat and get my torch out of my jacket pocket. In the stooping the pen may have slipped out of my pocket on to the drive; its clip was broken. It's the only time, at all events, that I remember stooping.'

It was possible, and for all French knew or could prove to the contrary, it might be true. He decided it would be politic to accept it.

'That would explain the whole thing,' he answered easily. 'Apparently it's what actually happened. Thank you, that's all I want about that. One other question: Did you ring up Dr Mallaby last evening?'

Plant stared, and this time French was sure that sudden emotion flickered in his eyes. ''Pon my soul, Chief Inspector, you've been busying yourself in my affairs to some purpose. May I ask what it portends?'

French drew himself up. 'You might know that, sir, for yourself. We're trying to find out everything about Dr Mallaby, and if you rang him up, it must have been close to the hour of his—er—misfortune. I should like to hear your account of the conversation.'

Plant remained silent, whistling tunelessly below his breath and shooting little speculative glances at French. Then he seemed to come to a decision.

'Since you ask it, I did ring him up about half-past nine last night. It was to ask him a question. He either couldn't or wouldn't answer it then, but shortly after he rang me up and answered it.'

'Did you form any opinion as to his frame of mind?'

'He seemed worried, but not more so than for some days previously. I noticed nothing which in any way suggested what afterwards happened.'

'What was the question, Mr Plant?'

Plant shook his head. 'I really don't see, Chief Inspector,

that you have any reason to ask that. It was a purely private matter and had nothing whatever to do with his death.'

'I'm sorry, Mr Plant, but I must press it. If I don't, and if Dr Mallaby dies, the coroner will. You must see that for yourself. I presume you were the last person to speak to the doctor. Of course the subject of the discussion will be demanded.'

'It was a confidential matter and not my secret.'

'Unless it proves to have been connected with either of the deaths, your confidence will be absolutely respected.'

Plant moved uneasily. 'You put me in an awkward position. If I answer you, I'll break my word to Mallaby, for he pledged me to silence. If I don't, no doubt you'll suspect the worst of everybody concerned.'

'Circumstances alter cases, sir; Dr Mallaby is now unable to speak for himself. You must agree that what has occurred relieves you of your promise.'

Plant shrugged. 'You have the authority behind you. I make a formal protest, but if you insist, I'll tell you.'

'I have no option, I'm afraid.'

'Very well. On Wednesday last—no, Thursday—Mallaby rang me up saying he wanted to consult me on an important and confidential matter. I invited him to dine in Town, and he came. He began, as I said, by pledging me to secrecy, and then he told me that he had been very much worried all the week by a remark which Bernard had made during his call on the Sunday evening. Mallaby said that on the previous evening, the Saturday of the birthday party, he had asked Miss Winnington to marry him. She had not given him a definite answer, but had asked for a week to consider it. You knew that, perhaps?'

'I knew it, sir.'

'On the Sunday evening during their talk Bernard had casually mentioned that he and Mrs Plant and Miss Winnington would each come in for a third of Clarence's money, amounting to some twenty thousand apiece after succession duty had been paid. This had terribly upset Mallaby's super-conscientious mind. He felt he could not expect an heiress to marry him and he did not know what to say to her. Perhaps you knew all that too?'

'Yes, sir.'

'I see there's not much I can tell you. Well, I naturally asked him why he had come to me about it, and he said that he wanted the advice of a man of the world on the whole question. First, was Bernard's summary of the situation correct? He said that while he would trust anything to Bernard's honour, he had little confidence in his business abilities, and as a brother-in-law I ought to know. Second, if it was correct, he would shrink from telling Miss Winnington of his change of view, and he wondered if Mrs Plant would let her know what was in his mind, so as to make his approach to her easier?'

'And what did you advise?'

'I told him I could not lay claim to being a man of the world, but that as far as my advice went, it was to follow the dictates of his own conscience. I told him I believed Bernard's figures were approximately correct and that I was sure Mrs Plant would help him, but that I thought Miss Winnington would prefer it if he approached her direct.'

'It sounds pretty good advice, if I may say so. Was that all?'

'Yes, except that I questioned his idea of renouncing the

proposal. I said he had acted in good faith when he made it and that I thought he ought to stand to it and let Miss Winnington decide.'

'Did he agree?'

'He seemed impressed, but he didn't say one way or the other.'

'I follow. And then?'

'Well, that was all. We chatted about other things, of course, but that is what he wanted to see me about.'

'Thank you. Then my other question: What did you ring him up about last night?'

'Simply to inquire what he had done. I thought some show of interest in his difficulties was called for.'

'And what did he answer?'

'At first he said shortly that he hadn't made up his mind, and rang off. Then he rang up again to say that he felt he hadn't been straight with me, and that he had decided to take my advice and tell Miss Winnington herself.'

'Decided to do it? But the week she had asked for was up before you spoke to him?'

'I didn't think of that all later. I suppose the tragedy caused a delay. I don't know, of course.'

More than this French could not get, but he felt he could scarcely expect more. Plant had answered his questions fully and he had no reason to doubt his statements. Indeed, for many of them there was some independent corroboration. But apart from the clearing up of suspicious incidents, the outstanding item, proved by Mrs Miggs and the telephone management, was that Plant had telephoned to Mallaby at a time which precluded all possibility of his being guilty of the attack. Further, if the same man had committed both crimes, this meant that he was not guilty of Clarence Winnington's murder either. French felt that he must remove Plant's name from his list of suspects.

The discovery that in all probability the same man was guilty of both crimes seemed also to tell against the professional burglar theory. Why should such a man attempt to murder Mallaby? French could see no possible reason.

Once again a deep depression filled his mind.

21

Guy Plant

When Guy Plant went up to bed on that Sunday night of his second adventure in crime, he felt that he should be well satisfied with the way in which he had carried out the ghastly enterprise. He had faced a dangerous situation, he had taken the necessary drastic action, and all had gone well. Nothing could ever be traced to him or proved against him.

Yet, in spite of these reassuring considerations, satisfaction was by no means uppermost in his mind. On the contrary, he was conscious of an unexpected feeling of anxiety and dread. He could not forget that the commission of a second crime more than doubled the likelihood of discovery. He realised that what he had done was definitely dangerous and that until the police investigation had taken place and a verdict of suicide had been registered he would not know real ease of mind. However, there was nothing that he could do about it, except to carry on normally, to know only the right amount when discussing the affair, to keep a stiff upper lip, and to hope for the best.

He tossed restlessly and wakefully until it was nearly

time to get up, when he fell into a troubled sleep. Short as this was, it rested him, and when he had bathed and shaved and had his morning coffee he felt much more his own man. He was able to greet his staff as usual, and each small encounter successfully met increased his assurance. He dictated his letters and got rid of Miss Beamish. Things were going well.

Then suddenly Fate hit him straight between the eyes. Bellissa rang up to tell him about Mallaby. As he listened, a sick and paralysing horror welled up in his mind.

Mallaby was not dead! Somehow he had bungled!

Plant had no illusions. He saw instantly that if Mallaby did not die, or if he recovered consciousness before the end, his own doom was sealed. He would hang!

For a moment the shock rendered him speechless, then he forced himself to murmur a reply and rang off. After that he sat like a block of stone, stunned and incapable of movement or thought.

Presently he rallied himself. At all costs he must shake off this ghastly panic. Fearfully he wondered if he was losing his nerve. If he did not pretend, and successfully, that nothing unusual had occurred, he would be doomed, irrespective of whether Mallaby lived or died. People would notice his manner, whispers would get about, that infernal chief inspector would hear them, he would probe and pry and delve—till he found something. If that happened, neither Clarence's money nor Mallaby's silence would avail him anything. He would have no more hope. The best left for him would be that he should take his own life—before they did . . .

Gradually his mind again began to work. Mallaby was unconscious and very low, and the doctors did not think he would recover. Well, in that there was hope. If he were to die without making a statement, all might yet be well . . .

His thoughts turned to his own plans for meeting just such an emergency. How thankful he was that he had worked them out in detail! Should he put them into operation immediately; fly the country at once before French could act? Or should he take the risk and hold on a little longer?

The difficulty of the choice made him positively ill. To stay was to risk his life; to go, to lose everything which he had worked for and which made life worth living.

At last he reached a decision. He would take the chance. He had a strong knife in his pocket with an edge like a razor, and if arrest seemed imminent he would cut his own wrist. If they got him, it would not be alive.

As luck would have it, he had an important conference that morning and this helped to keep him from thinking, but when on returning from lunch he learnt that French was calling to see *him* in a few minutes, his panic returned. Why coming to him? French would be occupied with Mallaby's attempted suicide. It couldn't be, it *couldn't* be that the man suspected some connection . . . ?

He must have something to steady him. Going to a cupboard, he took from it a bottle of whisky and poured out a stiff tot. Then he hesitated: would the smell of it give away that he feared the visit? He tossed it off. He could casually mention that he had had to entertain a client to lunch. Immediately he was filled with horror. An unnecessary lie was the one thing he must at all costs avoid! French would want to know who his guest had been, and he would go and interview whoever he said, and if he had not suspected before, he would then.

The whisky steadied him, and when French and Nelson appeared he had himself well in hand. Their manner was reassuring. They were evidently on a routine inquiry and not dealing with matters of importance. Besides, the sharp knife was in an open drawer ready to his hand.

All the same, French's first question reawakened all his panic, and it took every scrap of resolution that he possessed to avoid giving himself away. The pen! So the police had found it after all! This sly smooth-tongued serpent of a man knew about it all the time, but had said nothing! Plant felt doubly trapped. There was only one possible place where they could have found it. And they knew that before the murder it had been in his pocket!

Plant forced these ghastly thoughts from his mind and concentrated on his replies. If this was the end, he would meet it fighting. Again their reassuring manner struck him. Perhaps even now there was hope.

He had of course foreseen the possibility of this question and had thought out various replies. Now he chose what he believed was the best. He would admit without hesitation everything which French could find out for himself and confine his denials to a possible connection with the body. Thus he was able to answer without undue delay, and he hoped convincingly.

To his surprise, French appeared to accept his story. Of course with such a man you never knew, but at least the crisis was postponed. So far, though it was all most disquieting, he believed he had met the situation, but French's next question was a heavier blow. Had he rung up Mallaby on the previous evening?

Immediately an abyss seemed to be opening before him.

It had never entered his mind that French could learn of his messages, and he was horrified not only by the discovery that he had done so, but also by the dread of what else he might have ascertained. For the first time he temporised: he had to because here he had not thought out a reply. One thing was clear, his safety depended on how he answered, and he concentrated all his powers on finding a solution. Then just in the nick of time a plausible story occurred to him.

Once again Plant felt surprise, this time that his tale of Mallaby's matrimonial difficulties went so well. It seemed to convince French. Almost it convinced himself. A creditable performance certainly!

All the same it had been a near thing, and after the officers had gone he sank back in his chair, wiping his damp forehead. A near thing? It might soon be much worse than that! *Was* it so obvious that French had accepted it? These Scotland Yard men did not reveal their thoughts. Had he not just had an example of that? Might not French's manner simply mean that, while he suspected him, he had not yet completed his case against him? From all Plant had heard, police were like that: polite and reassuring in manner, while all the time they were probing and delving against one. They made no sign of any kind—and then suddenly they struck . . . With shaking hand he picked up his telephone and asked for his Weybridge number.

'I was expecting a caller today, Mrs Miggs: I forgot to tell you this morning. Has anyone been?'

So that was it! Had he been out last night? They were on to him! He sweated as he wondered what they knew. Was it a mere vague suspicion or had they definite evidence? It *could* not be the latter. He had been too careful. He had covered everything. He would have given ten years of his life to read French's mind.

While he had no idea how real his danger was, he felt that the situation called for firm handling. He dare not let things drift. Once again he reviewed his scheme for flight. All was ready. The suitcases he had packed with what he would require, and had kept them 'alive' by moving them from one station cloakroom to another. They were now back at Charing Cross, instantly available in case of need. Nor would he go empty-handed. Beneath a false bottom in one of them were the jewels.

He bent over his desk to complete one or two urgent matters before leaving to drive down to Hurst Lodge. As he did so there was a knock and Crossley entered. His face was white and strained, and his hands, as he carefully closed the door, twitched painfully. He moved jerkily towards the desk. Plant's heart sank as he looked at him.

'Crossley!' he whispered fiercely. 'Are you mad? What do you mean by coming in like this without being sent for? Do you want the whole office talking?'

Crossley wrung his hands. 'I must see you, Mr Plant! I must see you at once! I was afraid I'd miss you outside.'

'Pull yourself together, you fool!' Plant snarled. 'What do you think you look like?'

'I'm frightened! I've had enough of it! I can't stand any more!'

'Keep your voice down, will you! What's the matter?'

Horror and dread grew in the young man's eyes. 'At lunch,' he muttered, 'I saw—a *Standard*.'

With a sick qualm Plant understood. Here was danger again, pressing and imminent: more deadly even than French's possible suspicions. Whatever might have been the case before, he now knew that he was fighting for his life. He steeled himself to answer calmly.

'What of it? Explain yourself, and quickly.'

'I saw—Dr Mallaby's—suicide!'

'What do you know about Dr Mallaby?'

'That you killed him, or tried to!' Crossley's voice quavered up hysterically. 'And that I helped! I—' He was beginning to shout.

Plant stood up and deliberately slapped him across the face. 'You bloody fool,' he hissed, 'do you want both of us to hang? Pull yourself together! You're in it up to the neck and you know it! Your only hope is silence, now and always!'

Crossley stood and gulped. The blow had stopped his hysteria, at least for the moment.

'I'd be safe if I turned King's evidence,' he said in a low vicious voice.

Plant could only bluff. He laughed scornfully. 'You're not very complimentary, I will say. Do you imagine I'm such a fool as to have missed that possibility? What do you think your receipt was for? Eh, my fine fellow? You did the job for the money Winnington's death would bring. There was no accident or misunderstanding about it, nothing to sustain a plea for mercy. It was murder for money on your part. You can ruin me, I admit, but if you do, your receipt goes to the police and you'll hang too.' He paused, staring gloomily at the other, then changed his tactics. 'I did this for you as well as myself, Crossley. Mallaby had discovered the first job and it was necessary for our safety.'

Crossley gazed open-mouthed. 'But if he recovers?' he asked.

'He won't recover,' Plant declared firmly. 'I'm not unreasonable,' he went on in a pleasanter tone. 'I can understand you're scared; it's natural. But we can't settle the thing now. Let us meet tonight. What about Surbiton at eleven? Just outside the station entrance.'

He could see the youth was hesitating. He followed up his advantage.

'I'll fix you up somehow. As a matter of fact, I've got a proposal which I think would give you all the security you want. We'll talk about it tonight. Now you've been here long enough. Get back to the office.'

The colour had partly returned to Crossley's face and his left cheek was only very slightly redder than the other. Plant glanced round and seized a folder.

'Here's last month's cartage account. Take it with you and abstract it. If any question arises, say I had told you to come in for it at four o'clock.'

It was the best he could do, but if only his dupe kept his head it should suffice. Crossley, much steadied by the interview, quickly recovered his self-control. He left the room with the folder under his arm and walking normally.

With grim determination Plant forced himself to finish his work. Then he rang for his secretary.

'Here are the letters, Miss Beamish. I'm leaving a few minutes early this evening as I have to go down to the country. There's nothing else, I think?'

'Nothing else, Mr Plant.'

'Right.' He closed his desk and took his hat. 'Then good-night.'

'Good-night, Mr Plant.'

Plant's whole body ached with weariness as he got his car from an adjoining garage and started on the drive to

Little Wokeham. He had had a dreadful day and he was going to have a dreadful evening. The strain of appearing natural at Hurst Lodge, of talking endlessly about Mallaby, as he expected he would have to do, of showing enough but not too much concern, would take every ounce of his strength. And when he had done it the worst part of the day would only be beginning: the dealing with that sickly fool Crossley. How this was to be done he did not know. He had no proposal to put before him. Crossley, moreover, did not lack intelligence, and if in the interval he were to consult an encyclopaedia on King's evidence, he would see the exact worth of Plant's bluff.

His visit to Hurst Lodge passed off more smoothly than he could have hoped. Bernard was alone on his arrival, the sisters being upstairs and Horne having gone to the village.

'Good of you to come down,' Bernard greeted him.

This broke the ice. Plant was able to explain in detail why he had not come sooner, from which followed a natural transition to the cause of the visit. He heard with mixed feelings that Mallaby, though still alive, remained at death's door. It was easy to say how terribly shocked he had been by the affair and to glide off immediately into the question of the doctor's recent depression. This in turn could be quickly dismissed, for an early confidential query as to how Christina was taking it was only to be expected.

While talking to Bernard he had been thinking hard. The matter of the pen was bound to come out, and if he said nothing about it now, when he had so good an opportunity, it might afterwards look suspicious. At the first pause in the conversation he therefore went on: 'By the way, Bernard, that was an extraordinary business about your pen—I mean, Mallaby having it. You heard about it, of course?'

'Yes, French mentioned it. I was going to ask you about it. Have you any theory as to what happened?'

Plant shook his head. 'Well, no, not exactly. I did put up a theory to French, but it was only a suggestion, and as I told him, I don't know that it's correct. It was when I was taking out the car,' and he went on to repeat his story. Bernard's relief when he heard it was obvious, and it gave Plant an unpleasant jar to realise that he must have guessed the truth. Though now Bernard clearly accepted the tale, Plant found the whole episode extremely disquieting. Was there any reason to hope that French would be equally credulous?

Plant found it hard to concentrate on the conversation, but the others, when they came in, were themselves abstracted and he was sure his manner attracted no attention. He dined, but refused to stay the night, on the ground of avoiding an early start on the following morning. By half-past ten he was passing through Guildford on his way to Surbiton.

His thoughts turned wearily to the coming interview. This was what one got for dealing with a weak-minded fool! Curse Crossley and everything connected with him! He was one of those who would be more use dead.

This phrase, though purely rhetorical, made Plant shudder. Crossley dead! Was that the solution of his difficulties? If Crossley were dead no one would know of his alibi. If Crossley were dead he himself would be safe. Twice he had tried the method: what about a third time? He had been short of cash and he had tried it and he was, or would soon be, wealthy. He had been in danger and he had tried it again, and but for this ghastly mischance he would be safe. If Crossley were dead he—

With a cold shiver Plant woke up to what he was really contemplating. Was he mad, thinking such thoughts? To kill Crossley would be handing the truth to French on a salver. Besides, how could he do it? These things took thought and preparation. To attempt an improvisation would be to ask for discovery. No, no: not murder again! At least he must preserve his sanity.

With all the will-power at his command he switched his thoughts away from their insidious trend, concentrating his energies on evolving some more suitable plan. By the time he had reached Esher he believed he had found it.

One other matter caused him deep thought. His confidence in Crossley was exactly nil. What guarantee had he that the young fellow would not agree to his proposal and then in some renewed access of panic rush off to Scotland Yard?

He decided that next day he would ring up a firm of private detectives which he had frequently employed on behalf of his firm, and ask them to shadow Crossley, reporting immediately if he made any unusual moves.

He was deeply disturbed by all that had happened, but he felt he was dealing with the emergency adequately, indeed in the best way open to him.

22

Christina Winnington

In the meantime Christina had also been passing through a period of anxiety and stress. The murder of Clarence Winnington had of course begun it. The horror of the crime itself and the worry of having police in the home would alone have given ample cause for her feelings, but in addition certain personal worries oppressed her.

Of these the chief was the lurking fear that Bernard might be suspected and that Mallaby's evidence as to the time of the death might not be held to clear him. Bernard, she was positive, shared her alarm. He was plucky about the affair, as he would be about any trouble, but she could see that inwardly he was deeply worried and there could be little doubt as to the cause.

Anthony Mallaby was another perplexing problem. He had quite changed since the murder. Obviously some deep trouble was preying on his mind also. Further, she thought he avoided her. He came to Hurst Lodge less frequently, and only when he was unlikely to see her alone. When they did meet he seemed embarrassed, and this puzzled and hurt her. As a result, a faint doubt had sprung up in her mind which she found herself unable entirely to banish. Was it possible that he had killed her uncle? She loathed herself for harbouring the idea, but after all, what else could his very strange manner mean?

Her dread was not lessened by her complete ignorance of what the police were doing. They were certainly active enough. There was coming and going, walking about the grounds, photographing, and the asking of innumerable and, so far as she could see, completely pointless and irrelevant questions. When she met French she invariably asked him how he was getting on. Invariably he answered politely and with a show of completeness, but when she came afterwards to think over what he had said, she seldom found that she was very much the wiser.

The jewels constituted a smaller worry. Few women cared less for money and what money brings than Christina, but five thousand pounds' worth of jewels was five thousand pounds' worth of jewels, and she would have been less than human if she could have contemplated the loss with equanimity. Here again, though French said that everything possible was being done, he gave no details of his activities.

In this atmosphere of general misgiving not unmixed with actual fear there were occasional high spots of more acute distress. One of these was her uncle's funeral. Though private except for Mallaby, his solicitor and one or two others, it was for Christina rather an ordeal. She was glad when it was over. Only one relieving feature broke the depression of the day, though it was an important one. The will was satisfactory. Clarence had kept faith and she and Bellissa and Bernard would receive something like twenty thousand pounds apiece when death duties had been paid.

Then came this ghastly Monday morning with the news of Mallaby's attempted suicide. Josephs heard it from the milkman and told Bernard, who telephoned for details to Green Gables. Bernard came to Christina's room when she was dressing and told her.

Christina was at first completely numb from horror. Anthony Mallaby? Suicide! That good kind man! It did not seem possible. Surely, surely, there had been some mistake?

Then his worry and depression during the week recurred to her. She had already thought that some dreadful secret must be weighing on his mind. Now this proved it. Could it have concerned her? Surely not! Yet if not, why had he avoided her? She did not know, but she was sure it could have had nothing to do with her. Then what could it have been? Poor dear man! How unutterably horrible!

Once again that hideous suspicion crept into her mind. Had he, after all, killed Clarence, and was this his way of atonement?

No! She told herself that she was wrong. If he were guilty of the murder, he would never have shirked the consequences. Certainly he would not have died without having left a confession. But perhaps he had. Here also the police kept their own counsel.

Then Bernard had come back and they had sat talking over a pretence of breakfast, Horne having finished and Bellissa not yet being up. Bernard, who when things went well was sometimes a little trying, was now, as always when there was trouble, kind and helpful and sympathetic.

'I can't understand it,' he declared. 'I happened to meet him earlier in the day and he seemed absolutely normal. A little depressed, as indeed he has been during the week; I dare say you noticed it? But nothing to account for this.'

Christina began to sob gently. 'His trouble must have been simply unendurable,' she said brokenly, 'to have made him attempt such a thing. And now when he becomes conscious—if he does—it'll be the first thing he'll think of and it'll pull him down. I'll go in presently to the hospital: I must be there when he regains consciousness. He must not think I'd desert him because of—because of this.'

'I don't know whether I should ask, Christina, but were you—er—going to marry him?'

She sighed. 'I didn't know yesterday, I hadn't made up my mind. But I know now.' She spoke with sudden energy. 'I'll marry him, if only he lives and if—he still wants it.'

Bernard looked anxious. 'You're really sure about that?' he asked slowly. 'It's not idle curiosity: I have a reason for asking.'

'I'm glad to tell you, Bernard. I hesitated because I didn't know whether I loved him enough to make him happy. This has taught me. When I saw that I might lose him, I knew what I felt.'

Bernard fidgeted uneasily. 'Well, it's I who can't make up my mind this time,' he said uncertainly. 'I'm terribly afraid there may be trouble and I don't know whether it would be kinder to tell you or not to tell you. Better, I think, that you should hear it.'

She stared. 'There's no doubt now at all events,' she said quietly. 'When you've said so much you must go on.'

'There may be nothing in it, probably there isn't; but

again there may be. It's something French asked me about and he made me promise not to repeat it, even to you. But circumstances alter cases, and if you feel like that towards Mallaby, you ought to know. Briefly, Mallaby had found my pen.'

Again Christina stared, this time in frank amazement. 'Your pen? I don't follow. What about it?'

'He must have found it. It was locked in his safe. Just think, Christina; when and where could he have found it?'

She shook her head impatiently. 'I didn't even know you had lost it.'

'Well, I had. But where could he have found it? And why should he lock it up like that instead of returning it to me? Don't you see what I mean?'

She looked at him in sudden horror. 'You mean—when he came up to—to attend to Uncle Clarence?'

'That's it. Suppose he found it near the body? Isn't that the only thing that would account for his locking it up, and also for his anxiety and depression?'

'He thought you were guilty!'

'Well, that's what I imagine. It would explain everything.'

'But, Bernard, you're not guilty! How could it have got there?'

'Ah, that's just it. You see, I hadn't it on Sunday evening. I'd lent it to Guy. Don't you remember the battle of Blenheim controversy?'

Consternation showed on Christina's face. 'Then Guy . . . ?'

Bernard shook his head. 'We don't know that. We mustn't jump to conclusions. All we know is that there may be trouble. I thought you ought to hear it, so that in case something turns up it won't be such a shock.'

She thought for a while. 'But it's impossible,' she suddenly declared, and there was relief in her tones. 'Guy was at Ivy Cottage during the whole evening. It's not only that he said so himself. Mrs Miggs told Bellissa.'

'You're sure of that?'

'Absolutely. They were talking about what he had had for supper or something and it happened to come out. Bellissa didn't ask or anything.'

Bernard gave a sharp sigh. 'Good Lord, but that's a relief! I shouldn't have doubted the fellow, though I'm afraid I did. But then, how could Mallaby have got the pen?'

'I don't know, though I'm certain it wasn't as you imagined. What does Guy say?'

'I haven't an idea. I don't even know whether French asked him.'

They chatted on for some time, but without reaching any further conclusions, and then Christina took out the small car and drove to the County Hospital in Guildford. But she could not see Mallaby. Though he had regained consciousness, he was too weak to receive visitors. In fact, she was told that, while he was still breathing, she must be prepared for anything that might happen.

That Monday afternoon Guy Plant turned up and stayed for dinner. He seemed to have taken the second tragedy to heart, for his manner was abstracted and worried. In fact, it was not a very gay party which sat down to the meal.

One thing immensely relieved Christina's mind, and that was when Bernard repeated to her Plant's story of how he had probably dropped the pen on the Hurst Lodge drive. She accepted it at once, feeling ashamed of the suspicion which she had allowed to creep into her mind.

Two days later French rang up, asking for Bernard. As he was out, Christina replied.

'I wonder, Miss Winnington, if you all—yourself, Mrs Plant, Mr Winnington and Mr Horne—would do me a favour? I'm afraid it will give you a little trouble, but believe me it's in the interests of justice.'

'Of course we'll do anything we can.'

'It's to come up here to the Yard tomorrow. We've been going into the question of professional burglars and we're having an identification parade which I want all of you to see. I'm anxious to know if you recognise anyone in it.'

'That sounds promising, Mr French. Does it mean that you think you've got the person responsible for all this?'

'I shouldn't go so far as to say that, but I can tell you that the results may prove decisive. Now please don't ask me any more questions, for it wouldn't be fair to give you any hint of what to expect.'

Christina was impressed with this answer. She had heard that police methods were fair to the criminal, but this certainly showed a sense of scrupulous justice. Since Horne was to join them it was not a purely family affair, but something that concerned residence at Hurst Lodge.

She wondered if the experience would prove nerve-racking. If so, she was glad Horne was going with them. Since that day when he had suddenly thawed and told her of his work, she had got to know him very much better. They had begun by his describing to her the effect he hoped his book would have, and they had discussed socialism, literary propaganda and kindred subjects. Gradually their talks had taken on a more personal tone and she had found him a pleasant companion. He was well read, had travelled a little, and could express himself in an interesting way. She soon learned that, besides being intellectual and idealistic, he possessed considerable strength of character as well as natural kindliness. She was sorry he was going, and they had arranged to keep in touch with one another, so that she might read the typescript of the book when it was completed.

Next morning all four of them went up to Waterloo and soon found themselves at Scotland Yard. A little delay ensued while the constable at the door telephoned their arrival, then a young officer appeared and ushered them into a plainly furnished waiting-room. Seated morosely in a corner was Guy Plant. He looked up as they entered.

'A full house, it appears,' he said resentfully. 'What's it all about?'

'You know as much as we do,' Bernard answered, 'which is damn all.'

'Some stunt of French's,' Plant went on. 'Must be pretty important to have brought you all up.'

'An identification parade, he said,' put in Christina. 'He explained that they had been going into the question of professional burglars and we're to look at a lot of people and see if we recognise any of them.'

'Very inconvenient for me,' Plant grumbled. 'I had a conference.'

The discussion was brought to an end by the entrance of French.

'This is good of you all,' he greeted them. 'I'm sorry to have put you to so much trouble, but it's in a good cause and I'm sure you won't grudge it. Let me tell you what I want. We have an identification parade: it takes the form of a number of men standing in a row, and you have to walk along the line and see if you recognise any of them. That's all: it's perfectly simple. But I don't have to remind you that it may be important for one of the men, and to ask you to be very sure before you speak.'

'We can understand that,' said Bernard.

'Of course, sir, but we always mention it; matter of form in your case. Now we do this one by one. Who'll begin? Will you, Miss Winnington?'

'Much quicker if we could all do it together,' said Guy.

'No doubt, sir, but I'm afraid that's another of our rules. But if you're in a hurry, perhaps you'd like to come first?'

'Well, I'm rather busy this morning. Do you mind, Christina?'

'Of course not.'

'Then I'll come back for you, Miss Winnington, in a few minutes.'

'That's one thing Guy can't stand,' Bellissa remarked when they had gone; 'to be kept from his sacred office during working hours. I should have thought he'd be glad of any excuse to leave it.'

They carried on a desultory conversation till, after about ten minutes, French came back.

'Mr Plant's gone to his office,' he explained. 'Now, please, Miss Winnington.'

'Did he recognise anyone?' Christina asked as she got up.

'Ah,' French smiled, 'that would be telling. Can't give you any kind of help in this matter.'

They walked through corridors painted a drab green and out into a small courtyard surrounded by high buildings. Just at the door a constable was vigorously washing a car. He seemed an energetic young man. The whole place was running water, and as they entered he narrowly avoided deluging them both. It considerably annoyed French.

'Look what you're doing, Henderson!' he snapped. 'You're washing a car, not Scotland Yard.'

The young man cut off the water and sheepishly apologised as Christina stepped across the wet pavement. They passed through another building and in a further yard she saw the parade.

They were a sorry-looking crew, the dozen ill-dressed, woebegone, anxious-looking men who stood in an irregular line with a constable at each end. Directly Christina saw them she could feel nothing for them but pity. Devoutly she hoped she would not recognise any of them.

'Now, Miss Winnington,' said French, 'please walk along the line and look at each man. If you have seen any of them before, please say so. But you must be quite sure before you speak.'

There was a superficial resemblance between the men. All were of the same type. They looked down-and-outs, but they met her gaze with very different expressions. The eyes of some were lacklustre and expressionless, others were apprehensive, still others mocking. Christina hated it. It seemed indecent to be staring at them as if they were animals in a zoo. It was with immense relief that she reached the end of the line without having recognised anyone.

French thanked her and took her back to the waiting-room. Then Bellissa went, and in due course the men. None of them made an identification.

French was obviously disappointed. So indeed was the quartet. Bernard voiced their feelings.

'We seem to have wasted our morning, and I suppose it means the case is at a standstill. All the same, I'm glad none of those poor devils are for it.'

It was what Christina also felt.

23

Arthur Crossley

If the week following the murder of Clarence Winnington had been for Christina a period of anxiety and distress, for Arthur Crossley, save for the first day, it had been sheer hell.

That first day he had spent basking in a fools' paradise. Though he feared and hated his criminal association with his chief, the relief of freedom from the petty cash frauds and the unexpected glory of the hundred pounds had more than outweighed its drawbacks. All that Monday he looked forward with inexpressible delight to meeting Essie Howard and telling her his good news. She would be pleased and he would seize the opportunity to ask her to marry him. It seemed beyond the bounds of possibility that such a girl would accept a man like himself, yet hesitatingly he believed she might. What unspeakable joy that would be! He began building aerial castles. For the present they could get the unlet sitting-room adjoining his bedroom; then when he got a little more money they would move to a proper flat or even to a small house! He spent the day dreaming over his ledger, pictures of the future growing rosier and rosier with every hour that passed. Then the whole glorious house of cards suddenly collapsed, leaving him in a greater slough of despond than ever.

Just before the office closed on that Monday evening Plant called him into his room and told him to meet him at a secluded corner near St Paul's in half an hour. It was then that he handed to him the newspaper account of Clarence Winnington's murder and told him that he was an accessory before the fact, and that if the affair became known they would both hang.

Crossley was speechless from horror. Never in his wildest dreams had he imagined anything so dreadful. Bitterly he cursed the evil fate which had sent him the blank receipt form, his folly in making use of it, and above all, Plant for trapping him as he had. But regrets were of no avail. He was caught, and nothing that he could do would set him free. His only hope, as Plant had said, was to carry on as normally as he could, and if questions were asked, to brazen things out to the last. The knowledge of the precipice upon which he stood changed his whole outlook. Instead of his mind being filled with dreams of a future with Jessie Howard, the thought of her was now an intolerable pain. This development placed her utterly and for ever beyond his reach. He dared not ask her to marry him. He dared not even see her, lest she should notice the change in him and worm out his secret. He scarcely dared to see anyone or go anywhere. Human contacts were now dangerous. What was he to do? How could he live under such conditions? Very close to panic, he spent the evening trudging through street after street, only slinking back to his room when he knew his landlady would have gone to bed.

Next day it was a little better, though not much. He invented a toothache to account for his glum appearance, and that night, after much thought, he wrote to Jessie saying that he had been sent away to the north on the firm's business and would be unable to see her for some time. He could not bring himself to close down their association absolutely. He did not mean to deal unfairly with her, but only to gain time to see how things developed.

Then came his second interview with Plant, at the end of one of the Victoria platforms, when he was told that Mallaby had found some dangerous evidence which for their joint safety Plant was going to abstract. Bitterly as Crossley loathed helping with the faked alibi a second time, he had no alternative but to agree. Fortunately the affair passed off without difficulty, and when Plant returned he indicated that his expedition had been successful and that they were now safe.

On the Monday morning the cloud upon his spirits had lifted considerably, until at lunch—at a different restaurant—it descended upon him more heavily than ever. The man who had shared his table got up, leaving an early *Evening Standard* on his chair. Crossley picked it up.

Idly he noticed a paragraph headed in small capitals 'SURREY DOCTOR FOUND INJURED'. He glanced over it automatically and without interest till the name Mallaby caught his eye.

His blood ran absolutely cold. For a time everything went black, and he woke up to find his neighbours looking at him curiously. Summoning all his strength, he got up, paid and went to a bar, where he bought himself a double whisky. It steadied him.

The more he thought of what he had read, the more

frantic he grew. A theft of evidence! He ought to have known: how could anyone steal evidence—except in one way? And suicide! Plant was clever: that was all. Clever? He was a fiend, a devil! Crossley had been genuinely deceived by his lies, but who would believe that? If anything came out about this second affair he was finished, just as surely as his chief. And with two crimes the chance of discovery was twice as great . . .

He tried desperately to concentrate on his books, but it was quite hopeless. He felt thrown back on his own non-existent resources, and as the afternoon dragged on, his panic grew till he could bear it no longer. He must see Plant. Unfortunately two men were with him, but as soon as they went out he left the office and knocked at Plant's door. He had forgotten to take a book with him to explain his presence, but fortunately no one passed along the passage while he was there.

The interview steadied him. If Plant was a fiend, he was at least clever and competent and he did not get rattled. The promise of a scheme which would give him security convinced Crossley that all was not lost. The prospect of action that night went far towards completing the cure. He finished his day's work normally. No one had asked him about his visit to Plant, but if anyone had, he felt he could have given the cartage account excuse plausibly.

That evening he rode down to Surbiton. He was eager and nervous and much too early, and having hidden his bicycle on the drive of an empty house, he walked about till it was time to meet Plant. Exactly at eleven he approached the station and immediately saw him with his hat pulled forward and his collar turned high, walking forward from the opposite direction. They met and strolled off down one of the quieter streets. Plant wasted no time, coming to business directly they were alone.

'I recognise, Crossley,' he began in a pleasant enough tone, 'that you have been worried over this affair and I don't blame you; I should be if I were in your place. I have therefore thought out a scheme for your safety and ease of mind—and my own. But it may involve something that you won't like.'

What were likes and dislikes in a case of this kind? Crossley thought with exasperation. He was near to tears as he swore he would do anything, *anything*, to be free of his misery and fear.

'Very well, the scheme's this: you've got to get away from here and from the office, right away where no one will know you and you can start fresh with a clean sheet.'

Crossley had not expected this. Would it cut him off permanently from Jessie? Only in his first despair had he contemplated that: later he had hoped that their former relations might somehow be resumed. He began a half-hearted objection, but Plant cut him short.

'You must. You've no alternative. Your nerve will crack and you'll give us both away and we'll hang.'

This was unanswerable. It would be worth any sacrifice if that fear could be removed.

'What would it mean exactly?' he asked.

'I'll tell you. When you get home tonight, forge a letter to yourself from a hypothetical uncle in America, inviting you out. You can pad it up in any way you like. You could make him say, for instance, that now that he had retired he would like some of his own kith and kin in the house; or that now that he is getting old his conscience has been troubling him about his family and that he would like to end the: estrangement before it was too late. Anything you like, so long as you are offered a future in America and urged to go soon. See?'

The idea was so big that it took away Crossley's breath. 'Yes,' he answered, 'and then?'

'Finish the letter tonight. Tomorrow morning bring it in to me and say you've got this and want to go and when can I let you off? Then mention the story in the office, and for heaven's sake look pleased about it.'

Crossley wondered if this meant exactly what it said or if it was a trick to cover something else.

'What do I really do, Mr Plant?' he asked.

'Do? Why, go to America of course. I'll buy your ticket and I'll give you a hundred pounds in your pocket, and every month I'll send you a cheque for twenty pounds until you get your feet under you. Apart from leaving here, Crossley, it's a chance that ninety-nine young men out of a hundred would give their eyes for.'

It certainly sounded good, but Plant was a slippery devil. Could he be trusted? Would he simply get him out of the country and then leave him stranded without money? Crossley did not know what to say.

Plant made an impatient gesture. 'Well? What about it?'

Crossley found his difficulty hard to put into words. 'I'd agree, Mr Plant, like a shot only—only for—'

'For heaven's sake say what's in your mind. What's the trouble? Is it that girl?'

Crossley hung his head. 'No,' he mumbled, 'it's not that. I—I haven't been seeing her so much lately. It's—it's—'

'You doubt that I'd send the money?'

Crossley gasped with relief. 'Not at first, sir; I know you'd do what you say. But later—you might forget.'

Plant did not seem in the least offended. 'I'm glad you brought up the point. I don't intend to support you for the rest of your life, if that's what you mean. We'd better fix a limit. I'll pay you twenty pounds a month for a year, and if by that time you haven't got a job it'll be your own lookout.'

Crossley found the prospect a little terrifying. He would leave the country entirely dependent on the word of a proved liar and murderer. How did he know that Plant wouldn't work out some plan to save himself by throwing suspicion on him, and get him arrested and brought back? He wished he could get some better hold over Plant. Then the other's voice broke in on his thoughts.

'Don't let me urge you. It's entirely a matter for yourself. If you'd rather stay here and face the thing out, do so by all means.'

That did it. If he went, there was the fear of treachery by Plant; if he stayed, there was the practical certainty that sooner or later he would give himself away. He must choose the lesser evil.

'I'll go, sir.'

'Right.' Plant was almost genial. 'I believe you're doing the wise thing and I'm sure you won't be sorry. Then write that letter and let me have it in the morning.'

Crossley did not sleep much that night. It was after twelve when he reached his rooms, and well on to three before the letter was finished. He was proud of it, believing that he had considerably improved on Plant's suggestion. He had copied the writing of an old letter of his grandfather's, and done it well. His script looked like an old man's hand. In short, he felt that the whole thing was a work of art. It read:

FAR ROCKWAY, THOMASVILLE,
NEAR DALLAS, TEXAS, U.S.A.

Dear Nephew,

After the unhappy breach between your side of the family and mine, you will be surprised to receive this letter. But the fact is that I am coming to the end of my time here, and before I go I should like to see the hatchet buried between us. I met with an accident some time ago from which complications have set in, and the doctors give me only a few weeks more to live.

This is to ask you if you will come out and see me as a visible token that the breach is healed. I enclose $250 for your fare, and if you must return to England I will give you more. But perhaps you may decide to stay here: I have no doubt that you could easily get a job and there will be a little for you after I am gone. However, more of that when we meet, as I hope we shall.

Trusting that you will not refuse the request of an old man,

Your Uncle,
Jasper Crossley.

Unrefreshed but excited, Crossley turned up next morning at the office and took an early opportunity of seeing Plant.

'Not at all bad,' was that gentleman's comment. 'It'll do. Did you get the letters out of the box this morning?'

'Yes, sir.'

'That's right. Then don't forget that it was among them and that you've destroyed the envelope. Now when do you want to go? This is Tuesday. What about Saturday? Can you carry on till then?'

'Oh yes, sir. Saturday'll do first-rate.'

'Then I'll fix it up. In the meantime, let the thing be known in the office, but don't talk too much about it. Don't mention your uncle's name and only give his approximate address.'

Crossley nodded. 'I thought of near Dallas, as you see.'

'Dallas or anywhere else will do, so long as it's only near it. You were right not to put it in a town. If anyone knows the country you can say it's some village near Dallas, but you've left the letter with me and have forgotten the name. See?'

'I'll manage.'

'You're the one who'll suffer if you don't. But you'll be all right. Now about money. You may want to buy one or two things, and here's ten pounds. I'll give you the other ninety and your tickets on Friday. You haven't a passport, I suppose?'

'No, sir.'

'I think I can get one in time. Slip out now and get me necessary photographs and bring them to me.'

'Thank you, Mr Plant.'

'One word more. Don't think about what has happened. That's past, and as far as you're concerned, done with. Banish it from your mind and fix your thoughts on the future, your journey, what you'll do in New York, where you'll go to look for a job.'

'Can you help me there, sir?'

'Yes, I'll give you a first-class testimonial and a list of firms who might want a man of your type. I've no doubt you'll get fixed up without trouble.'

'Thank you again.'

'You don't need to: I'm doing this for myself as well as you. Now, good luck, Crossley. Keep a stiff upper lip and a closed mouth and you'll be all right.'

The men in the office were interested in his story, most of them enviously. They chaffed him good-humouredly, but he was both relieved and disappointed to find that none of them really cared whether he went or stayed, and they dropped the subject without having asked any awkward questions.

One matter now began to worry Crossley. Should he see Jessie before leaving? It was all over between them, both because of what had happened and of what was going to happen. He could never come back to England again, and to meet her would only be painful to both. Would a letter meet the case? He could say what he wanted better in writing and it would save embarrassment on both sides.

Then he saw that he had no choice in the matter. He dared not meet her. It would be dangerous. In her presence he could not answer for himself. If she began to ask questions he might blurt out the truth. No, there was no chance of his ever seeing her again. This was part of the price he was going to pay for what he had done.

He wrote a good letter, and spending some of his ten pounds on railway fares, posted it in Northampton. Though still a little uneasy, he felt he had now done all that was required of him. After all, there had been nothing definite between them. The word marriage had never been mentioned.

On the Thursday he noticed a chubby-faced young man closeted with Mr Hargreave, the chief clerk. On the Friday morning, his last day, the man reappeared, and after speaking to Mr Hargreave went round and had a word with each of the others, presently coming to Crossley.

'My name's Thompson,' he said, 'and I'm a detective inspector from Scotland Yard. I'm investigating a case of robbery in this area. I want to ask you whether you've ever seen about this building or in the street near by a short stooped man with a limp? He has a little black moustache and wears a khaki raincoat and soft grey hat. You could hardly mistake him.'

Crossley, whose heart had given a leap as his visitor announced his calling, quickly again became normal.

'I'm afraid not,' he said. 'I haven't noticed him!'

'Oh well,' said the young man, 'there was just the chance. Can't be helped.' He paused, then looked a little strangely at Crossley.

'You're the man who's going to America, aren't you?' he asked. 'Mr Hargreave mentioned it.'

'Yes, my uncle has sent for me.'

'Some people have all the luck. I bet there's no one in the place who doesn't envy you. What part of the States, if I may ask?'

'Near Dallas, Texas.'

'Ah yes. Nice part, I'm told. Going soon?'

'I'm leaving the office this evening and sailing tomorrow.'

'I wish it was me.' The young man nodded and moved on to one of the typists.

Though the conversation had been perfectly innocuous, Crossley felt vaguely disquieted. Why should Thompson have been interested in his movements? There could be nothing in it, and yet was it not a little strange?

However, everything went on as usual till after lunch, but then a blow fell which left Crossley livid and gasping with sheer terror. As he entered the office hall on his return from the meal he saw the same young man standing at the bottom of the stairs. He came over at once.

'I'm afraid I did not tell you my real business this morning,' he said, and Crossley noticed that his expression was now anything but friendly. 'I shall do so now. As a detective inspector from Scotland Yard I have to ask you to come with me there to answer some questions. If you come quietly no one need be any the wiser, but if you make a fuss I have constables outside.'

Crossley stood turned to stone, staring stupidly at the man. Then, feeling almost too numbed to think, he slowly turned and staggered out to a waiting car.

24

Joseph French

After his interview with Plant at the latter's office on the Monday afternoon, French felt that he had reached a deadlock in his case. Plant had been his only real suspect, but now that the man had accounted reasonably for all the incidents which had caused French to doubt him, the justification for that suspicion had disappeared. French must look elsewhere. But where? He could think of no one else who might be guilty.

He was exasperated beyond words that he could not see Mallaby. The man had regained consciousness on the morning after the affair, but had remained so weak that the doctors positively refused to allow him to be interviewed. All they would say was that he had made no statement of any kind.

Some items of news were waiting for him when he reached the Yard next morning. The analyst had reported on the specimens sent him from Green Gables and the hospital. The dregs in the glass found beside Mallaby contained a trace of a well-known soporific of which the formula was attached, and this drug was also present in the system. The quantity was small, though the actual amount was unknown. In the water from the sink trap were traces of blood of the same group as Mallaby's.

Here was final and absolute proof that French's reconstruction was correct and that murder had been attempted. Further, the information would be useful when he came to prepare the case for the Public Prosecutor—if he ever did so—though it gave no help towards identifying the criminal.

While he was considering the matter Nelson rang up.

'I learnt something last night, Mr French, which may interest you, though I don't think it will exactly help in the case. When I got back to Guildford I went up to the hospital to inquire for Mallaby. I saw one of the surgeons and he told me the doctor ought by rights to have been killed by that cut in his wrist. He owes his life to a strange chance.'

French expressed the required interest.

'The murderer knew what he was about when he made his cut, for it was in the right place and to sever the radial artery is a pretty serious matter. No doubt when he made it he saw the blood spurting out and was sure he had got it. But there was something else he didn't know—couldn't have known, of course—and it upset his plan. The surgeon explained it like this. The radial artery divides in the wrist into two branches. The junction is usually below where the murderer made his cut, and if it had been there in Mallaby's case, his number would have been up. But occasionally the junction occurs a little higher up the arm. Aberrant, the surgeon called it.'

'I know; it means diverging from the normal type.'

'That's right, I looked it up. Well, Mallaby's was one of these cases. The junction happened to be above the cut, so, instead of severing the whole artery, the murderer only got one of the branches. It meant a lot less serious haemorrhage.'

The point had puzzled French. He knew that the cutting of an artery such as the radial would usually be fatal unless it was dealt with pretty quickly, and he had been unable to understand how Mallaby had survived while the murderer was completing the preparations for his getaway. This was now clear.

But French was still perplexed by another point. If Mallaby had been sent to sleep by this dope, would the opening of his wrist not have awakened him? French could scarcely believe that a mere double dose of a sleeping-draught would have produced a state of sufficient unconsciousness to neutralise the reaction to such a shock. On the other hand, if Mallaby had been awakened he would undoubtedly have struggled, which he had not done. French determined to put the point to Henry on the first opportunity. An attempt to follow up the purchase or theft of the sleeping-draught must also be made.

As he opened the file to note what he had just learnt, his thoughts swung back to Plant. Suddenly he saw that on the previous afternoon he had made a mistake. He had assumed that Plant's statement was satisfactory. Now he was by no means so sure. Second thoughts made him wonder whether the story was as probable as had at first appeared.

Suppose Plant had dropped the pen outside the front door at Hurst Lodge as he suggested: when could Mallaby have picked it up?

French turned over the file till he came to the tabulated movements of the various members of the party. Plant had left for Ivy Cottage on that fatal Sunday at about 6.30. Mallaby was not at Hurst Lodge that day until summoned, by Josephs, when he arrived about 10.40 at night. It was then dark and he was hurrying with his mind full of the tragedy, and it was therefore unlikely in the extreme that he had seen the pen, not to speak of stopping to pick it up. He had left for home about 3.00 a.m., while it was still dark. He did not return till long after daybreak on the following morning.

As soon as it became light on that morning the Surrey police began to search the grounds, and if the pen had been there they would certainly have found it. Therefore if Mallaby found it, it must have been during the night.

Could he have picked it up when he was leaving at 3.00 a.m.? French did not believe it possible. If he had, would he not have handed it to Josephs? Or if Josephs had not been there, would he have locked it in his safe and said nothing about it?

Never! He would have returned it at the first opportunity. With a sharp revulsion of feeling French swung back to his previous hypothesis. Mallaby had seen the pen near the body, had recognised it as Bernard's, had believed Bernard was guilty and had removed it to try to save him. This view, French now once again believed, was overwhelmingly confirmed by the falsification of the time of the death.

A thought struck him, and he lifted his telephone and put through a call to Hurst Lodge. Josephs answered it.

'I forgot to ask you a question when I was down,' said

French. 'On the Sunday of Mr Winnington's death did you see Mr Plant off when he left about half-past six?'

'Yes, sir. He drove his own car.'

'Quite. And that same night when Dr Mallaby left, I think about three in the morning, were you present?'

'Yes, sir. I didn't go to bed at all.'

French considered asking the direct questions whether Plant had dropped a glove and whether Mallaby had picked up a pen, then decided these could keep. He did not want Josephs to put Plant on his guard by mentioning the matter.

But without these questions he thought he had obtained his information. If Josephs had been there he would never have let Plant grovel for his glove and Mallaby would certainly have handed him the pen. Both men had lied, Plant to save himself, Mallaby to save Bernard.

Though Plant's guilt at last seemed demonstrated, French did not stop his systematic analysis, turning to the second question he had asked Plant: why he had rung up Mallaby? Here Plant's reply was more plausible, but French's reawakened critical faculty attacked it with vigour.

It was obvious that the two men were discussing some private and important business: this was proved by the dinner in Town. Plant had incidentally said that his telephone message was on the same business, and this might well be the fact. What then was that business? Was it really likely that Mallaby would have consulted a man like Plant on the perplexities of his courtship? Had he any reason to doubt Bernard's business ability or his statement about the legacy? If he had wanted Mrs Plant's help, would he not have asked her for it? Most important of all, instead of trying to enlist the assistance of outsiders, would he not have gone himself to Christina? From what he knew of Mallaby's character, French believed he would.

On the face of it, therefore, it was unlikely that Plant's statement as to the nature of his business with Mallaby was true. What then could they have discussed?

Suddenly an idea shot into French's mind. The pen! Suppose Mallaby knew that Plant had borrowed the pen and that it was in his pocket on that fatal Sunday evening. Suppose he had met Plant to ask for an explanation as to how it had come to be near the body? If this were so— French's interest quickened still further—Plant must have seen his danger. Here was all the motive that any jury could require for the murder of Mallaby!

French was delighted with his progress. More and more it looked as if Plant was his man. Was there any further test which he could apply to clinch the matter?

Nelson's discovery of the footprints at Green Gables suggested an obvious one: to obtain Plant's walking trace. This could not prove him guilty—it might on the contrary prove him innocent—but if his trace corresponded to those found, French would himself be satisfied.

Being anxious to avoid putting the man on his guard, French spent some time considering how he could best obtain the information. Then a method occurred to him. He would invite the Hurst Lodge party and Plant to the Yard and by some excuse get them to walk singly over some wet pavement. The footprints of each on the dry concrete beyond could be quickly measured and photographed, and the ground dried off with a plumber's blow-lamp, ready for the next comer. It was perhaps a little elaborate, but he could think of nothing simpler.

It worked well. Plant's trace exactly corresponded with those on the scenes of the two crimes.

Though technically inconclusive, this result swept away French's last doubt. Plant was guilty. His motive was powerful, his opportunity adequate, and there was strong independent evidence to connect him with both affairs.

Everything now hinged on the alibi. If French could break it he would not be far from his goal, for the mere existence of a faked alibi was in itself next thing to proof of guilt.

It was of course abundantly clear that *someone* was in Plant's study when both the crimes were committed, but there was no real proof that this was Plant. The occupant had not been seen. Anyone could smoke, walk about, turn on the radio, and make all the other sounds which were heard. French had recognised this from the first, but up till now it had not seemed necessary to develop the idea.

Was there any way of finding out who such a confederate might have been? He rang for two assistants.

'In this Little Wokeham case there is reason to believe that Guy Plant is guilty of both murders, and that he had an accomplice in his house to build up his alibi. I want that accomplice. Will you, Cleaver, go down to Weybridge and find out what you can about his friends. You'll see all known particulars about him in the file. Thompson, I want you to work his office in the same way. I can't give you detailed instructions, you'll both have to use your wits and do your best.' He paused, then called Cleaver back. 'Wait for me. I'll go with you.'

It had occurred to French that a difficulty in his slowly crystallising theory was the interchange of the men at the beginning and end of each episode. Plant would scarcely have risked the accomplice entering by the front door, lest Mrs Miggs should come into the hall and see him. It would therefore be worth while considering the possibilities of another approach.

As has been said, the Ivy Cottage study was immediately above the kitchen, both occupying the full width of the rear extension, but the windows looked out in opposite directions, the kitchen giving on the yard and the study on the grounds. The study window was therefore well hidden, and French wondered if it could have been used.

Taking with them a light folding ladder, he and Cleaver reached Weybridge and reconnoitred the house. Being the last in its suburban avenue, and the study looking towards open country, their area of approach was very secluded.

'Wait for me here,' said French, as ladder in hand he slipped through a gap in the hedge. Taking cover behind shrubs, he crept up to the wall beneath the window. Though several days had elapsed since the last time surreptitious entry might have been required, marks of a ladder should still show on the sward. He searched with care. There were none.

Baffled, he began to wonder was he on the wrong track? Then an almost invisible stain of mud on the brickwork caught his eye. Another! And another! All the way up from ground to sill the faint marks showed. With satisfaction he diagnosed them. Someone had climbed a rope ladder. This would swing his feet against the wall at every step.

Here was final proof. French waved for Cleaver and told him to photograph the marks. Then with the same caution they crept out of the grounds. French left Cleaver to carry on, and having rung up Nelson to explain what was in the wind, he returned to the Yard.

Next day he had reports from both men. Cleaver's was written and negative, but Thompson came to make his in person.

'I think I'm on to your man, sir,' he began. 'Chap named Crossley, a clerk in Plant's office.'

'Good work,' said French. 'Tell me about it.'

'I went to the office in Queen Victoria Street and asked if there was a man there called Lyons. This enabled me to have a squint round the clerks and fix on one who looked as if he could put away a pint of beer. I hung about the street till closing time, and when the clerk came out I spoke to him. I told him I'd seen him in the office and I wanted a favour for which I could pay, and would he come and have a drink while I explained.

'As I expected, he was ready enough for the drink. Then I told him I was out of a job and I'd heard his was a good office and what were the chances of getting taken on? I said that if the boss's private secretary recommended a man it usually carried weight, and would he introduce me? I promised him ten shillings a week for the first ten weeks if I got a job.'

French's eye twinkled. 'Dirty dog's trick,' he commented.

Thompson knew his chief. 'Fair exchange, sir,' he said with an innocent air, 'he's all that beer to the good for what cost him nothing. I suppose it may go down in my expenses?'

'Keep to the point. You're telling me a story.'

'Quite, sir. I kept him putting down pint after pint till he began to talk. Then I just sat and listened.'

'Your morals are a danger to the community. What did he say?'

'I steered him in due course to the office staff: what sort they'd be to work with and all that. He told me a lot of things, but only one that was interesting. One clerk, a man of about thirty, had been badly worried for the last ten days or fortnight, something cruel on his mind, as my friend put it. Then on last Tuesday he seemed excited and told them he'd had a letter from his uncle in America asking him to go out, and that he was leaving the office on Friday—that's today—and sailing tomorrow.'

'You've been running it a bit close.'

'Close, sir, but not late. It interested me that the uneasiness had come just before the first murder and the call to America just after the second.'

'Yes, that's certainly suggestive.'

'There was another point. The whole business of the journey to America seemed to have been arranged at a pretty breathless speed. There was no time for the uncle to hear whether Crossley would go, and one would think he'd have wanted to know that before sending the money for the fare.'

'Quite sound. What did you do?'

'Tried a little experiment. Went in and had an individual word with the clerks, asking each had they seen a certain person in the corridor. With Crossley I began by saying I was from the Yard, and I got the reaction I expected. He was scared stiff. I saw it in his eyes.'

'Promising enough. Yes?'

''Fraid that's all, sir. I thought I had enough to bring him in.

'For questioning only. Yes, I think you have.' Thompson stood up. 'Of course, sir, only for questioning. Very good, I'll see to it.'

'You haven't much time.'

'I'll get back to the office now and pick him up as he comes in after lunch.'

'Bring him here and put him in a waiting-room; a little solitary meditation won't do him any harm. Then go to wherever he lives and have a look round. Afterwards I'll see him here.'

About four that afternoon an informal meeting took place in French's room. French was at his desk, in front of which sat Crossley, his face pale and drawn and fear in his eyes. Beside him was Nelson, for whom French had telephoned. At a side table sat Thompson, alertly ready to take notes. French leant back in his chair and eyed his unwilling guest.

French was in no hurry to start and the silence grew oppressive. Crossley was obviously finding it increasingly irksome. He licked his dry lips and little beads of perspiration glistened on his forehead.

'I'm sorry, Mr Crossley,' French said at last, 'to have had to ask you here, but we're in the middle of an inquiry and we think you can give us some help. It's a rather serious matter, in fact a case of murder and attempted murder, and before I begin I have to tell you two things. First, you need not answer my questions unless you like. If you think it might incriminate you to do so, then don't reply, though of course in this case you must remember that a failure may raise unfortunate suspicions in our minds. You may, if you like, have a solicitor present to advise you. Second, you must be very sure of anything you do say, because your statement may be given in evidence in court. You understand the position?'

This did not tend to set Crossley at his case. He nodded. French thought he would not trust himself to speak.

'Then I want to tell you a little story; please follow it carefully. On last Sunday week a young man took out his bicycle and rode from his rooms in London down to Weybridge.' (Thompson had reported that Crossley had a bicycle, and from earlier researches French knew that Plant had not, hence the deduction.) 'He was employed in a London office and he went to call on the head of his department, who lived down there. He had his own ideas of procedure, had this young man. Instead of going to the front door and knocking, he hid his bicycle and crept across the grass to beneath his chief's study-window, which was on the first floor. Believe it or not, he then began very carefully and silently to climb a rope ladder which was hanging down from the sill. Eh, did you speak?'

Crossley, absolutely ghastly, had given a faint moan. He shook his head, again remaining silent.

'No?' said French. 'Well, to continue. He sat there, did this young man, for two or three hours, keeping guard, as one might say, while his chief was away. During that time he busied himself in a variety of ways; he typed, slowly and incompetently, he stirred the fire, he turned on and off the radio and he smoked, above all he smoked. Then when his chief had got back he left the study with the same care and went home.'

Crossley was frozen motionless. He stared at French as if hypnotised, horror and despair stamped on every line of his face. French obviously did not observe his distress, but went on with a cheerful interest in the story.

'Then last Sunday night, just a week later, the young man did the same thing all over again, or practically the same thing. This time he did not type, but instead he used the telephone. And what do you think was the young man's name? Eh? I'm sure you said something?'

French paused, then leant forward and spoke more gravely. 'The game's up, Crossley. As you see, we know everything. Hold up, man! Don't give way like that. Thompson, get him a drink.'

A dash of whisky brought a faint colour back into Crossley's cheeks.

'Now,' went on French, 'you've got yourself into a nasty hole, but I don't wish to make it worse for you than I can help. You must think carefully: Would you like to make a statement or would you rather send for a solicitor? He would advise you what it was wise for you to say. You're free to do either, and neither course will count against you.'

Crossley made an emphatic gesture. 'I don't want a solicitor,' he declared earnestly. 'All I want is to tell the truth. I wanted to directly I found out what Mr Plant had done, but he frightened me out of it.'

'I can't advise you,' French answered, 'but don't refuse the solicitor unless you're quite sure you don't want him.'

Crossley was quite sure; nothing but immediate confession would satisfy him. At French's suggestion he began his statement by saying so, and then went on to tell all that had happened to him, his falling in love (French did not press him to reveal Jessie's name), his finding the blank receipt form, his petty cash frauds, Plant's proposal and his acceptance of it because he was not strong enough to do anything else. He stressed his complete ignorance of

Plant's purpose and his horror when he discovered it, and swore that only fear forced him to assist on the second occasion. He was wise enough to keep nothing back, even to the acceptance of the hundred pounds.

From the young man's manner it was obvious to French that the story was true.

'I accept your statement, Crossley,' he said not unkindly, 'but it's only fair to tell you that you're in serious trouble. I shall have to arrest you and you'll be tried as an accessory to Plant. You'll have to take your medicine, but while I can promise nothing, I won't make it worse for you than I can help.'

When Crossley was removed French got busy. A warrant for Plant's arrest was quickly obtained, and with Nelson and Thompson he drove to the Yellow Star Line offices.

'Mr Plant has gone out,' he was told. 'Would you like to see his secretary?'

'Yes,' Miss Beamish confirmed, 'he went out a couple of hours ago to call on Friar & Talbot, our solicitors. I thought it rather strange. He came in here and said he had met the City Surveyor at lunch and he had told him they were bringing in new regulations about office fire-escapes, and he wanted to refresh his memory about ours to see if it would require alteration. He went out,' she pointed to the window with the iron staircase beyond, 'and said I might close the window after him, as he would leave through the yard. He hasn't come back yet, but he shouldn't be long, because it's nearly time for the office to close.'

As French expected, a call to Friar & Talbot established the fact that Plant had not been there. With a sinking heart French glanced at his helpers.

'We'll come back later, thank you,' he said to Miss Beamish.

That evening furious activity radiated from the Yard. A description was circulated, all Plant's known haunts were picketed, the port officers were warned: everything possible was done to find the missing man.

But all was of no avail. Plant had gone down that fire-escape, and as far as French was concerned, had walked from there right off the human stage.

25

Guy Plant

As Guy Plant returned to the office after lunch on that same Friday on which French interviewed Crossley at the Yard, he felt the clouds which had overshadowed him were lifting slightly. His position was still precarious in the extreme, though not so utterly hopeless as it had seemed a day or two earlier. With one of his most urgent problems he had dealt satisfactorily, that of Crossley. Crossley had been the weak link in his scheme, and to all intents and purposes Crossley had been eliminated. In three and a half hours the young man would leave the office for the last time, and after another day England would see him no more. He might consider that any danger from Crossley was at an end.

French's discoveries also had been a gnawing anxiety. They had come dangerously near the truth, and at first Plant was by no means certain that his efforts to hoodwink the man had succeeded. Now he felt easier on this point. French had obviously accepted his explanations. No move had been made against him, and if French had doubted his statement, he would unquestionably have shown his hand. Indeed, so far from hitting on the truth, French had gone completely off on the wrong track. He had evidently accepted the professional burglar theory, for he had asked Plant and the Winningtons to a parade at the Yard. Doubtless a suspected burglar was among the men, and French had probably hoped to prove that he had been reconnoitring at Hurst Lodge before making his coup.

There remained, of course, the hideous peril of Mallaby, who, so far as he could hear—he dared not make too frequent inquiries—still lingered on. If Mallaby would only die he believed he would be safe, but as long as a flicker of vitality remained in him, his own life hung by a thread. Frequently he slipped his hand into his pocket to reassure himself by the feel of the knife, if the word reassure can be used in such a ghastly connection. Again and again he thought of flight, but he was convinced that Mallaby could not recover, and always he decided to remain on and take his chance. That French had not moved showed that he had not heard Mallaby's statement, and if the man had been going to recover, he surely would have been fit to make it before this.

His growing optimism made the blow, when it fell, all the more devastating. About half-past two, not many minutes after he had reached the office, his telephone rang.

'Is that Mr Plant? Cutler speaking.'

Cutler was the private detective whom Plant had employed to shadow Crossley, lest an urge for confession should lead that young man in undesirable directions. With a sudden foreboding Plant acknowledged the call.

'I've some news, Mr Plant. Our friend has just been

arrested in the hall of your office. I followed the police car. He's been taken to Scotland Yard.'

For a moment Plant lost the power of movement. Then he forced himself to reply:

'Thanks, Cutler. Thanks very much. That's what I wanted to know. I'll see you later.'

He rang off and sat staring blankly before him into vacancy. So this was the end! That wily devil French had known all the time! If they had got on to Crossley they must have wormed out the whole thing. The fool of course would blurt out the truth, and that would finish them both. Crossley might get off with penal servitude, but he would not. Nothing could now save him—but his own efforts.

In a state of semi-coma he dully wondered how French could have picked on Crossley. To suspect himself was natural: he was Clarence's nephew by marriage and Clarence's money would come to his wife. That was an obvious clue. But between Crossley and either Clarence or Mallaby there was no connection whatever. Plant would have sworn it was utterly impossible that any detective could have found him.

Then he reminded himself that he could not afford time for the consideration of what was now only of academic interest. If he were to save himself he must act, and at once. His chances of escape were not too good at the best, but if he delayed they would be nil. Fortunately he knew what to do. He had worked out every step of his plan in the closest detail, and had made all possible preparations for carrying it out. Nothing now remained but to put it into action.

The building might be watched, and his first step must

therefore be to leave it unseen. He began by taking a stiff double whisky and filling up his pocket flask from the office bottle. Then, putting on hat and coat and taking a small suitcase in which he had packed his disguises, he went into Miss Beamish's room adjoining and told her of his call on Friar & Talbot and his discussion on fire-escapes with the City Surveyor. That any alteration to the office escape was the business of the technical staff, not of the accountant, would have struck most of the clerks as an inconsistency in his tale. Not so Miss Beamish. He knew that she would accept without question anything he said.

He walked deliberately down the escape, pausing at intervals to examine it for the benefit of chance observers. It led into an area surrounded by high buildings. This was used not only as a light well but also as a yard into which were carted various stores and coal for the central heating. It was connected with a lane behind Queen Victoria Street by a large gate containing a wicket. Fortunately at the moment the yard was empty and the gate locked. This of course w'as its normal condition, but it might have happened that coal or other stores were being unloaded, in which case Plant would have had to risk walking out without his disguise.

In the exit cartway beneath a wing of the building, hidden by its cover from the office windows, he quickly put on his less dressy overcoat, his shapeless hat, his old shoes, his glasses and his cheek pads, packing those discarded in the suitcase. Also he smeared coal-dust on his hands and lit a pipe. He had already obtained a key for the wicket on the excuse that he might sometimes wish to park his car in the yard in the evenings. Now he opened it, passed outside, locked it behind him, and set off eastwards. He took care to shuffle along instead of walking with his normal briskness. Though he dared not look round, he saw no watcher and he believed he had got away unseen.

He slouched along through Upper Thames Street and into Cannon Street Station. There in a lavatory he reversed his coat, straightened his hat, and washed his hands. Booking to a station in the suburbs, he took the next train, which left in a few minutes. At London Bridge he got out and dodged about the station, keeping as much as possible out of sight. His other three suitcases were at Charing Cross, and about a quarter to four he took a train there.

He had kept a sharp lookout at London Bridge and was convinced that he was not being shadowed. All the same, as a precaution he walked casually down the Tube steps from the circulating area at Charing Cross, then turned quickly out of the Villiers Street entrance and so back into the Main Line Station. There he called a porter, gave him his cloakroom tickets, and had all his suitcases put into a taxi.

He drove to Victoria, arriving about a quarter past four. A couple of days earlier he had bought a return ticket to Berne, and showing this, he took a leisurely seat in the 4.30 boat train. No one paid him any special attention and he felt satisfied that so far his plans had gone well.

Of course, up till now it had all been plain sailing. The real difficulties would begin at Folkestone. Well, one thing at a time. He could only hope for the best.

In one particular he was being unexpectedly, indeed extraordinarily lucky: the weather was assisting his plan. A cold wind had been blowing all afternoon, and now it rose still further, while a thin rain began to fall. At the ports it would be wet and stormy. Nothing could be better!

The train ran through to Folkestone Harbour, stopping only for the reverse near Folkestone Central. As they went slowly down the steep incline through the town, he took a comforting nip from his flask in preparation for what was to come.

He had, he assured himself, no reason for alarm, though of course in an unrehearsed plan there was always danger. The smallest hitch indeed might lead to unrelieved disaster.

At last the train drew into the station. Directly it stopped Plant got out, and disdaining the proffered aid of a porter, stacked three of his four suitcases against one of the platform buildings. With the fourth he hurried to a lavatory, and taking out the clothes he had purchased at the London theatrical supplies shop, he quickly changed. In three or four minutes he emerged in the uniform of an English luggage porter.

Now he reaped the benefit of his prevision in bringing four suitcases. In themselves they made a reasonable load, thus enabling him to avoid contact with other passengers. Carrying them all, he got into the line of porters hurrying on board. His heart was in his mouth lest there should be some check on luggage of which he was unaware, but though they passed a policeman at the shed door, he made no move. Here it was that the weather helped. Plant could keep his head down, fighting in the half-light against the gale.

Almost to his surprise, he found himself on board the ship. He followed the others to where they were stacking the luggage and put three of his suitcases at the end of the pile, where he could get them easily.

One of the difficult moments of his scheme followed. He had to hide somewhere on board. Watching his chance, he slipped away from the others and went out on the after well deck. No passengers had braved the weather on this wet and windswept area, but he knew that members of the crew would be to starboard on the poop, dealing with the stern mooring ropes. Crouching in the almost complete darkness beneath the port stepladder leading to the boat deck, he took his overcoat, hat and shoes from the suitcase and put them on. This was an improvement on his original plan. Had the evening been fine and the deck been occupied, he would have made for the second-class lavatory, a much more dangerous proceeding. Transformed now into a passenger, he regained the shelter, placed his suitcase beside the other three, and returned to the deck.

Though his reason told him that until they reached the other side he was fairly safe, his anxiety grew as the need for action diminished. The next hour would be nerve-racking. He felt that his plan was to keep out of sight, but this was easier said than done. In the end he spent most of his time in the semi-darkness of the deck, moving from one shadowed corner to another as seemed desirable. Needless to say, he did not go to get his passport stamped, and he kept a careful eye on the examiner, dodging him to avoid showing his ticket. If a landing card were given out which was not returned at the gangway, an investigation would inevitably follow.

The crossing proved gratifyingly bad. A choppy sea was running from the south-west and the ship pitched and rolled with a thoroughly satisfactory corkscrew motion. It gave Plant practically undisputed possession of the deck.

Under normal circumstances he would probably have been ill, but his anxiety saved him from this disaster.

Even the longest hour eventually comes to an end, and at last the lights of Boulogne loomed up ahead. Now was approaching another period of stress, and once more Plant steadied himself with a nip from his flask. As they reached the moles he picked up his suitcase and again made his way to his hiding-place beneath the ladder. This time he had to carry out a more drastic change of clothes, but in the dark and storm he managed it without discovery. Having donned the uniform he had bought in Paris, he became a typical French *porteur*.

His nerves tense, he now waited while the engines stopped, reversed, and stopped again. Then came the gentle bump as the ship touched the side of the wharf. Some more leaden moments crawled by, and then he heard what he was waiting for: the rush of the French porters coming on like a boarding party. He remained where he was for a few moments, so as not to be among the first ashore, then quietly slipped out and joined them.

Now, he told himself, he had only to remain calm and watch his opportunity. He fixed his eyes on a huge man who was putting his strap through the handles of a pile of luggage. He had a strap too, a well-worn one dark with age, and he immediately began linking his own four suit-cases together and slinging them over his shoulder in the approved manner. When the big man moved off under his load, he followed.

Here also the wind was high and the rain heavy, so that he could hide his face in a natural way. As he had hoped, he got ashore without difficulty. So far, so good, but the worst was yet to come; the ugly business of the customs was still to be negotiated. Well, he had thought that out as carefully as the rest of the plan, and if his luck held he should pull it off.

Crossing the wind-swept wharf, he entered the customs shed. Owing to his delay it was full, as he had intended it should be. The central counter was jammed up with luggage and a crowd three deep stood round it. Plant put his suitcases down behind the passengers, ostensibly to wait for a place, but really to observe the shape of the chalk-mark the examiners were making. Then he stooped, obviously to adjust his strap. With a piece of chalk which he had secreted in his pocket, be marked his suitcases similarly.

Now for the crux of his entire plan! Could he get past the gendarmes on to the platform? He waited till a number of porters were going out together and joined them. They moved towards the door, doubly guarded by men whose entire duty was to prevent persons doing what he was attempting. He felt his heart turn to water, but with his head down he pushed on. Then once again he broke into a cold sweat. He was on the platform!

Though the worst was now over, he was not even yet completely through with his adventure. Leaving the suitcase containing his clothes on the platform, he climbed into the train and placed the other three in a compartment. Then with the fourth he went into the station lavatory, for the last time changing. When he emerged he was Guy Plant, except for his original disguise. Doing his utmost to appear normal, he returned to the train and took his place.

Fortunately the three other travellers occupying his compartment were French, and when a discussion arose between one of them and the conductor about a sleeping-berth, in which the others joined, he was careful to know only English. Finally the complaining one vanished in the wake of the official, and the others settled down to sleep.

Plant, though aching with weariness, dared not sleep. In a sort of coma, the miles passed till, shortly after twelve, they drew into Chalons. Here he got out, put three of his suitcases in the cloakroom and with the fourth left the station. At that hour of the night he thought a traveller without luggage might arouse comment. He had previously ascertained that he could break his journey on the Berne ticket.

Walking round by road to the other side of the station, he bought a single to Paris. His train did not leave for some three hours and he filled in the time by getting a meal in the refreshment-room, retrieving his remaining suitcases, and dozing in the waiting-room.

The train he boarded was an international express from Germany and Austria, and on the way to Paris he slept from sheer exhaustion. His roundabout route had been very tiring, but he had at least the satisfaction of arriving at the Gare de l'Est instead of the Gate du Nord, where, had the hue and cry started, English passengers might have received embarrassing attention from the police.

He drove to the rooms he had engaged, where, pleading the fatigue of a night journey, he spent most of the day in bed. It was getting dusk, indeed, before he went out. He was now Roy Beane, to suit his altered passport, an English author come to Paris to obtain local colour for his new book. All the same, when he left his rooms he did not advertise his nationality. While he was out he was a visitor from Provence, his French being fluent from his three years in the Marseilles office.

Over a leisurely dinner in an obscure restaurant he took stock of his position. So far he had done magnificently. He had given French the slip and he was satisfied that he had left no trace of his movements. When one other matter was disposed of he would be safe, as safe as if those two ghastly incidents had never taken place. The immediate future was also provided for. He had with him a fair sum in francs, not to speak of a fortune in jewels.

The outstanding matter he dealt with later that evening. Taking his various uniforms and unwanted clothes, he went down on one of the quays along the Seine, and hidden beneath a bridge, he weighted the pockets with stones from a pile along the bank, and threw the garments one by one into the river. A careful look round assured him that he was unobserved, and with a sigh of relief he returned to his rooms.

Next morning he gave his landlady his doctored passport, believing that the inspection it was likely to receive would be insufficient to reveal his forgery. In this he was correct. The passport was returned to him later without comment.

A more difficult problem was the turning of his jewels into money. For this he would have liked to go to Amsterdam, but he dared not risk exhibiting his passport at the frontier. He decided he would get some tools and cut a few of the smaller stones from their settings, then try the jewellers of the Rue de la Paix or the Rue de Rivoli.

Next day he began his writing, copying out for the benefit of a curious landlady the opening pages of *A Tale of Two Cities*, though had Charles Dickens looked over his shoulder, that famous man would have scratched his head in bewilderment over the strange names of his characters.

So passed a number of days, days of apparent safety, and yet Plant knew no case of mind. On the contrary, his life began to grow increasingly irksome. He feared and hated solitude, but he feared and hated the company of others more. Lest he should give himself away he could make no friends. He was afraid to go out in the daytime in case through some hideous chance he should meet someone he knew. The leaden hours dragged slowly by while he read and wrote and wished for the dusk. Then, with his coat collar turned up about his ears and his hat pulled down over his eyes, he would take his exercise, an interminable solitary tramp through the lesser known streets, with nothing to look forward to at the end but the further dreary isolation of his rooms.

The endless lonely days gradually became a long-drawn-out misery. He began to brood. Thoughts of his crimes took possession of his mind. He could not blot out the look of Clarence Winnington and Anthony Mallaby as they lay, the one on the floor in that ghastly room, the other in his chair with his bleeding wrist. He could not forget their trustfulness and how he had rewarded it. His whole soul revolted from his thoughts, from his entire way of living. But he could neither get rid of the one nor alter the other. Nor could he see how his condition might be improved. Sometimes he thought it would always remain its present nightmare, and hope faded. Sometimes he wondered would his brain stand the stress? Slowly the fear of madness grew in his mind.

Then to his horror he began to notice a change in himself.

His nerve was failing him. He now simply did not dare to accept risks which formerly he had taken in his stride. His imagination began to play tricks with him. When a policeman glanced at him casually he read into it an accusing stare and shrank back. Sometimes it took all his strength to prevent himself turning and rushing away. He began to think policemen were staring at him, and if he saw one in the distance he would hurriedly enter a shop or turn the nearest corner.

Then one evening what he had vaguely dreaded at last crystallised into fact. He was passing along the Rue de La Fayette when just in front of him a policeman appeared suddenly from a side street. The man glanced at him, then looked more searchingly. His face changed and he stepped forward with upraised arm. This was real: this was no imagination. Plant's nerve went to shreds. In sudden uncontrollable panic he turned and fled.

The policeman blew a whistle and gave chase, while the passers-by looked on with interest. Then in front Plant saw another policeman, hurrying to meet him. He was just passing a Metro staircase. Automatically he turned in and raced down the steps. If his luck held, he might get a train before they appeared. Perhaps there was still hope.

But the police were gaining. When he reached the platform, dashing past the surprised ticket-examiner, they were only a few yards behind. Then Plant's heart sank and he knew it really was the end. On the platform was a third policeman. He turned and ran forward, his arms out in a rugby tackle.

Just then a train thundered into the station. Plant saw it approaching like some huge juggernaut. He glanced at the police in front and behind, and in a moment of time saw a cell, a court, another cell, and then—

Swinging aside, he plunged off the platform just as that monstrous roaring shape swept by.

26

Joseph French

When French found that Guy Plant had slipped through his fingers, his feelings can be better imagined than described. At first he did not believe that the man could have escaped, but as day succeeded day without any trace of him coming to light, he could no longer evade the mortifying conclusion. The fault, he knew only too well, was his own. He had under-estimated Plant. He had not believed either that he knew he was seriously suspected, or that, had he done so, he could so expertly have got away.

French, of course, had taken reasonable precautions, precautions which normally would have been amply sufficient. He had had Plant shadowed, but, as he now saw, inadequately. He had detailed only one officer for the job, and this man naturally kept a watch on the front door of the office. There was no reason to suppose Plant would have panicked in the way he had. The only thing which could have advised him of his danger was the detention of Crossley, and there was no time for him to have learnt of that. A piece of sheer bad luck! Obviously someone had seen Crossley being picked up and warned Plant. Beyond measure exasperating! French felt it was going to prove a severe blow to his prestige.

Apart from the puzzle of Plant's prescience, there remained the problem of where the man had hidden himself. The entire resources of the British police force were mobilised to find him: without result. French indeed had done more than make the routine inquiries usual under such circumstances. He had interviewed the booking-clerks at the main London stations and airports, as well as issuing a questionnaire to bus conductors and taximen. Nor had he overlooked the possibility that Plant might be dead. He had instituted a search for the body, requiring that refuse dumps and such like should be examined, and that the river police should keep a special lookout along Suicide Alley, as he was wont to call the Thames.

A whole week of concentrated effort passed before he received the slightest encouragement. On the following Friday he was rung up by an official of the Audit Department at Victoria. Some information had come into his hands which might or might not bear on French's inquiries, and if he cared to call round, he could judge the matter for himself.

Fifteen minutes later French was talking to the man himself, who proved to be the clerk in charge.

'I don't say this has anything to do with your business,' he began, 'but it's something just a bit out of the ordinary and it's at the time you mentioned. I thought I'd better tell you.'

'I'm grateful to you, Mr Bryson. If it helps us it will be worth any trouble, and if it doesn't there's no harm done.'

'I'm glad you take that view. It's really quite a simple matter. On Wednesday week we sold a second return to Berne. It was one of those books which have a page for each section of the journey. There was Victoria to Dover or Folkestone, Dover to Calais or Folkestone to Boulogne, Calais or Boulogne to Laon, Laon to Basle and Basle to Berne. That's done, you know, because of all the different interests which get a share of the spoils.'

'So I understood,' said French, before whom the point, had often come up.

'Well, on Friday, two days after the ticket was purchased, the Victoria-Folkestone section was collected on the 4.30 p.m. service. But the passenger must have left the station at Folkestone, for the steamer portion was not collected. I made special inquiries and he has not crossed since. Now why would a man buy a ticket to Berne and stop off at Folkestone?'

French was keenly interested. He had already seen that if Plant had been making a bolt for the Continent the 4.30 service from Victoria was the first he could get.

'That certainly wants looking into,' he answered heartily. 'Does the non-collection of the steamer portion necessarily mean that the holder did not cross?'

'I should say so. He could not have got ashore at Boulogne without a landing ticket, and he could only have got a landing ticket by surrendering his book ticket.'

French had known this, but he liked to have things confirmed. It was obvious that he must go into the matter thoroughly. Telephoning to the Folkestone police, he went down by the next train, and with a local sergeant interviewed the staff at the Harbour Station.

The information they received contradicted that of the clerk at Victoria, though it sounded equally conclusive.

Few passengers travelled to Folkestone by the boat train, but the tickets of such as did were not collected on the train, but by the man at the station barrier. These tickets, moreover, were invariably of card and not out of a book. On the day in question no ticket of any kind had been collected, and the staff was satisfied that everyone who arrived by the train had gone on by the boat.

It was a mystery to French, but all the more valuable for that, because mystery plus the coincidence of time made it by no means unlikely that the ghost passenger was Plant.

He turned into a bar and over a pint of bitter thought the matter out. He could not see his way clear, but at least it seemed certain that inquiries should be made on the French side. He therefore rang up the Yard, asking to be put through to Sir Mortimer Ellison, the Assistant Commissioner.

As a result, an envelope containing French's passport, letters of introduction, tickets and money arrived by the 4.30 from Victoria, and obtaining these from the guard, he crossed to Boulogne. He waited till the disembarkation was over and the trains had left, then saw the officials at the Gare Maritime.

They could tell him nothing except that no traveller had left the station from the service in question. All who crossed had gone on somewhere by train.

French felt very much up against it. In fact, he did not know what to do next. The evidence of the Victoria clerk suggested that the mysterious traveller had not crossed the Channel, while that of the Folkestone staff was that he must have done so. Here at Boulogne the facts would fit in with either theory, which did not help a great deal.

French wondered if there was any way in which the

point could be settled? If the evidence from the ports was true, and there could be little doubt of this, the traveller had not only crossed, but had gone on by train. He might, of course, have travelled on some other ticket, though if he had another ticket, French did not see why he should have taken that to Berne. At all events, that to Berne was the only one known of, and the first question therefore was, Had the traveller gone to Berne?

French looked up a timetable and glanced at his watch. If he were quick he could get a train to Paris that night. He hurried to the town station and just caught it. It gave him plenty of time to think over his case, not reaching Paris till after seven next morning.

He called at the Sûreté, and obtaining the help of an inspector, M. Pinet, drove to the Gare du Nord. There, after a deal of search, they found the Audit Department and stated their case. Were any leaves of Book Ticket Number So-and-so collected on the 20.39 train from Boulogne to Berne on Friday night the 25th ultimo?

The search took some time, but at last the official returned with a scrap of yellow paper. It was the leaf Calais or Boulogne to Laon.

'Laon is as far as the Northern Section extends,' he explained. 'If you want further information you must go to the Eastern Section.'

'The Gare de l'Est,' said Pinet. 'It is quite near. We walk? Yes?'

'I'm getting quite hopeful that it's my man,' said French as they left the station. 'He played some trick on the steamer, presumably to avoid the passport men. When you add that to the time he left London, I don't think there can be much doubt.'

'But yes. It is likely, is it not? Myself, I do not see how he could have done the trick. My faith, it is not easy to cross the Channel without tickets and passports. No?'

'I agree; I don't see it either. However, let's carry on and perhaps we'll learn something.'

The Eastern Section covered the journey from Laon to Basle, and at the Gare de l'Est they learnt that no corresponding page had been collected.

'*Eh bien*,' said Pinet, 'it is then that he left the train at Laon or between Laon and Basle. The ticket permitted the break of journey, is it not, monsieur?'

The clerk agreed that this could be done at any of the principal stations.

'Then we telephone our men in the towns *en route*: Laon, Reims, Chalons, Chaumont, Vesoul, Belfort? There are others? We shall get our friend to make the list.'

He beamed on the clerk, then turned to French. 'It is not needful, monsieur, that you weary yourself with the telephoning. Myself, I see to it. Doubtless you can enjoy yourself in our beautiful Paris for a few hours while we wait for a reply? It is so? Yes?'

Late that afternoon news came in. The ticket-examiner at Chalons remembered that a man had left the train in question at his station. He had shown his ticket, which was a book return London to Basle, saying he was breaking the journey for a few hours. The examiner had noted the episode because he expected to see the man again on the resumption of the journey. But he had not done so, and no trace of any such resumption could be found. Of course, this in itself was not proof that it did not occur.

'It does not prove it, no, but the absence of the ticket

does,' Pinet commented. 'He travel to Chalons on a Basle ticket. Why?'

'A roundabout journey to hide his tracks,' French suggested. 'He has doubled off somewhere from Chalons. Where would you say?'

Pinet shrugged. 'From Chalons one could go to anywhere in France.'

'What about Paris?' French said quietly.

The Frenchman looked at him and made an emphatic gesture. 'You are right, monsieur. He avoids the Gare du Nord. But yes! He has come to Paris.'

'Losing himself in a large town? Yes, I think that's it. There's another thing which points in the same direction. He spoke French well, but no other foreign language. He would therefore be likely to stick to France or some French-speaking country. And where in a French-speaking country could he hide himself better than in Paris?'

It was as a result of these views that the description of Plant was put into the hands of every policeman in the city, which led, as sooner or later it inevitably must, to the man's discovery.

After the tragic finale at the Metro station the conclusion of the case was soon reached. Bernard Winnington was sent for and formally identified Plant's remains. The address of the dead man's rooms was amongst those noted in his pocket engagement book, and there in one of his suitcases were found the jewels, intact save for one or two small pieces from which he had extracted the stones. Police charities benefited considerably from a reward for the discovery, which Christina insisted should be paid.

Crossley's full confession and the fact that he had been

little more than the tool of the older man were taken into favourable consideration at the young fellow's trial, and he received the comparatively light sentence of two years' imprisonment.

As a result of the case, French found his prestige enhanced rather than diminished. It was true that the murderer's death had been brought about only indirectly by the law. But it had been brought about, and the entire affair had been cleared up. Sir Mortimer was satisfyingly complimentary in his references to it.

Nearly a year later French had an interesting reminder of the case. He had been sent to Biarritz, to obtain evidence from a visitor there in connection with some City frauds, and when walking down the main street he met Christina and Mallaby, the latter quite recovered from his distressing experience. They stopped, and after a chat Christina invited him to dine at their hotel that evening.

He had already told them how he discovered Plant's guilt, and in return they gave him their news. Now that the case was over, Mallaby admitted that for Christina's sake he had in the hospital pretended to be worse than he really was, so as to avoid being questioned by French until he knew what had happened to Plant. It was only when he heard from Christina of the man's flight that he regained sufficient strength to undergo a police examination. On his slow return to health he had told Christina that he must withdraw his proposal, giving his reason. She had absolutely declined to release him, and after a long discussion had managed to overcome his scruples. She had insisted that he should give up his practice and, with her money added to his own, undertake some of the original research which had always lain near his heart. They had just had a three months' honeymoon and were now on their way back to London.

Of the other residents at Hurst Lodge, Bernard had joined with a friend in setting up a racing stables in Hampshire, and Bellissa, for the time being at least, was going to housekeep for him. Horne had settled down to write. His book had been a success, insomuch that he had determined to try to live by his pen.

French, who had liked all four, though particularly admiring Christina, was glad that after their time of stress a happier period seemed to be opening out for them. 'We owe a lot to you, Mr French,' Christina told him as they were saying good-night. 'You certainly made everything as easy for us as you could.'

He could have wished for no better epitaph to the case.

By the same author

Inspector French's Greatest Case

At the offices of the Hatton Garden diamond merchant *Duke & Peabody*, the body of old Mr Gething is discovered beside a now-empty safe. With multiple suspects, the robbery and murder is clearly the work of a master criminal, and requires a master detective to solve it. Meticulous as ever, Inspector Joseph French of Scotland Yard embarks on an investigation that takes him from the streets of London to Holland, France and Spain, and finally to a ship bound for South America . . .

'Because he is so austerely realistic, Freeman Wills Croft is deservedly a first favourite with all who want a real puzzle.'
                                                                     TIMES LITERARY SUPPLEMENT

By the same author

Inspector French and the Cheyne Mystery

When young Maxwell Cheyne discovers that a series of mishaps are the result of unwelcome attention from a dangerous gang of criminals, he teams up with a young woman who is determined to help him outwit them. But when she disappears, he finally decides to go to Scotland Yard for help. Concerned by the developing situation, Inspector Joseph French takes charge of the investigation and applies his trademark methods to track down the kidnappers and thwart their intentions . . .

'Freeman Wills Crofts is among the few muscular writers of detective fiction. He has never let me down.'
                                        DAILY EXPRESS

By the same author

Inspector French and the Starvel Hollow Tragedy

A chance invitation from friends saves Ruth Averill's life on the night her uncle's old house in Starvel Hollow is consumed by fire, killing him and incinerating the fortune he kept in cash. Dismissed at the inquest as a tragic accident, the case is closed—until Scotland Yard is alerted to the circulation of bank-notes supposedly destroyed in the inferno. Inspector Joseph French suspects that dark deeds were done in the Hollow that night and begins to uncover a brutal crime involving arson, murder and body snatching . . .

'Freeman Wills Crofts is the only author who gives us intricate crime in fiction as it might really be, and not as the irreflective would like it to be.'   OBSERVER

By the same author

Inspector French and the Sea Mystery

Off the coast of Burry Port in south Wales, two fishermen discover a shipping crate and manage to haul it ashore. Inside is the decomposing body of a brutally murdered man. With nothing to indicate who he is or where it came from, the local police decide to call in Scotland Yard. Fortunately Inspector Joseph French does not believe in insoluble cases—there are always clues to be found if you know what to look for. Testing his theories with his accustomed thoroughness, French's ingenuity sets him off on another investigation . . .

'Inspector French is as near the real thing as any sleuth in fiction.'
                                                    SUNDAY TIMES

By the same author

Inspector French: Found Floating

The Carrington family, victims of a strange poisoning, take an Olympic cruise from Glasgow to help them recover. At Creuta one member goes ashore and does not return. Their body is next day found floating in the Straits of Gibraltar. Joining the ship at Marseilles, can Inspector French solve the mystery before they reach Athens?

Introduced by Tony Medawar, this classic Inspector French novel includes unique interludes by Superintendent Walter Hambrook of Scotland Yard, who provides a real-life detective commentary on the case as the mystery unfolds.

'I doubt whether Inspector French has had a more difficult problem to solve than that of the body 'Found Floating' in the Mediterranean.' SUNDAY TIMES

By the same author

Inspector French:
The End of Andrew Harrison

Becoming the social secretary for millionaire financier
Andrew Harrison sounded like the dream job: just writing
a few letters and making amiable conversation, with luxu-
rious accommodation thrown in. But Markham Crewe had
not reckoned on the unpopularity of his employer, especially
within his own household, where animosity bordered on
sheer hatred. When Harrison is found dead on his Henley
houseboat, Crewe is not the only one to doubt the verdict
of suicide. Inspector French is another...

'A really satisfying puzzle ... With every fresh detective story
Crofts displays new fields of specialised knowledge.'
DAILY MAIL